The New Har

Central Av
New Har

(800)

Little

Little

by
David Treuer

GRAYWOLF PRESS
SAINT PAUL

Publication of this volume is made possible in part by a grant provided by the Minnesota State Arts Board through an appropriation by the Minnesota State Legislature, and by a grant from the National Endowment for the Arts. Significant additional support has been provided by the Andrew W. Mellon Foundation, the Lila Wallace-Reader's Digest Fund, the McKnight Foundation, and other generous contributions from foundations, corporations, and individuals. Graywolf Press is a member agency of United Arts, Saint Paul. To these organizations and individuals who make our work possible, we offer heartfelt thanks.

Published by Graywolf Press
2402 University Avenue, Suite 203
Saint Paul, Minnesota 55114

Printed in the United States of America.

ISBN 1-55597-231-4

2 4 6 8 9 7 5 3
First Graywolf Printing, 1995
Library of Congress Catalog Card Number 95–077949

This is dedicated to the one who showed me that I could
and to the one who gave me the reason

Robert Treuer & Margaret Seelye Treuer

Little

I

A Whole Heart

Donovan
1980

The grave we dug for my brother Little remained empty even after we filled it back in. And nobody was going to admit it. Everyone at the housing tract we called Poverty avoided the bare fact, the empty grave. Tucked back up in the woods, Poverty had no witness, and since there were only seven of us living in the two remaining houses that hadn't been gutted or broken, we had no one to explain it all to. We had no one to hand it to, fact by fact. So, even without the body, everything remained the same.

Stan still thought he was Little's father. During the wake he shuffled between the empty coffin wedged in the corner of the living room and the front steps that sagged under the weight of the clustered beer drinkers.

"My boy," he slurred. "My boy, my boy, my boy."

He still believed the signs. His six fingers and Little's. He thought it meant that they were blood related. Little's hands had been deformed since birth, his fingers fused into huge claws, three clubby fingers on each hand, ready to grab onto anyone who entered his orbit. Stan still believed the signs, though he had six fingers on his left hand. His right had been blown off in Vietnam, which is why we called Little, Little. Little Stan, that is.

"My boy's gone," Stan mumbled into Jeannette's hair, which hung in a gray knotty braid. She grimaced and turned the frying-pan handle inward on the stove so he wouldn't spill the hot grease from the fry bread on himself. Protecting him like a child.

3

When he swerved outside, the old twins, Duke and Ellis, tried to swoop him up in the stories they always told on end, tried to lure him into sleeping off the Black Label in the back seat of their Catalina. They tried to still him under their wings. When that didn't work, they blocked him physically from going down to the lake where he stared across the cold April water to where the water tower blinked its red eye next to town.

Celia just sat on the torn plaid couch. Her arms crossed, her foot kicking out from under the ruffled eave of her dress. She didn't comfort Stan or respond to Ellis's hugs or Duke's jokes. She didn't look at the empty coffin where her son, my brother, was supposed to lie.

Everyone from our housing tract that we called Poverty was there. We only numbered seven.

We didn't even have the body, not even his clothes, his hair, no memories of anything he ever said. Nothing but his one word, "You."

No pipe man came, though the Catholic priest stopped by. With quivering red-knuckled hands he came to deliver his condolences and a frozen ham wrapped in tinfoil. Jeannette met him on the front steps and he handed her the ham, its metal skin winking in the April light. He said he would give Little the last rites.

We stood, Duke in midjoke, Jeannette with her hands on her hips, Violet leaning to see out the door from where she was scooping Jell-O salad into a bowl. Our eyes were bleary with menthol smoke, our hands busy with caffeine, squinting at the priest who sawed back and forth on the front steps.

"Not in my house," Jeannette said.

"But . . ." he stammered.

"No."

"His soul," said the priest, toeing a bottle cap on the lowest step.

I imagined holy water arcing onto the lace curtains, the priest bending over an empty coffin, creasing the egg-smooth satin pillow with his baby-soft thumb. Ham was one thing, but irony was something we would not take from a white priest from Iowa.

He turned and walked slowly back to where the car waited.

The pale blue car crunched its way back to the highway. We never saw him again.

On the second day of the wake Duke and I drove to town to borrow a bigger coffeemaker from the bingo hall. The Pontiac Catalina that Duke and Ellis claimed was their "mobile home" hummed along the pitted asphalt, lifting and diving along the frost heaves. Anyone at Poverty would have put them up in their house, even Jeannette would have let them in ours, though it was crammed with Stan, Celia, and me. Stan's sister, Violet, was living in their mother's house across Poverty. No one lived there now except Violet and Jackie. Their mother Rose left when I was small. The other houses were all in various stages of ruin; two had burned, one was sagging slowly to the ground from water damage, and the other was split in two by a white pine knocked down in a storm. But Duke and Ellis stuck to their car.

"Are you sure they've got a pot to spare at the hall?" I asked.

"It don't matter who it was, Donovan," said Duke.

"What?"

"It don't matter."

"What doesn't matter?"

Duke gripped the steering wheel with his left hand as he fished around in his front shirt pocket for his cigarettes.

"Little's father," he said carefully as he bent his head down from the wind to light his cigarette.

"Do you know?" I asked, shifting in my seat.

He nodded, but kept his eyes straight ahead.

"Just like it don't matter who left you by the road. Take care of your ma, that's all."

The wind swept in and I looked out at the tan fields. The snow was finally gone. One match would be all it would take and the smoke would curl off the fields, lick the fence posts, and jump into the trees. Sparks would whip up in the sky, far far overhead.

We never shut off the coffeepot during the four days before we buried the empty coffin. At night the "on" switch glowed red, blurred by the cigarette smoke that hung in the house like river fog.

Violet kept it going, filling cups when they were getting low, banging the grounds into the plastic garbage can and filling the coffeepot up again. Duke joked her, saying that Poverty alone was keeping an entire nation of Colombians in work. She kept the coffee hot, ran to the store for more powdered creamer, and stalked the house emptying ashtrays. She washed them and they were never dry enough. When people rested their cigarettes in the grooves, they sizzled and burned unevenly, the white paper leeching brown.

She straightened the sheet thrown over the only table, put half-eaten ham sandwiches in the fridge, and made sure that her daughter Jackie was with me.

I picked around slowly, moving from person to person like I was shuffling from room to empty room in a house swept clean. Everyone was in storage.

My ma ruffled my hair.

"It's not your fault," she said, picking the ratty couch apart with her eyes. Celia. The one who raised me after Duke and Ellis found me cast-off, half-frozen in an abandoned car.

I picked around. The rest of the summer Jackie and I spent scuffing our feet, stealing beer to drink at the dam. Stan watched us from the fishery window where he worked as we threw the empties over the cement spillway.

But that day, that bright funeral day, we didn't go to the dam. We couldn't bring ourselves to trust the water. We didn't even have the body to put in the grave, no words of his to remember, to turn over like river rocks looking for something skittering away in the murk like the orange dart of a crayfish.

Little didn't speak. It wasn't that he couldn't. All he had ever said was "you." He was deformed, not retarded. It was a choice. Like Duke, he chose not to tell what he knew.

That day, when the grass was still dead, we took the opportunity not to lie to ourselves, but to lie to everyone else. As we dug the hole, it was a relief to know that although we had nothing to put in it, on the outside we could show our determination.

On a rise by the lake behind Poverty we dug the hole. We pushed the shovels, shiny and slick with use, past the mat of pine needles. They scraped away easily like so much skin. We cut the black soil off first, soil not close or thick enough to be real sod, and it crumbled in a heap. Then we cut through the sand that warmed and slid past our shovels. It kept slipping back into the opening. It leveled at the bottom and we patiently lifted it out. It reminded me of a joke Ma told me once: What gets bigger the more you take out? A hole.

A heart, maybe.

That's what it seemed like, though I didn't get it at the time. Little had offered his one word, like punctuation after the punch line. You. It wasn't that Little couldn't speak, he just didn't. Except for "you."

A hole. A heart. A whole heart, it kept on getting bigger and bigger. We dug with the sun on our backs. It warmed its way through our shirts though the wind off the lake was still cold. The ice had gone out the week before.

Duke told me to climb down inside and lift out the shifting sand with a bucket. I scooped the sand into the plastic ice-cream pail and handed it to them where they piled it in a shifting heap. The hole got bigger but the sun couldn't get down inside. Right there at the bottom I knew the joke was right. The more sand, the more rocks I moved, the more roots I chopped out with a dull hatchet, the emptier it got. I knew from down there where we dug for Little, but couldn't put him, that there had to *be* something we were digging for.

We dug and dug, looking for reasons. We would have kept on except Jeannette came outside, wrapped in one of Stan's flannel shirts, wondering what was taking us half the day. At seventy she had that old-lady way of making everything you do seem so stupid, as coarse and plain as rough lumber.

"That there hole's big enough to drive your shitty car into," she said to Duke and Ellis.

We stopped digging then.

Everyone came out of the house and stood around, pretending discomfort when the discomfort wasn't at his death. It was at the why of his short, speechless life.

The older ones, Duke, Ellis, Jeannette, Violet, Stan, and Celia kept lying to each other, shifting their weight from foot to foot, squinting at the sun. Jackie and I stood too, until they out-patienced us, until we split and ran to the hay field across the road from Poverty where we raced the giant dandelions like the three of us used to.

The dandelion heads were as big as oranges. Each seed looked like a miniature parachute, like what Stan said he had jumped with in the marines. Clustered together at the end of the stalk they were like spider-webbed umbrellas. We plucked them off a plant that had escaped the winter underneath a turned-over water trough and held them between our fingers, high above our heads, and let them go.

We raced them across the fields, over the turned-in hay and clods of dead grass and up, up over the trees, the bent, twisted jack pine and red pine. We raced them that day as we did every summer, holding the seeds up and just letting the wind take them. I felt as though they went further, were carried higher than ever before. Past all the old places, beyond the old lines and boundaries of the reservation, the lousy jobs, the no-money, the beer. We flung them as far as we could because we knew that we had nothing to do with it, no control over where they landed. We never could do anything with those silk-spun dandelion seeds. They were too light.

It was the wind that took them, carried them across the sky up into that pale blue, powder blue like my ma's faded-out dress. Up into that color the wind took them and I don't believe they ever settled down, but scattered away.

Jackie fell asleep with her head on my stomach. I looked where those seeds were blowing. Not because I wanted to know, but because I knew I couldn't.

In later years all of us at Poverty dressed up our stories about Little, gave them wings, and let them go. And since there was so little to tell, they took off, circled higher, and like the dandelions, never touched the ground again.

After it got dark we walked back to Poverty, toward houses where beer tops were already popped and the televisions were on. Jackie went home where Violet tucked her into bed even though Jackie was nine. I went out to the hole.

I stood at the edge of the grave. It was just as they left it; gaping and empty. The sand looked crustier and the topsoil had lost its deep black glitter. It was still empty because they hadn't filled it in yet; there was nothing to cover.

All of the talk: Stan claiming that he was the father, Violet thanking God because *her* child wasn't like that, Jeannette suffering us with her silence, the twins' balance in which Duke jabbered and Ellis thought. It was all open and out, but like the dandelions we threw, there was nothing stable about us. All the talk and the silence, the secrets kept or known gradually changed shape. They acquired new habits and grew beyond what Poverty and the reservation had previously allowed. Even later when I knew the truth and held it to me like a long lost friend it gave no comfort, offered nothing of itself, and passed on. The importance of knowing had long since faded. The hole got bigger the more we dug.

I stood there that night at the edge and then, finally, did what I had been waiting to do for ten years. I buried Little.

Wisconsin
November 1968

The winter of 1968 was the last winter it snowed deeper than three feet and the branches of birch, aspen, and jack pine snapped under the weight. The ditches leveled off at the top with blowing snow, connecting with the fields that stretched from central Minnesota all the way to the Rocky Mountains. The Rockies stared across the barren plains to Minnesota and judged the nakedness that lay out for all to see.

During the summer months the leaves and grass could hide what shouldn't be seen. When the heat came in those months the surface growth, whether pine or brush, grass or weeds, could cover the deficiencies of right, the diminishing borders, even the history. This could not be done when it snowed and the living growth had retreated or died. But just the same, in November the weather delivered so much that was unexpected, when everyone had assumed that they had seen it all before. The flakes and jumble of snow that fell so hard and so thick was out of place in November. The weather had been too cold for the snow and for the winds that came from the south, blowing off Lake Michigan and across Wisconsin. When it warmed to zero and the red alcohol thermometers began to work again, the winds swept over the lakes and rivers, blending them with the fields. The November winds blew the snow from the ground, shook it from its frozen place on the bare branches of trees, and broke it from the crested drifts along the sides of barns and ditches. It was swept from the fields that used to yield wheat second only to the Nile valley, but that had long before given up their last bit of topsoil to spring oats and winter wheat. The fields that used to yield corn, beets, soybean, and sunflower to farmers who came from Germany, Sweden, and Norway were choked with quack grass. The descendants of the Germans, Swedes, and Norwegians now worked as auto mechanics, store owners, policemen, telephone repairmen, truckers, pipeline supervisors, carpenters, plumbers, roofers, welders, sheet-metal workers, and as agents of history. As the snow lifted and swirled through the air they remembered for their fathers and mothers, and remembered to their children who sat at kitchen tables in Levis, their blond hair under greasy baseball caps. The gusts reached in and shook the window panes from where they sat in their sashes, as the sons and daughters of immigrants remembered the day the Iron Range had produced more iron ore and taconite than any other mine in the United States. They remembered before iron was discovered, when the great pine logs were loaded on trains and shipped north to Winnipeg and south to Minneapolis. They remembered before the railroads, when the logs were hauled by steamship up the Red River and down the Mississippi, and before that when they were sledged out in the winter on sleds pulled by horses, and in the summer on carts pulled by oxen.

They put more wood in their stoves, and staggered a bit as their arthritis kicked in, or the continual pinch of a sciatic nerve jerked along the run of a back. Lowering themselves into squeaky aluminum chairs they remembered before the logging, when their ancestors first arrived by boat and quarreled with the French for the land of Minnesota. They remembered the French trappers who, escaping from a life of crime, played out their fantasies trading with the Indians.

Then they remembered their great-great-grandparents who left the famines of Europe. They remembered that their ancestors brought with them only a few plates that had been decorated with painted rose petals and laurels during the long Scandinavian winters in which the sun would never set, in which it would hover at the edge of the horizon taunting them with its simultaneous presence and distance. They remembered those plates standing next

to the ones painted by their great-grandparents during the long,
dark, and bone-cracking cold Minnesota winters. They even remembered why there were no others. Why, where there should
have been similarly decorated plates painted by their parents,
even themselves, there were only empty spaces. There were only
empty spaces, gaping holes where there should have been some
porcelain history because they and their parents had been too
busy with the farm — with the construction of the silo, with fix-
ing the far wall of the barn that had begun to lean — to spend
time weaving paint onto something that was used to eat off. And
now, now they did not know how to create the arc of vine and leaf
along porcelain rims.

They remembered it all to their children in dirty jeans, clean
blond hair, and greasy baseball caps who still lived at home.
Their children lived at home and kept odd hours because they
worked in town as grocery baggers, pizza-delivery boys, gas-
pump attendants, and night janitors. They remembered to their
daughters whose skin was clean and whose hair was done with
large waves of bangs, supported by patience and hair spray. They
worked as hairstylists, waitresses, and girlfriends who were too
alone to say no to their overanxious boyfriends, and too Lutheran to say yes above a whisper in the back seat of a car.

They remembered their past and constructed the present with
mortgages and loans to pay the property taxes on their fathers'
land in whose fields and pastures stood rusted skeletons of farm
machinery too broken down with age to be sold at the county
auction. They told these stories in earnest at kitchen tables over
potbellies and Pabst Blue Ribbon, sometimes coffee, to their children who had long ago quit listening.

They remembered to children who took loans they could never
pay back on pickup trucks. These were children who grew up
under the floodlights that attracted moths, june bugs, and fish-
flies at the Dairy Queen just off the main streets of small towns
with names like Dent, Durkel, Deadwood, Badger, Armistice,
and Hope. And who in the winter went to the Thursday night
hockey games played by their teams who were always hopelessly
outmatched by their rivals from the rich suburbs of Minneapolis:
Edina, Minnetonka, and St. Louis Park.

But there were places where their memory could not go. When this happened they smoothed over the gaps and jumps of what life was like before they got there. They couldn't remember what the land looked like before it was logged the very first time. They couldn't let themselves guess. These memories had no place next to the kitchen tables and they couldn't be spoken over bowls of peeled potatoes still steaming into the damp kitchen light. Conversations about before their arrival, about who had lived there before were never given audience when fathers and sons squinted together under the belly of the tractor tightening the crank shaft or securing a cowling with bailing wire so the dirt that was knifed up wouldn't cake in the gears.

When they padded the bottom of the pickup truck with hay and then placed the crated eggs on top so they wouldn't break down the rutted roads, the talk and remembering was always about last year's hay, or this batch of eggs. During the slow ride to town the talk shifted between the here and now and the not so here and now; about the hen that strutted the yard in front of the barn protecting what she thought were her eggs but were only a few pebbles or rocks that had been loosened from the packed dirt by boots or the hooves of the cows. It didn't go much further than before the crossing-over, because their memory wasn't made for that, couldn't contain who had lived and walked before, and who was beginning to emerge again, to speak again.

So they stitched and sewed, smoothing over the spaces that to them appeared as silences, though that was a sentiment far from the truth. What they could remember was how the boats pitched and sloughed through the waves and how it was dark down in the third-class compartments that were wet and smelled of urine and mildew. If it had been a freight then the memories were of whatever the boat had held before them. Sometimes it was coal, and the passengers scrubbed for weeks to get rid of the smudges that had worked under their skin from chaffing against the metal walls. Some of the dirt never went away. Other times the cargo had been potatoes or beets and the conversation was less rueful about the washing because the great-great-grandparents were never able to enjoy those foods again. The smell never washed out and there had been too many rats. The cattle freight spoke of rotting hay and the sloshing of urine and shit, because the crew knew that they would still have boarders even if it was rotten and dark.

These conversations could be accommodated because when the mother peeled potatoes, they were reminded because the potatoes were right there, safely being disassembled in the family's own kitchen. They were reminded of these modern stories when the father hosed out the cattle trailer because it was new and because there was a loan that would always be newer than the trailer. The father would remember only as far back as the crossing because if he remembered further back he would be forced to go back even before the tractor and its use. His son was there, hosing, wishing he wasn't. The father's conversation found no purchase with his son, and as soon as the last of the manure left the trailer the boy went to shoot mourning doves with his BB gun or to go with his friends to the bridge where they dared each other to jump off into the river.

There were memories longer and deeper than these that touched the land, especially when the snow got deep or the drought brought not only heat but also wind. The topsoil was lifted off and it looked so easy, it left so readily while the farmer just watched it go into the wind. When he looked windward he saw that the horizon was hazy and the sun was blood red because of all the dirt in the sky that had been stolen by the winds from everyone's fields. When this happened the farmer thought back and counted how many times this had happened to him, or his uncle, or his father. He kept searching for a time when the soil stayed neat and the rows were crusty and straight, glistening with just the right mixture of loam, sand, and clay so that there was neither too much water nor too little and it stayed topside neither too briefly nor too long. The farmer would have to think back behind the farms to the logging days, but then the barges broke or the band on the saw melted from the heat. While out logging in the bush there had been the times when the wind blew from the wrong side just when the last wedge had been cut from the trunk. As the tree fell the other men couldn't hear the sound of its fall, so the warnings didn't help, the frantic waves and yells that were shouted from a distance did little good. They fell on the unlucky ones, splitting bone and lopping off arms. The blood spilled onto the floor of pine needles thicker than any of their memories and seeped through.

On a Thursday night of rememberings, forgettings, and hand jobs under blankets on the plastic seats at local hockey games, a car was driving north and west from Wisconsin. The car had no story to tell of sex that had been gotten after conquering the high school's cutest cheerleader. It spoke of no nights out shining deer during the summer. It had never had children begging to ride on the hood, their sticky hands plastered with the remnants of Push-Ups or Mr. Freezees. It had never had teenagers spilling beer on the seats, worrying if their parents would smell it. It had never drag raced other cars down the many straight side streets in Sheboygan.

The brown Impala had been first purchased by an old woman named Myrtle Jacobsen who never used it to go to faraway places. She used it to drive from home to the grocery store and back, or to the hospital for her weekly checkups. She thought she was dying of cancer and she longed to go through the living agony of chemotherapy, but the doctors told her again and again that she didn't have cancer and that she was in good health.

The woman named Myrtle who first owned the brown car lived like that for eight years until one day she dropped dead while feeding her cat. The car was sold by her son who flew all the way from Oakland to tie up the loose ends of her meager estate. It was an estate that consisted of a small house in Sheboygan filled with pictures, a doll collection of no value, and a brown Chevy Impala. He really had to get back to Oakland so he sold the house to a Century 21 realtor and he sold the car to the first used-car dealer he saw on his drive back to the airport.

The used-car dealer, Bill Henderson, paid more than he should have for the car partly because the son from Oakland was greedy and partly because Mr. Henderson was thinking of the necklace this deal would buy for the nineteen-year-old with whom he was having an affair.

The nondescript car sat in Bill's lot for a year, until an Indian man and his shaggy-headed boy came looking for a car. Normally Bill Henderson would have waved them away, or showed them the most expensive car so they were cowed and wouldn't waste his time, or he would have feigned activity of great import. However, his mind was on other things, on secrets of his own, so he did not see the Indian until it was too late to assemble his defense, and then he saw that the Indian in fact had money in his pocket. The Indian had enough money because he sold Rubbermaid household products door-to-door. It was a job that usually didn't pay so well, but the Indian had the knack for finding women who really wanted nothing more than a spotlessly clean floor. They wanted a clean floor and brooms with straight straws because their husbands were having affairs and there was nothing they could do about it. They couldn't leave their husbands because they couldn't market their skills as housewives. Their once-proud breasts and firm thighs — Scandinavian through and through — sagged, and their blue eyes were clouded from advancing age. They wanted to spite their husbands with toilet bowls that sparkled a dewy white, like ivory. They wanted to caress the linoleum with firm sponge mops and smooth the counters with unfrayed dish towels, as they imagined their husbands caressing and touching younger women with firm breasts that their husbands oohed over and likened to chamois or silk, neither of which they had ever seen. The wives who hated their own wrinkles and stretch marks somehow loved their husbands. Their love was coupled with spite, so they wanted to scour frying pans thick with crusted grease, just as their husbands devoured the inner thighs of other women so white and smooth that they spent their money just to get to the tight, wet, forgiving sex, flesh that they had purchased with their treats of movies, rings, and flowers.

It was because of this that the Indian and his small boy had enough money to buy the brown Impala. They didn't have to pay as much as they might have, considering the age of the car and the race of the used-car dealer. But Bill Henderson's mind wasn't on the price of the car. He had found out that his wife was having an affair too, with the father of the nineteen-year-old girl he was fucking in the back seats of all the cars he owned. The brown

Impala that had stood at the end of the lot was the sole exception. Surprisingly, given its obscure location under the branches
of a leaning oak tree and its expansive back seat, they had never
used its seats for anything. Bill used subcompacts and compacts,
working his way across the lot, but he had never reached the
Impala. Bill Henderson got a kick out of fucking in cars during
the A.M. and test-driving them with prospective buyers during
the P.M., but the Impala was a decidedly unappealing car. So the
Indian with his three-year-old boy bought the car with very little
interesting history, got in, inserted the key, turned the motor
over, and pulled out and away.

Once out of the lot, they didn't go back to an apartment to
gather belongings. They didn't stop at a Perkins or a Country
Kitchen to have a nice waffle breakfast. They didn't drop by anyone's house to say good-bye over three or four cups of good coffee
with lots of condensed milk and sugar. The Indian got behind the
wheel and his little boy sat in the passenger seat and stared out
the window as the low buildings and cement sidewalks ended and
the fields began.

At first the car was cold, but the heater was good so the car
became warm and the frost on the windows started to disappear.
The little boy, impatient for his view, scraped off a patch of frost
from his window and stuck his fingers and the ice shavings in his
mouth. The fields rolled on and then stopped every few miles
when the maple and oak forests closed in on the sides of the highway. These soon gave way to pine and rolling hills as the brown
Impala passed Black River Falls and Tomah, where the old
Indian boarding school had been. The man drove past it and he
never knew of its history or even its existence, curtained as it was
from the road by sloping ditches and windbreaks of large blue
spruce.

The man and the boy stopped in Superior, Wisconsin, where
they ate in a small diner. There were only a few people eating;
it was after dinner hours and there was a single waitress serv-
ing. She carried a frown, her mind on how to avoid the glances of
the short-order cook who had a missing tooth, half a growth of
beard, and nice wrinkled eyes. Anyone else might have liked
those eyes, but she couldn't appreciate them. They were too soft,

perhaps they could see too much. She wanted a man with hard eyes. A man with steel blue eyes. Outside the temperature began to drop and snow started down in lazy circles, lightly covering the dirty gray sidewalks as the man sat with his boy and deliberated only a little. The man ordered for himself and his boy, while the child took no notice of what was going on around him. He never asked where they were going or even why. He preferred instead to play with the crayons left for him on the table. As the waitress took their order she was aware of her left hand, with its empty ring finger. She wondered as the man ordered the egg skillet and black coffee and as he ordered pancakes for his boy. She wondered why no one courted her. Why no one brought her home at four in the morning, begging her to let him come upstairs so she could smile demurely and swing her backside, just a little, as she ascended the stairs alone, in full confidence that they would make love in the future, and that it would be so good that she would cry. She wondered as the boy drew on his place mat why it was that no one got her flowers in the middle of the winter, the petals just a little brown from the frost. She would have liked that. Flowers in the winter. Flowers in the wintertime, even slightly browned ones would have spoken of devotion. Devotion from a steel blue-eyed man would have been priceless to her.

That was why after the Indians left she gave the short-order cook a smile that was only a little like defeat. It was like this that she went home with him and wondered at his softness and his hands that patched her and shored up her sides. No one would have thought that hands used to caressing frozen hamburger patties and hash browns could show her how low she hung and lift her up, just a little bit, enough to know that it was better than nothing. It made her cry, but just a little bit.

It was like this that the Indian and his boy crossed into Minnesota, leaving nothing behind. The apartment they had lived in was almost empty. There were no family heirlooms to put in storage, or to wrap in newspaper and pack into boxes, to carefully fit in a trunk. There was no furniture to sell at a rummage sale or to give to friends in a fit of charity. The apartment itself was situated above a Woolworth five-and-dime store. It used to be storage space for the Woolworth's but the heyday of five-and-dimes was long over and the owner needed the rent money just to float his store. The apartment wasn't decorated. The very idea of hanging pictures or putting up curtains seemed to defy what the apartment was about. It was about temporary things; a halfway place between jobs, wives, husbands, or the streets and jail. It was about peeling paint that no one wanted to fix and that some even liked that way. To the Indian it was about another home that wasn't really, and another job that was. So he left with his son, taking with him the only memory that he dared let pin him down. His son wasn't a link or an arrow that he'd fashioned. His son was a weight that would hold him under the water. His son would be the one who held his hand as the snow drifted into his mouth while he drowned. His son was the one who showed him exactly who he was, which served to remind him of what he was not.

In most men this would serve to instill a hatred of the boy. The violent aggressions that the boy's living generated would have been taken out on him. To this Indian, though, it was different. He didn't hate his son. This is not to say that he loved him either — the boy's mother had been a woman who worked in the Woolworth's below the apartment and they had fucked exactly five times before they both lost interest. Nine months later she dropped the baby boy off at the apartment and left without a word. The man could see her through the window as she got into a light blue pickup truck, a truck the color of leaving.

He couldn't hate the boy, just as he couldn't hate the apartment because it was just a temporary stage, between lives. The boy, too, was just a place devoid of pictures and curtains. He was merely a time between leavings and arrivals. The man had never met his own father, had never been told of the funny things his father had done when he was a young man. He had never been hit by his father or held on his lap. He couldn't hate his father either.

In this absence of feeling he drove west through the snow that now was driving down in gusts and blanketing the roads, the ditches, and the fields. He bent his head close to the windshield and tried to find the yellow lines in the middle of the road. The map said that the highway would go straight through the middle of the reservation. He had never been there, the reser-

vation his father was from. His mother admitted she wasn't
exactly sure who his father was, but she had narrowed it down
to two men. They were identical twins, she had said. She had
had sex with both of them the same night in the same car. What
she didn't tell her son was that once she had passed out, the
twins had stolen the car and she had never seen them again. She
felt that it really didn't matter. She never exhibited any need or
desire to go find them, those two opposites; one quiet, one full of
stories and jokes. Regardless of their differences, she had said,
they were both good in the sack. That had been the end of it for
her. She also said that at the time they had been working in the
steel mills in Sheboygan, Wisconsin, where she met them at a
bar. As he drove, he kept hold of these absences of memory, held
them at a distance, and pulled them close; it really didn't matter
which, because he had nothing to know. But he wondered
whether his father would have laughed and joked, whether he
had enough confidence so that upon making a mistake he would
simply laugh, or if he held his coffee cup in both hands or
between a single finger and a thumb. Whether he whistled in the
morning.

It was with rememberings like these that the Indian man and
his boy drove west. The brown Impala split the snow and it
swirled even thicker around the car and across the road. The boy
was asleep on the seat, wrapped in an old quilt that the father
had purchased at a rummage sale. No kind grandmother had
sewn it for the boy out of love or loneliness. None of his aunts,
sitting around smoking Benson & Hedges menthols, drinking coffee, had sewn it for his birthday. It was a discard thrown away at
a rummage sale after all the children had grown and gone to college on the East Coast. It was a rag with all of the memories
laundered out.

The car slowed to twenty miles an hour and crawled past the
sign announcing the reservation boundary without even a pause
or a sigh of recognition. The sign, like any state line, marked no
change at all, marked changes that couldn't be seen with the eye.
So the sign went unnoticed by the Indian and his boy just as they
went unnoticed by the sign and the pines that grew close to the
road. They didn't notice the snow getting deeper and deeper,

trapping the car. The Impala carried a cache of nonmemories in a place where every tree, ditch, gully, river, lake, house, field, and person was remembered.

The car hit some ice the grader had missed and was swept smoothly into the ditch. It slid while the father wondered at the smoothness of the ride and his inability to steer. It hit a power box. The boy stayed on the seat but the man hit his head against the steering wheel. He slipped sideways and under the steering wheel and lay bunched down by the gas pedal and the brake, knocked out cold.

It went unnoticed like this: a brown Chevy Impala sat in the ditch with a sleeping boy and an unconscious father. The snow kept on getting deeper, piling around the car and the temperature dropped lower and lower. There was no sound but the sound of the wind prying at the windows and door handles, creeping under the hood and through the floor. Even that was muted by the glass and metal surrounding them. It was late and most people nursed cups of coffee or tea made with a generous amount of sugar in the comfort of their own homes. Most people sat in their kitchens and told stories about the last time it had snowed so much and so hard, which was close to twenty years ago this coming April.

The father managed to rouse himself. He crawled out from the nest on the floor and the first thing he noticed was that the window on the passenger's side had been smashed in, something he didn't remember from before. The second thing he noticed was that the bundle of quilt and little boy that was his, was gone. The seat next to him was bare and the back seat, too, was empty. His eyes searched the ditch and along the road because he had heard of people being thrown from cars when they crashed. He found nothing but snow and ice. He looked for tracks leading away from the car, and they were there — muffled dents in the blowing snow.

He kicked around in the drifts, scraped with his booted foot under the front bumper and leaned on the grill, breathing in the wet snow.

The man knew that this was the end. It was the end of a long string of apartments where the little boy slept on the couch, or under the kitchen table. This was the end of more than four years of nonmemories and secondhand clothes.

This end was also the beginning of more than Donovan could ever have imagined. When the headlights of a westbound truck came into view, the man opened his door, pushed the snow out of the way, and staggered onto the highway. The truck slowed and the Indian man got in. The truck started up again and traveled west toward Grand Forks. In its turn it would travel through many small towns and larger cities whose names were too numerous and full of people alive and warm to be said out loud.

Duke and Ellis

The November night we found young Donovan, the snow dropped hard and drifted tight around the reservation. It snows different on the rez than it does off. Maybe it's our cars: all broken down, held together with duct tape. Or maybe it's our houses, shacks, and tract housing, like out at Poverty. It fell hard and drifted tight. The flakes started down like the scraps of paper Ellis and me covered our bingo cards with, lighting over numbers and trees, blank spaces and wrecked-out cars, numbers we didn't have, empty fields. The more snow that fell the fewer the possibilities. Though we didn't know where it would land we knew one thing for sure: the coverings and flutter would never stay put like they do on bingo cards, which we liked to keep clean and square. Now with big casinos the bingo cards aren't cards anymore, they're newsprint. The dabbers soak through and it looks awful.

We've never used the dabbers they sell at the bingo hall. We didn't use the Tiddly-Winky red plastic chips either.

The night we found Donovan half-frozen, wrapped in a beat-up quilt, we had packed up our house and drove it into town from where we parked it at Poverty. Our house had a V-8, four wheels, maroon paint, rust, half a muffler, and everything we claimed as our own in the world. We live in our car; we talk there, eat, smoke, fuck, tell dirty jokes, smile, and lie. The Catalina is a good eleven feet long and wide enough to stretch out full on the seats.

We can squeeze everybody who needs to be in with just enough extra room to pass a bottle or a smoke.

We could live in one of the cardboard excuses for a house at Poverty. They weren't even five years old by the time we drove from Sheboygan and parked down at the end of Poverty. Not even five years old and already two houses had burnt down and another split in two during a storm.

The other houses just grew old faster than we did and looked worse. There's only so many times you can call the RTC about broken windows, drains that don't drain, roofs that were shingled without tar paper under the shingles, and foundations laid over roots above the frost line so they buckle and heave in the spring and you feel like you're living right over a fault line. Only so many times you can use duct tape to fix the problem yourself unless it's an election year and they send a whole crew with orange vests on just to caulk a bead around the shower surround. Then it's a ceremony, like when Poverty was first built.

Back in the bush, where basswood and maple used to shoulder each other for a view of the lake, is where they decided to build Poverty in '65. Tucked away in a backwater bay near where the river whines into the lake, they poured kerosene on the two tar-paper shacks that leaned into the jack pine, and built the first housing tract on the reservation. No one remembers this except Jeannette, but the first house, before Poverty and even before the tar-paper shacks, was built by us, Ellis and me. It had sighed back into the ground years before, a rectangular lump in the weak soil. The tribal chairman was there when they opened Poverty up. So was the assistant secretary of the interior. He was there smiling into the sun, shaking hands to plug for Johnson's War on Poverty.

So we named it Poverty and people moved in for the novelty that wore off as fast as the paint did. They moved out as quick as the cheap frames squeaked on the shifting foundations and a new batch moved in just as the pipes burst in the first winter.

Poverty was a joke. So Ellis and I parked our car there, used Jeannette's bathroom, and never slept under one of those leaky roofs.

We built the first house where Poverty is now; me, Ellis, and

Jeannette. That lump in the ground they bulldozed used to be made of logs, reservation pine we knocked to the ground while working for the logging company after we stole Jeannette from Iowa. Even though it was rez pine that we sweated over, nickled down, and helped skid out to the camps, even though it was technically our pine, we had to steal it log by log from the lumber company until we could build our shack.

At that time, before Poverty, there was a low rise where the river emptied into the lake, halfway between the logging camp and town. There were all kinds of trees; maple and basswood back from the lake, white and red pine up next to shore. Even though the path from the camp ran right by where we were building with contraband lumber we weren't too worried about being caught. It was 1923 and, since booze was illegal, no one was worrying about a few trees that fell off the skidder. It was hard to turn it around, the long wooden runners yoked to stubborn and ill-treated Clydesdales or oxen. No one looked back. When we dropped trees next to shore and came back with fewer than the others, they thought it was because we were Indians, fifteen years old and lazy.

We dragged them through the snow in the winter and floated them along the shore in the summer so that within a year we moved from the lean-to we were huddled in to our cabin. Jeannette was pregnant.

Our cabin. *Our* home. It was drafty so we plugged the cracks with moss. The roof only sloped a little so the water worked its way inside. The floor was dirt and the cold ate our feet away, but it was ours, and Jeannette was fourteen years old and pregnant.

Every day we got up and walked with our axes to where we were logging. Every day early we left her as she threw up and then got dressed to check the snares for rabbits. It's not like today when you can get in your car and be there. From where we sweated down the trees miles away we'd stop, huffing steam into the air and ask ourselves: Is she okay? Has she eaten? We leaned on our axes or sat on stumps and wondered as we gnawed on our frozen camp bread with cramped fingers. We couldn't be there, couldn't walk the snare line with her, or help her carry the commodities back from town.

We warned her not to go to town for them because people would see her. The priest would take her and sell her to those white women from Iowa again.

By the time spring rolled around she was too big to make the walk from town. There wasn't any snow, so we couldn't set snares. Jeannette was too weak to sugar by herself, and all the sugar maples around the lake had been cut down anyway. There was no way to get our commodities because Ellis and I had to fill a quota of trees every day. Instead, we stole what food we could from the camp. We stole what we could, but it was never enough. We could never steal enough flour, lard, and bacon to feed the four of us. There was only so much that could go unnoticed. We set snares for deer, but they were set too high, or too low, or in the wrong place, and we went hungry. And hungrier. Now even when we were with Jeannette we worried about her. She fainted all the time, sweated when it was cold, and said she could feel the baby kicking her out of anger.

We came back from the bush one night and she was asleep.

We shook her.

"Jeannette. Jeannette."

Ellis used her name to try and wake her up. She only moaned and tried to roll over on the spruce boughs we had laid out for her on the floor. She was too far along to do anything more than twist from side to side, swearing at us to leave her alone.

We didn't know what to do. So the next day when we went out in the bush to cut, Ellis gave me his axe, took off his boots, and started to run to town. It was March and warm. The ice was creeping away from the lake edge. There was no snow. The ground was crisp with dead grass and leaves.

Jeannette was seven months pregnant with Ellis's child, or my child. I was using an axe to cut down 200-year-old pine and Ellis was running the ten miles to town barefoot so Jeannette wouldn't die or lose the child.

I stopped chopping after the first three trees and sharpened my axe. I took the rasp from my belt and filed the edge. My heart was slowing, the woods sounds coming slowly back. The sun was out and I was sweating through my shirt. I could feel the shudder of trees falling far away. I listened and thought I could hear the sound of Ellis's feet thumping down the path to town.

By midday I'd dropped twenty trees and I stopped again to chew on a stale piece of camp bread I'd stuck in my coat pocket. The others had moved off. I could barely feel the thump of trees hitting the ground. There wasn't any wind and the sweat dripped along my neck where it attracted blackflies and mosquitoes, out of place in March. Ellis had probably reached town a couple of hours ago. We didn't know where to go in town for help. All of the other Indians were as bad off as us. The white people — the agent, priest, bar owner, lumber wholesaler, railroad men, and surveyors — had no reason to care, nothing in it for them.

I closed my eyes and tried to imagine what it would look like if time went by a lot faster. If I stood on high ground and could see the trees being logged off in fast motion. If I looked toward our cabin and the trees fell away like dominoes I could see Jeannette. See if she woke up, if she lost the baby, or died. If I could just know something then it would be all right. I could cry or laugh or run. So I imagined hard, tried to melt the trees away, push the brush away and find the cabin. I couldn't. They kept springing up thicker, closer together. The bark kept on coming into focus, the scaly cracked-mud look of red-pine bark.

I chewed the bread and opened my eyes. Everything was the same. The downed trees and the trampled brush spread away from where I sat on a stump. The bugs still battered their way to where they haloed my sweaty head. My toes curled and uncurled in my boots, my fingers flexed and unflexed. I could hear the river spill over the dam miles away.

Ellis came back in the afternoon right after I'd crossed the river and walked the path down to the lake. His feet were swollen and cut, but his breathing was regular as he led the priest and the doctor into our cabin.

I leaned my axe against the cabin wall by the door and touched Ellis on the arm as he let them in. I held him there with the pressure of my fingers so he would look at me, so I could read there what he did or said to get them to help us. He gave me a quick look and shouldered past me into where they were kneeling by Jeannette. Ellis and I stood over them to the side, letting the sun light up the interior so the doctor could see what he was doing.

Jeannette was still asleep. She moved and moaned a little as the doctor listened to her heart, took her temperature, and put his ear to her rounded stomach, catching the stutter of the little baby's heart.

The priest stood next to us.

"How far along?" he asked.

"Seven," we said, not taking our eyes off Jeannette.

"Who's the father," he asked.

"We are," we said.

He laughed.

"You both can't be the father," he chuckled. "Which one, really?"

We turned to look at him.

"Both," we said.

Maybe it was our look, the way we didn't smile or look down, toeing dust. He saw something in our identical eyes, our broad shoulders. We were only fifteen but we were already six feet tall and strong from chopping and sawing.

We looked back at Jeannette. The doctor was giving her a shot of something in her arm. He stood up and wiped his hands with a white kerchief.

"She won't die," he said. "She won't lose her baby either. But she has to eat."

"The agent will bring food tomorrow," the priest said. "He promised me."

The doctor packed his bag carefully and walked gingerly out of the cabin, followed by the priest.

We bent close and knelt, finally, where Jeannette slept soundly.

The agent came with a wagon the next day with three months of commodities: flour, lard, sugar, bacon, salt, yeast, raisins. Jeannette grew stronger. Her fever broke within a week and Ellis and I went back to cutting, letting our axes bite into something we could see and touch, knowing the trees were there and real.

When Jeannette gave birth to a little boy she was strong

enough to do it with only me and Ellis to help. It was summer full, and the water in the lake was warm and calm. We figured the hard part was over. Two weeks after the baby was born the agent and the priest showed up in a wagon.

Jeannette sat on the ground in front of the cabin nursing the baby. Ellis and I were coming around the house with fresh spruce boughs for the floor.

"Are they bringing more food?" I asked Ellis.

He shrugged and dropped the spruce next to the front door and stuck his hatchet in his belt.

"Are you ready?" asked the priest.

"Ready for what?" I asked, looking at Ellis and Jeannette. Ellis ignored me and stood in front of her.

"Ready for what?" I repeated.

The priest was looking at Jeannette and the baby. The agent had his hands on his hips and looked from Ellis to me and back.

"That's the agreement," said the priest.

We didn't move.

"That's the deal," he said, trying to use smaller words.

"No deal," said Ellis.

I moved to the side next to Jeannette. She was glaring from under her hair, the baby sucking contentedly at her tit.

"We gave you the food, Ellis," said the agent. He shifted his weight onto one leg.

"No deal," said Ellis. "We'll give the food back."

"You ate it," said the agent, his voice rising, leaning into his words. Sweat dripped off his nose.

"We'll give up our next three months of food," said Ellis.

"But you agreed," the priest said earnestly. "You agreed," he said again, looking at the agent nervously, then back to Ellis.

"The baby's going to be Christian," said the priest.

And finally I understood; Ellis had agreed to give up the baby to the church for three months of food. Jeannette jumped up and moved toward the cabin.

"You ain't getting him," she hissed. You come here? You come here?

She was screaming and backing toward the cabin.

In a blur, the priest ran past Ellis and up to Jeannette. He grabbed her arm. She tried to jerk away from him, shielding the boy with her shoulders.

Ellis started toward him to tear the priest away from Jeannette, but the agent grabbed and held him from behind. Ellis was stronger but the agent was big and fat.

I stood between the two struggles looking back and forth until I saw the agent reaching for his gun. I took three steps and punched him as hard as I could at the base of his skull. His head snapped forward and his grip loosened on Ellis. I turned and ran toward the priest.

I was only three steps away, maybe four. So close. He jerked on Jeannette's arm again and she lost her grip on our baby, swaddled in the scraps of one of my flannel shirts.

Jeannette tried to grab for him but the priest still held her arms. The baby fell.

He was only two weeks old, so soft; his skull as tender as a turtle's egg. The dirt was hard-packed with rocks and wood chips.

I could've caught him if I'd moved faster, been just a little bit smarter.

But his head hit the ground. There wasn't any sound, though you'd think you'd hear something, some small rip, a crushing sound. But there was nothing. His fat little legs twitched. He tried to cry and then lay still, the scuffle dust settling on his fresh skin.

The priest let go of Jeannette and stumbled back, falling into a sitting position, his arms flopped loosely on his legs like he was begging for something.

Ellis screamed and pushed the agent away from him. He pulled the hatchet from his belt. Before I had time to call out he raised it up and buried it just above the agent's collarbone, deep into his neck. His head snapped back and blood spurted from his neck in a long arc. He fell on the ground and rolled and rolled. He gurgled and splashed around in his own blood, his arms lifting and smashing down, the fat of his stomach jiggling, his heels gouging the dirt. Then he quit moving too.

The priest just sat there. Ellis stood over the agent while he coughed and spat. I looked over at Jeannette. She was cradling our dead baby.

I kicked the priest.

"Run," I said.

He looked up at me, dazed.

"Run, you fucker!"

He jumped to his feet and took off, his robes flapping, his black-shoed feet spitting up dust as he disappeared in the trees along the lake.

I took the baby from Jeannette and wrapped him in my shirt. There was no weight to him at all as I set him in the darkened cabin.

That night, after burying our baby by the lake, we threw the agent in the wagon and unhitched the horse. We took the agent's gun and rode northeast along the lake until we hit the rail line and jumped a train heading to Superior, then Ashland and south to Sheboygan.

We didn't see Jeannette or our lake for thirty years. We didn't know that she had burned the cabin after we left, that they put her in jail so she'd tell them where we went. She never did, and we vowed never to live in a house again, never to give anything a hold over us, ever.

The night we found Donovan we up and drove our car to the parking lot of the community hall, which doubled as a bingo hall on Thursdays. This was 1968, years and years before they started building casinos, before high-stakes blackjack and video poker. The community center was a cinder-blocked, thinly-insulated, cheap-paneled, linoleum-tiled, one-room building. But the air was warm, heated with space heaters every few yards, thick with smoke and gossip, where jackets were tossed over plastic-backed chairs, where people slowly folded and unfolded tattered stories and new jokes. We left our home in the parking lot and crunched our way through the few inches of new snow that had already fallen by seven o'clock. Clenching our arms and pushing our hands across our chests to opposite pockets, we tried to beat the cold from our jackets. We hit the toes of our boots against the wall, but it was too cold for the snow to stick.

Opening the doors with numb hands, we went inside to gamble our government checks. We nodded our way past the others

who were halfway through their first card. We squeaked down
into two chairs in the back. Shifting our weight as much as we
could, we made the plastic seats sing out against the metal.

A couple of heads turned.

"Excuse me," I said loudly. A couple more heads turned.

Ellis and I began to take off our coats. The cold, stiff cloth
snapped loudly in the hush. Ellis pushed his chair back to work
on loosening his boots. His chair screamed across the linoleum.

No one said anything but I could almost hear all the bingo
players sigh in exasperation. Jeannette used to bingo with us
when she lived in town at the old-age home. She went into the
home just before she turned sixty. She only lived there a couple of
years. She says that Celia put her in. Celia says that Jeannette
wanted to go on her own. We think that it was too much for Jeannette to live at Poverty, to live in the tract housing slammed down
over the cabin we built when we brought her back from Iowa. It
was too much because the three of us used to live there and it was
too much for her to live with Celia when Ellis and I were away. I
say this because she moved back from retirement housing within a
year of our return and just months after Celia got pregnant. She
quit playing bingo with us and would lock her door at the old-age
home when we came by. She said we embarrassed her.

Really it was because she never ever in her life bingoed. She
was too impatient, even at sixty.

"B 3," she'd hiss. "B 3, god damn it!"

The caller drew out the ball.

"B 12," he said, glaring at her.

"Jesus," she said, snapping a Salem from her beaded cigarette
case.

"Keep it down," I said. "We're trying to win some money
here."

"You're the loud one," she said sideways, trying to keep her
eyes on the caller.

"If you think I'm loud here you should hear my bed springs
groan."

Ellis snickered.

"You're too broke to even have a bed," she said. "You sleep in
your car."

"That's true," I had to admit. "But that's only because I wore 'em out."

I was winning.

"Don't make me laugh," she said, frowning around her cigarette. "The only thing that's wore out is the joke you keep hid in your pants."

I was calm, as I leaned back in my chair.

"Well," I drawled, "you'd know. You're the one that did the wearing."

"That's it!" she raged, pushing her chair back. "I ain't ever playing bingo with you again."

She got up, whisked her purse off the table, and blew out the door.

She kept her promise. So the night we found Donovan we settled down in our chairs without her while the wind groaned around the building. Jeannette fretted over her pregnant daughter back at Poverty, and we laid our cards out.

The hum of the space heaters mixed with the rattle of the numbered Ping-Pong balls that tossed around and around in the plastic bowl. The coffeepot ticked away in the corner. No one talked, thinking of bingo, or of snow.

But the same wind that brought the snow and Donovan carried our luck away so that all we had left after our last card were the bits of paper we used. We tried to blot out the numbers but they showed through too much sometimes, not enough other times, and always in the wrong place.

We shouldered on our coats and stumbled through the snow out to the Catalina. Ellis was driving. He hunched himself around the wheel and squinted through the bottom of the windshield as we pulled out of the parking lot.

When enough snow blew off the windshield and we realized just how hard it was coming down, we were too far from the bingo hall to turn around. The snow drifted across the highway in long snaking lines and blew into the ditches on either side so we didn't know where the road ended and the woods began. Ellis was driving and he knew better than to stare into the snow. He knew he would be hypnotized by the flakes streaking toward the windshield so he searched for the white line on the shoulder, keeping his eyes away from the light. The ice lifted off the asphalt and into the air so it seemed the whole car was being driven clear into the white sky. Ellis drove with the right wheels in the softer snow of the ditch so we kept straight on our path. We had to go slow; the wind was tearing at the car, forcing its fingers into the cracks of the door, into the seam where the windshield meets the hood, through the door handles. Even with the heaters on, its breath mixed with ours and drove us further into our coats and boots, which we had lifted from the winter giveaway at St. Mary's in late October. It pushed us further down in our seats and Ellis looked out from under his eyebrows just enough to see the white stretch in front of the headlights and his ears stuck up just enough above the turned-up collar of his coat so he could hear, faintly, the crunch of thicker snow under the right tires forcing a line in the powdered shoulder of the ditch.

It was like this, picking our way slowly toward Poverty, that we almost wrecked our home on the car parked along the side of the highway. The front end was buried in the deep drifts that completely covered the front bumper and crept up across the hood. It sloped into the ditch almost touching the tree line. The black bark was chipping off the jack pine in the wind and their cones were clenched tight, frozen solid. Even in the summer, in the heat of July, jack pinecones don't open. Spruce, red pine, and white pine will open for anyone and anything. When they sprout they grow tall, straight up. Jack pine are never like that. It takes a fire to open them, to curl back the flaps on the cone, so the trees can lay their seed. Sometimes the new trees grow straight, other times they grow crooked and wobbly. I've even seen them grow straight down with the roots sticking up in the air. You can never tell until they've grown.

Like the jack pine the car was held tight. It could have sprouted anything, growing in any direction. Stalled-out cars aren't strange, especially on the reservation, but there was something about the way the snow held and covered it that made me wonder. It was as if the snow and ice were trying to hide something, push it away until it was too late; too late to save anything inside or to track where it came from. Already the snow was over the tires. It would have been buried in another hour and the banks would have crawled past the door handles, then over the windows, the roof, and on, and on. The snow did keep on blowing over and down and piled deep around us until morning, but we found the car in time.

For a while, Ellis and I just sat there and stared at our find. We didn't get out; we just ate the wind as it tore around our car. Ellis stared ahead and I glanced around, first at the car and then into the sky and back again. Finally I jerked myself awake and pulled myself from the Catalina in a tumble, knee-deep in snow. There was someone in the car.

Ellis sat in the driver's seat and kept the engine of our home running as I fought my way over to the cocoon that could have held anything. It was tightly wrapped and it could have been a present sitting there, waiting to be claimed. It might have been an empty shell filled to the top with birch chalk, dust, and snow. A winning bingo card. Or bones and spirits could have come spilling from the doors. I didn't know, and that was my protection. I pulled on the door handle glazed with ice, but the door didn't open. It was frozen shut from the snow that edged in the cracks and froze when it met the heat inside. The ice caked the whole door, and it even attached itself underneath the handle, latching onto the paint.

I pulled my hand from the handle and the skin ripped from the pads of my fingers. My hand had frozen to the ice and my fingers were bloody and raw, left bare in the whip of the wind. I could feel them bleeding down past my jacket cuffs and I winced as I cupped them against the window, trying to peer inside. Ice froze across the plate glass and distorted everything I saw. It was like the glass they put in public bathroom windows, bubbled and waved, so all you see is vague shapes, like you're underwater, or real drunk. I breathed against the glass and rubbed away the ice with my clothed elbow but I didn't see the future in that stalled-out car.

What I did see was a jumble of rags in the front seat. They were quilts worn and wrapped into tatters of cloth. I hurried. The cold swept through the bottom of my coat and the open tops of my boots were filled with snow, numbing my shins where my sockless legs met the cuffs of my pants, which were too high to shut out the snow.

I leaned back and hit the window with my elbow. The window was so slick it sent me spinning away. I smashed again with my elbow; my arm went numb. Looking in again I thought I saw a small form on the front seat, curled deep into the rags. Strips of cloth were wrapped around a small head tucked away from where the wind crept in the door.

I ran back through the ridges of snow to the Catalina and opened the back door. I looked to where Ellis sat in the front seat. He was hunched over and the green lights from the dashboard lit up his face. He didn't even turn his head as the ice blew in through the open door as I searched around in the mess for the tire iron.

"Leave it be, Duke." I glanced up as my hand wrapped around the cold iron.

"Leave him in the car; let's go."

He guessed I found someone and he knew whoever it was would slip away if we left him there. His dreams would get fuzzier and he would die.

I lifted the iron out of the back seat and slammed the door, running back to the car in the ditch. I could see the plates were out of state, and there wasn't enough mud or dirt caked on them for it to be from any reservation. They were yellow Wisconsin plates, the decal next to the fender read Henderson's Cars, Madison. It was an Impala and even though the wheels were almost buried to the top I could see that they were worn smooth, probably never changed.

The cold iron stung my fingers where the skin had been ripped off, the iced metal stuck to the blood that coated my palms. My cheeks were already numb. I hefted the metal above my head with both hands, almost tipping back in the snow. I was dizzy and my ears burned from the constant wind.

Once. Twice. The glass crinkled and dropped down, splashing onto the door, into the snow, and covering the blanketed form with flashing bangles glittering in the headlights. I threw the iron in the snow without thinking and cleared the glass from the opening with my forearm. I found the tire iron later in the spring, a rusted patch against the dead grass.

Now I only thought of reaching through the open window. My arms broke more of the glass from the edges of the door and I slid my hands under the small bundle in the front seat. I pulled it toward me across the space and it slid easily: there was no weight to it at all.

Even as I took it in my arms and saw that it was a child, it remained light. So much like the long lines in the snow that took the road into itself. I hugged the body close to my chest as I struggled for breath and the energy to move toward where Ellis sat waiting. The way the snow crept over the car made me think of a sinking ship as I waded through the deepening snow to the warmth of our car just a few yards away.

I unwrapped what turned out to be a small boy as Ellis put the Catalina into gear and edged around the abandoned car, moving us back to Poverty. I expected him to be frozen stiff, covered only in a small quilt, brown corduroy pants, and a Dallas Cowboys sweatshirt.

Once I turned the heat up and took off the ragged quilt I was shocked by the feel of his skin; he was so hot to the touch that I had to take my hands away. I lost the tip of my little finger to the cold because of that night. My hands were numb to everything, but when I touched the four-year-old boy's head and rubbed his hands in mine, I didn't warm him. I burned my own hands.

We pulled into Celia's.

Celia's house was at the end of Poverty. It was almost identical to the other four houses, almost and not exactly, because of us. Celia's house was different. It wasn't that the pipes froze, they froze in all the houses. Nor the water stains in the pressed cardboard paneled ceiling, they all had that too. Her house at the end of Poverty wasn't yellow, well, almost not yellow. The metal siding *used* to be painted yellow. A sick yellow like fever or poison. But when her mother Jeannette had moved in after running away from the nursing home, Jeannette demanded a new color. She came puffing up to the door, only minutes after Ellis and I decided to park our car next door for good. Strange as it was, it never felt like coincidence. She stepped up to the front door and her shoulders sagged.

"Can't live in no nursing home. My own daughter's gonna let me rot in some place where I don't belong. I'm as healthy as I ever was." Truth was, Celia was pregnant with Little. Jeannette had her bags in her hand and she was flushed from having walked the seven miles from the old-age center. She took one look at the peeling yellow paint and the weeds up to the front step and shook her head.

"And I can't live in no piss-yellow house neither." She walked in and put her bags in the empty room reserved for boxes and old newspapers, for empty cans and children that hadn't been born yet.

So the next day Ellis and I drove into town and went to RJ's Hardware store. We checked out the whole place and then when the clerk was busy we stole four cans of paint. We grabbed the gallon cans that were closest to the door and ran them out to where the Catalina was still running in the parking lot. It must have been a funny sight, two seventy-year-old men running, bent over four cans of paint. We were charging like we were the Minnesota Vikings, carrying the ball across the goal line in the last ten seconds of the fourth quarter.

We didn't notice the color until we were driving back to Poverty, cackling about the slow-eyed store clerk, and arguing over which one of us was Joe Namath. Three cans were purple. The label on the side said "Lilac." This wasn't so bad, but the last can was labeled "Orange Flame."

There was nothing we could do. We couldn't let the paint go, and Jeannette couldn't live in her faded-canary, sun-bleached construction-paper, piss-yellow house.

So we did what any sensible Indians would do. We started painting the front of the house from the top down.

We did it all in one night so Jeannette would have a nice surprise in the morning. We had been afraid that she would wake up while we were painting, so during dinner we slipped a shot or two of Southern Comfort into her iced tea. As we painted we could hear her snoring straight through the walls. By three A.M., we got about two feet from the bottom when we ran out of Lilac. We couldn't just leave the rest yellow so we slathered on the remaining can of Flame.

It was too dark to step back and appreciate our work so we crept back to our home, me in the front seat and Ellis in the back, and went to sleep.

I woke up just after sunrise and looked over at Jeannette and Celia's house just as the sun hit our masterpiece. I jumped and woke Ellis from the back seat. I saw the front of the house catch on fire as the mid-June sun rose.

We stumbled out and scratched at the crusted corners of our eyes. The house wasn't on fire, but the border of orange below was slapped on with uneven strokes. There hadn't been enough paint to cover the yellow. It looked like orange and yellow flames licking up the sides of the house. We squinted closer and saw Jeannette standing in her nightgown of pink flannel. She stood on the front step with her hands on her hips and shook her head.

She saw us across the way, next to our Pontiac.

"Jesus Christ."

We stood straighter and quit smiling.

"Will you look at this house? Just look at it." She swung her head back to the Lilac and Flame.

"Were you boys drinking last night? This looks more like one of those whorehouses in Minneapolis you go to. This ain't no respectable-looking house, even for the reservation."

She spat on the ground.

"First I run away from the nursing home to a piss-yellow house. I wake up the next morning and I'm living in a brothel."

But I know she liked it 'cause later on she got some lilac cuttings and put them in a Ball jar on the front windowsill. Probably just for a little bit of color. At the time all she did was step up, wipe off her bunny slippers before she went inside, and pull the door hard enough to skip over the last catch where the metal stripping had come up off the linoleum.

It was through that door that we carried Donovan. We nearly dropped him as Jeannette jumped up from the game of old maid she was playing by herself and rushed forward. We nearly dropped him. Our hands, numbed like they were, could barely juggle him from the car into the heat of the house.

"Watch out you fools," she snapped. "This ain't a bottle of whiskey."

We nodded. Jeannette had always been sharp. She knew a baby when she saw one.

We stood back as she laid him out on the kitchen table. I went over to the gas stove, and since it didn't have a pilot light I took out a blue-tip match and tried to strike it on the edge of the cast-iron inset of the front burner. My hands were frozen so hard I could barely hold the match between my two fingers. I struck once and completely missed. I tried again and skinned my knuckle on the ridge of metal right above the oven door. No blood came out, I just carved a white patch from my skin.

"Move over," Jeannette commanded. She pushed me away, lit the match with her thumbnail, and started the burner. She took a stick of commodity butter from the refrigerator and put it in a pan. She added sugar to it and set it on the stove until it dissolved into liquid. Then with a wooden spoon, she stirred and lifted a gob of it out and over to the little boy's mouth. He sucked it in. It was the first move he had made. His mouth worked as he swallowed it. Jeannette gave him another spoonful.

My cheeks were raw and puffy red as the heat from the house warmed them. I could move my fingers better, but the missing pads burned when I pressed them against the flesh of my palm. I put the coffeepot — still half full from breakfast — back on the burner. Jeannette had taken the melted butter off the stove and put it next to Donovan's head. He moved some more and Jeannette rubbed his hands and feet. He cried and this woke Celia. She came shuffling out of the back room in a T-shirt and a pair of cream-colored long johns. Her eyes opened wide when she saw what was happening. She hadn't been much more than a zombie since Stan and Pick had left for Vietnam but she moved to her mother's side fast when she heard that baby cry.

Ellis and I sipped coffee as they worked. Rubbing, washing, feeding, singing, and clothing his body, they stood over him. My face became warm and I began to feel dizzy. The coffee roiled in my stomach and my hands could barely hold my cup. The room spun and I figured it must have been from going cold-warm, warm-cold all night. I put the cup I was holding down while Celia and Jeannette worked over the child and Ellis stood over them. I had nothing to do. Ellis just watched, gradually moving closer until he stood directly behind Celia, towering over her in the lamplight. He put his hand on her shoulder and peered down at the little boy. There was nothing for me, nothing for me in that house. I walked to the door.

I grabbed the extension cord and the space heater from the wood box. No one moved and the lights went dim and flared again as I turned on the heater.

Opening the door I carried it out to the car, the red coils of wire glowed, marking my path red as I fought my way to the Catalina where I fell asleep alone under the wash of the snow piling flake by flake over the hood.

Jeannette

On my sixtieth birthday I want no more rhubarb. It was one of those wake-up-early days. One when you notice it's raining outside your window but it doesn't shut all the way so the wet air gets in your room. It was one of those pull-your-legs-out-from-under-the-covers mornings to find that you have no slippers for your feet. You used them to plug the crack in the other window the night before when the rain started. Your moccasins were sold at the last powwow so there would be real oranges to eat for a whole week. Breakfast, dinner, and supper, there were real, not-so-fresh, but oh-so-orange oranges to eat. Not in a can or on a picture but full of real juice and little pulpy capsules that burst just right when you sucked them from the rind.

The first time I ever tasted an orange was when I was a little girl and a white woman from Iowa gave one to me. Ever since, I wanted that little bit of sunshine that had been passed hand to hand across the United States only to reach me. All different colored hands just so I could use my thumbnail to tear off the thick peel. Right when I peeled the orange open I checked to see if I nicked or dented the fruit and I separated it carefully. I pulled it into sections like I was separating the only three one-dollar bills I had ever seen only to forget them in a skirt pocket that got washed, the bills nestling comfortably and damply together.

I sucked the sections and let the juice roll down my tongue while I closed my eyes. With my eyes closed I could ignore whose kitchen I sat in and who actually gave me that little bit of music on my tongue. With my eyes closed I didn't have to see the pile of dishes in the sink and the china balanced on the table covered in a white-and-red-checkered cloth, china that I was whipped over when I broke it.

After one whipping the hat-and-shoe ladies must have felt bad, must have felt guilty, because they gave me an orange. With my eyes closed, and my mouth full of that sweet orange, I sat and heard the grasshoppers rubbing their wings together in the field and heard the killdeer scream when the men came close to their nests in the meadows, where they tilled up to the edge of town. I sat and heard all of that as I sucked the sections until the clumps of pulp gave way and I emptied the skin until it was a dry sack that I chewed quickly and thoughtlessly because there was no flavor in it anymore.

That was the first orange I ate. But the whole bag of them that I traded my moccasins for I ate quickly, tearing them apart with no caution for juice or rind until I had jammed my mouth full and my fingernails hurt where the rind had worked its way into the flesh. I ate those with no patience because then I had Celia, my girl, and Duke and Ellis were gone working the steel mills in Sheboygan. I had my daughter and mothering sucked out all the gentleness I had saved for myself.

It rained hard and then soft and then just drizzled, frosting my window that usually doesn't have a view at all. However, with mist or light rain, if I squint hard I can pretend that it is the highest tower on Crazy Ludwig's castle in Germany. I saw a picture of it once. With a good mist and fog I can see that lake at the bottom of the valley, glittering in the sun. I read, there where I saw the picture, that the lake was made by slaves and that Ludwig was crazy as a nut. That could be, but he sure appreciated a nice view; the way the pine trees go right down to the edge of the lake, and the bridge that goes over the gorge looks so delicate and fragile even though it's made from solid stone. Huge windows that can look out to see these things, that can see swans arching their necks on the lake, are much better than my view without fog or rain. If it's frosted over I got a good view but if it's not then all I see are the sawed-off bodies of the black spruce trees, cropped because they got too close to the electrical wires that hung low overhead. Those, and the stubby whitewashed Catholic church across the street.

It was a morning with rememberings of oranges and castles and rain that cleared up too soon to expose my view of amputated trees. It was my birthday morning, and I knew that I couldn't stay in the old-age home. I was sixty. Sixty years old in a rainy room with a disappearing view and no slippers. It's true that I signed myself in, committed myself to bad food and a bad view. In less than a year with a bad view I knew I couldn't stay there anymore. I needed a little taste of kindness on my birthday. I wanted just a little bit of orange so I could go on with the business of being sixty.

Being sixty isn't like turning from nineteen to twenty. From nineteen to twenty there was nothing but an intake of air and a quick look around to see if anything'd changed. The only difference is that you hold your cigarette more loosely in your hand and your legs are crossed a little higher up. Your casual intake of smoke can be followed by draping your arm over your crossed legs so you can drop ash on the floor.

From nineteen to twenty you wear your skirt a little shorter and put on a darker shade of lipstick. You say "shit." You complain about your aching feet, but not too loudly. You speak about what you read in the papers and you can even shrug and laugh while the word "bullshit" rides on your laughter. When you laugh you pause before it comes and in its wake you let silence fall before you and you take another drag on your unfiltered Camels. Cigarettes that you can now smoke one after another without getting sick.

You sit with your friends and watch the men watching you. You and all of your friends lean together conspiratorially and laugh at one of them, pretending that you haven't grown up with him and all of his cousins your whole life, and that it wasn't him that you first kissed behind the honeysuckle on the south side of the clapboard reservation schoolhouse.

Turning from fifty-nine to sixty isn't anything like that. That just means that your age is easier to say and harder to hide. It means that it is expected that you have had your fill of sweetness and softness, and wetness between your legs. It means that no one will give you an orange while you sit in their kitchen ready to do their and God's work. Turning sixty allows me to walk over behind the old weighing shed next to the railroad tracks where the rhubarb still grows in weedy clumps. The red stalks are thick and the broad green leaves on top sometimes hide everything until I take hold of the base and rip them up. I tuck them under my arm and walk back to my little kitchen in the old-age home where I peel them carefully, my fingers turning raspberry red. Being sixty means that I can eat them plain and let them pucker up my whole mouth. I am allowed to enjoy the feeling of tartness.

Turning sixty also lets me know that the only reason I can enjoy the puckered feeling in my mouth is that I know that no one will bring me oranges anymore. Everyone is content to let me chew the stringiness of life while I wilt in the memory of an orange that is so simple and pure. Oranges are too simple for a woman who has turned sixty. The outside is too smooth and the inside too sticky and sweet. Save the sweet stickiness for the younger ones as the rain lifts, exposing the power lines and the church outside my window.

But on my sixtieth birthday I want no more rhubarb. On my sixtieth birthday I would give anything for the bitter peel of an orange. I would give anything for the sting of sticky acid just for a glimpse of the whole fruit underneath. On my sixtieth birthday I would like to sit in a white woman's kitchen eating an orange with my eyes closed listening to the grasshoppers and the killdeer only to open my eyes to see my beloveds standing on the other side of the screen door, to the side of the back porch. On my sixtieth birthday I would like to see them, my beloveds, standing in smeared clothing and matted hair holding a dirty loaf of bread and a torn quilt. I would like to see them, each one an exact duplication of each other. Each of them standing with those eyes wet like they were going to cry.

I was a baby, born in 1908, when some say history ended up here where the real woods used to stand. Though from where I sit now, in the last house at the end of Poverty, I see it differently. From where I sit and watch Donovan, Jackie, and Little play, streaking past the windows chasing each other, or tumbling around Duke and Ellis's Catalina I see it differently. Who would have guessed that the seeds cast and broken open by fire would have opened this way, these ways. So I watch them, and they think me mean, they think me bitter, only because there is so much they don't know. Donovan doesn't know who left him by the side of the road; Jackie knows that Lyle is her father, but she doesn't know why he left. And Little. Little knows, he knows but refuses to speak about his past, a wisdom those of us who lived through the old times, those of us who snuck through the nets of smallpox and influenza learned long ago. Long ago in 1908. And on the reservation, 1908 was a naked year, devoid of any warmth. That was the year the last big trees were knocked to the ground. The last three-hundred-year-old red pine was cut from the center of Manitou Island in the middle of our lake. All we had left was second growth and when we stood naked, the truth about us was revealed in stands of slashed poplar and scarred jack pine. The fish dove to the deepest part of the lake to avoid the logs that clotted its surface in a sticky mass before they were floated down to Minneapolis, where they were skinned and sliced into boards the settlers liked to use to build their houses.

The bear had left long before, but now the deer left us too. They were always so shy, them and the rabbits. The deer never made much noise and were too gentle to call attention to our condition. It was too much for them to watch us drown in the dust that settled across everything.

In 1918 the last buffalo died, and now no one believes that they ever even lived up here. It didn't die from gun or arrow, but from an intense loneliness. It staggered into the center of town and died on the streets as everyone stood around and watched through half-lidded eyes, lazy with whiskey. When its last breath left it, and it lay in the dust without even its own voice, some men came to cut what flesh they could from its body. As they cut it open they were forced back by the smell of rotting flesh. The skin disintegrated under the prod of axe handles and steel-toed work boots. No one wanted to touch it with their own hands so it stayed there all night. When in the morning someone brought a flatbed trailer pulled by two logging horses to remove it, they found that it had already left. Its outline stained the sand for another half a year, until the snow came.

In 1918 my mother was dreaming of a mink wrap until all thoughts of going down to the Agency to get her rations of flour and lard were driven clear from her head. I stood there and listened as she lay wrapped in a wool blanket in mid-June. It was dark and she lay against the wall in a pile of quilts made from rotting panels of fabric that I had cut from the pants legs of drunken loggers as they lay passed out along the boarded walls of the town bar. Her eyes were closed and a sweat from hunger clung to her face as she turned from side to side.

"Baby?" She didn't open her eyes but she reached out with her voice because she couldn't lift her arms anymore.

"Yes, Mama." I sat next to her and straightened the tangles in my hair, my fingers catching in the sticks and tangles. She didn't brush it like she used to.

"All I ever wanted was a mink wrap. Your daddy never gave one to me, did he?"

"No, Mama." Daddy was long gone and we figured that he moved off with the lumber camps, the only place where there was predictable food. My hair hung down my back and it got smoother and smoother the more I picked the sticks and burrs, stuck there from the raspberry patch behind the church.

"They soft, you know. Like hundreds of feathers all close together." I nodded, my head bobbing from weakness. My stomach had been empty since the last week. The only food I'd had were the green raspberries that I picked from the one patch that still bore fruit, which was against the woodpile behind St. Mary's.

"Them ladies in Italy have 'em. But they don't grow mink over there. Mink come from right here. How come I don't got one around my neck?" Her voice was cracked and I remembered when it used to sing me songs. When we were out in the bush, collecting Indian tea that cut the hunger, or pulling the shriveled blueberries coated with dust, she would sing to me.

Don't be sad, little girl.
Don't cry little girl.
Don't cry anymore, little girl.
Because the birds still love you.
And I can hear them calling you
tonight.

I bent my head close to hers and I wrapped my hair around her neck. I reached all the way around until I could grab it on the other side. It was oily smooth and it was thick.

"Is this how it is?" I whispered in her ear.

"Yeah. You found one. That feels so good."

I tightened my grip twisting the extra hair around my hand and turned my shoulder in, taking up the slack.

"Is this how it is?"

She nodded and a breath brushed past her cracked lips. I dug my feet into the dirt floor and pulled harder with my hand.

"Is this how it is?"

She said nothing now and her body grew tense, and then relaxed bit by bit as I held her wrap as tightly as I could around her neck.

"Is this how it is?" I whispered at last and hugged her.

"You don't need to cry anymore, Mama. *Gego mawiken, Gaawiin gimanezisiin ji-mawiyan.* You don't got to cry no more."

But she was far away so I got up and walked through the one-room shack to the flapping door. I opened it and stepped out into the dust and heat of June. Not looking up at the sun I headed north, to the lumber camps where Duke and Ellis were stripping logs for one penny per stick.

ى ﺭ

West of town and along the river just north of where Poverty sits now: that's where the logging camp was; long low log shacks tossed in an ever-growing clearing like matchboxes strewn across a scratched table. Every day at five the men got up and spit on their hands to seal the still-bleeding blisters and cuts. Spitting again on the floor as they stamped their feet into cracked hobnail boots, they shrugged off the morning cold.

I had never been to the camp before. But I knew where it was. In the fall when the leaves had dropped from the maple and basswood, before the ice stopped the water solid, the sounds flew down along the river and across the lake: an axe patiently nickling slivers from a huge pine, the singing of a hammer against a horseshoe and the horseshoe against the anvil. Sometimes when the wind was just right a short laugh stole to where I sat with my mother huddled in the quilt as our clothes lay drying on top of the barrel stove in our shack. Sometimes there was an explosion. A deep trembling below the register of ice cracking on the lakes.

From the shack we lived in I could see the men come into town, bent and dirty men who came out of the woods like the slow trickle of sap. Crossing the river at the dam they stumbled into town, loaded up on whiskey, and passed out along the road or under the shallow eaves of the bar. Duke and Ellis came too, and even though they weren't older than ten, they worked the camps following the food.

They had come from one of the Indian camps where they found work even though they were so young because the old men were dead and the young ones were still busy dying overseas. Duke and Ellis left the northern camps in the winter of 1916, walking over the lake and into town. Their toes frozen, mute and identical, they were smart enough to pry open the coal chute at the back of the church and slip inside, falling asleep behind the coal furnace, sleeping off the cold while the frostbitten skin blistered and peeled. That's where I met them — not in the basement of the church where they slept that winter and where they carefully pried open boxes of communion wafers, nibbling like mice, but in the coat room where they hid during the services, tapping coat pockets for forgotten change.

My mother went to church during the winter when she could still walk. Not because of God, but because of the cold. She only spoke Indian, so even though I was eight when we started going to the wooden white church I knew it was for the same reasons that we walked from the bush and lived in town; for food, warmth, and company. She knew what I didn't know. She was dying and she had to find somebody to pass me off to, someone to push her only living child into the act of living.

All of her brothers and sisters had died, my father had left. I don't even remember my own brothers and sisters, though my mother told me I had had three of each. I don't remember them, at least not exactly. I can bring back voices, the swish of a braid over the woven cedar-bark mat I played on in the sugar bush, a thin hand tying me tighter on the travois as we broke camp. I remember a worn trouser knee when I sat on my father's lap as he chewed venison soft in his mouth before placing it gently between my lips.

My mother never talked about my brothers and sisters, though she said my father left for the logging camps when they were still up north where the biggest trees had not yet been beaten down. She spoke about him, recalled his hands as we wove mattresses from cattail fronds, his singing voice while we struggled back to our shack in town loaded down with salt, lard, and flour. When she spoke of him then, a little more came back; the shape of his knotted calf as I clung to his leg, the weight of his palm on the crown of my head as he stood and spoke.

Since she spoke of him and not of the others I assumed he was alive and the others weren't. When I met Duke and Ellis I asked them if they knew my father. They told me in whispers between hanging coats in the church that they did, and when they last saw him he was still alive.

We left the woods when I was eight, when the game left for the most isolated swamps and the few remote stands of ancient trees. There hadn't been much food for a while, but there had been others around to help with the sugaring, to untangle the nets and rice the river. The Indian agent had been trying to get us to move, to get the few remaining families out of the bush and into town, or even better, to move south where they were opening up the prairies for us. That agent was trying hard. He trekked upriver to where we camped, red in the face, batting mosquitoes and deerflies. He pleaded. He begged. He brought the priest.

"For your children's sake," they said.

"For their education."

Knowing that my mother knew no English they spoke Indian,

chopping at the words, stumbling around like two bears in a single-seat outhouse.

"Who are they?" I asked, peeking from behind the sap-boiling kettle.

"Evil," she said.

"What do they want?"

"Evil."

My mother wouldn't listen and I imitated her, crossing my arms and drawing deep breaths. When we heard them coming we hid in the sumac, under the drooping canopy of black spruce, in tall grass, in whatever and wherever. But the high fire, the brim-full kettle and still-gasping fish told them we weren't far.

So they left us alone. Instead, they gave out annuity payments in town. They knew we would come, that we had to come in, caught by the gills while they slowly drained the water away. Our numbers shrank; some made the walks to town and back, others cashed in and moved to where there was open field, where the trees never shouldered, and where they said grain grew as far as the eye could see. They knew they would die if they abandoned their lakes, but they thought they would die with full stomachs, not knowing that they would be gnawed to death by the wind and have their eyes go wide at the sight of the endless open.

My mother and I were the last to leave. By that time we were stretched tight, no longer able to pull the nets by ourselves, to tip the copper kettle. We were being peeled back from the land the way the skin of smoking fish curls over to expose what is soft and white, what can be flaked away by the wind, by even the softest, weakest hands. Finally, finally, we rolled the nets and stashed them in a tree, coated the kettle in mud and turned it with a thunk on its heavy rim, put what we had in empty flour sacks and walked to town. Don't look back, don't look back.

꿍 꿍

Town. A bar, a church, a store that even at that time was owned by that no-good Marshall family, and a scattering of shacks built from tar paper, cardboard, and roofing tin. All the lumber that crept in a steady trickle from our woods never stopped for us who had so recently belonged to it, but kept on going south to Minneapolis. There were among those pitiful shacks a few lodges in the old style.

We had no home, nothing to trade except for a few weak summer furs, though we could have used the boiling kettle if we had been strong enough to lug it to town or set it in a canoe. We ended up staying in a woodshed that, having no wood to hold, was open to us; me, my mother, and an oil-barrel stove. We went to church in the winter months when my mother could do more than moan and beg for my father. We went for warmth, food, and company. Church, where I met Duke and Ellis, those who were to save my life three times and give me two brand new ones, though only one would survive.

Holding my mother's rough hand and pulling at the ends of my hair, which had been braided too tight, we crunched through the snow toward the church. Painted white and set against the snow, it looked like a huge drift, a cave of ice lit from within by kerosene lanterns that gave off a yellow light the way walleyes' eggs drip out of their smooth white bellies in the spring. My mother walked fast, her skirt blowing back, the stiff wool scratching my face. I turned my chin in toward the folds of the blanket wrapped around me, an edge dragging a wavy line in the snow like the track of a turtle's tail in the sand.

Pulling me up the steps by my arm, my mother shouldered the heavy door open and stood me in the entry. The heat washed over us. Not trusting her only coat in the coatroom, she made her way to a pew close to one of the heat vents.

Something made me pause, pulled me from the wake of my mother's strong walk. Something. A rustle in the curtain maybe. A quick flash like a walleye struggling in a net deep in clear running water.

I pushed the curtain back and stepped in, letting the thick red fall in place behind me. Except for a wedge of buttery light the coatroom remained dark. The greasy smell of wet wool, wood smoke, and sun-dried fish jerked lazily in the half-light. In the knife of light a coat swayed on a wooden peg. I stopped. The heavy velour curtain tapped at the back of my legs.

The sound of the church filling up distracted me. Thick boots thumping the pine floor. Laughs, the brush of fabric against skin, cloth against cloth. Then, I heard the thud of a boot against wood. I stopped. Squatting down I peered into the row of coats. In the dim I saw a wet-bright spot. An eye. I shuffled forward on my hands and knees. I saw two heads, the gloss of straight black hair.

"Who's that?" I said in Indian.

The heads backed against the wall, and a finger floated up to a pair of lips, shushing me.

Still on my hands and knees I crawled into the arbor of wool. I lifted my knee and set it down, not on the pine planking but on something warm, rubbery, and flat.

"Ow!"

It was a hand. It jerked from underneath my knee and slapped me open across the face.

"Dog," I hissed, thrusting my hand out, trying to claw the face that bobbed in front of me. I missed and fell forward.

They grabbed my hands, clamped theirs around my wrists, and I sprawled on my back, my head cushioned on someone's thigh.

I blinked. I blinked again. Peering over me, identical bangs hanging into identical sets of eyes, were two faces, exactly alike. They had delicately arched noses, but flared. Narrow eyes, skin the color of walnut but whisper smooth like basswood. I laughed a low whispering laugh.

"You're just boys," I said, trying to cover my surprise. They *were* boys, a couple of years older and holding me with hands that were strong.

"Shut up little girl," one of them said. The one with the big mouth who I later learned was Duke.

"Shut up or we'll get caught."

"Caught what?"

His hand flashed up with a bright Indian-head penny between his thumb and forefinger. They had been rummaging pockets for change and food.

"Where you from?" I asked.

Duke pointed his lower lip toward the north, whispering that they had been at the camps.

"Do you know my dad?" I told them his name.

They nodded.

"Is he alive?"

Ellis pressed a thin finger up against my chapped lips and spoke. Not whispering, but in a voice meant only to travel the short distance between us.

"He was when I last saw him."

Out in the body of the church they were beginning the hymns, translated into Indian.

"I'd better go."

I stood and placed my blanket and hat in the corner so my mother would have fewer suspicions. I lifted the curtain.

"Look for change in my stuff and I'll bust you over the head."

I heard a snicker. Duke spoke up.

"Knock on the coal chute around back later."

I left and when I walked from the service with my mother four large pieces of coal rattled in my hat as I pulled it tight over my ears.

∽ ∾

Later on I snuck away from our woodshed with one of the five potatoes we'd bought with the rabbit furs we had sold at the Marshall's store. Rabbits that still hopped, only to be strangled with stove wire, close to the edge of town. Taking one of the five potatoes, shriveled and dotted with eyes, brown like the neck skin of old men, I jogged to the church and banged the coal chute with the toe of my shoe.

Having left the blanket with my mother I shivered in the cold. One side of my dress hung lower than the other because the potato hung heavy in my pocket, thumping against my thigh as I stamped my feet into the wind-packed snow. The cast-iron chute door opened a crack, squeaking loudly in the night chill.

"Lift it, it's heavy," Duke whispered through the opening.

I tucked my fingers under the cold lip and heaved up.

"What now?" I asked, impatient. Freezing.

Just before I was going to drop it, Duke wedged a piece of

splintered axe handle between the door and the lip. It hung open and he motioned for me to slide down.

"I can't, my dress'll get dirty. My mother will know."

Duke nodded and disappeared, returning with the lid of a wooden crate that he placed at the top of the chute. Grabbing onto the sides of the chute I stepped onto the crate lid and slid down, careful not to smush the potato that, once I was standing, I pulled out of my skirt with a flourish.

We sat there that night, wedged between the stone foundation wall and the wide back of the furnace. Absorbing the heat we picked at the potato, which we had roasted by putting it on a coal scoop that we shoved into the ash box. Duke took a cloth pouch of "Dukes" tobacco and rolled the dry shreds in a scrap of newspaper, and this, he told me, was how he got his English name, being they didn't speak any English except for the little bit he and Ellis picked up from loggers. It was mostly swear words anyway. Ellis got his because of his silence, the way he sat still, not rocking or flexing his toes the way Duke did. The way I do. The English-speaking loggers, without any foothold or clues to his personality, called him the same name as the island they first set foot on, the first place of dry America that they had seen.

Duke and Ellis had only spent a little time at those camps, having logged mostly with the Indian crews, one of which had been headed by their uncle.

"Is he alive?" I asked.

"When I last saw him," said Duke.

"Your father?"

"When I last saw him," said Duke again.

"My daddy, too." Not a question. I wanted to hear them say it again. So I could tell my mother. So she would know.

"Everyone," said Duke, "everyone was still alive."

But Ellis shook his head, holding my eyes and shaking, shaking. No.

"What?" I asked, looking back at him. "What?"

"Everyone was —," said Duke, but Ellis cut him short.

"Everyone was dying. He was dying when we left."

"Why didn't you stay? Why didn't you help them?"

Duke picked at his charred potato, bobbing his head down to his hands.

"They wouldn't let us," he said. He was crying.

Smallpox had gotten into the camp and there was no way to get help. All the roads and trails were snowed in. Town and a doctor, who wouldn't have come even if it were right next door, were fifteen miles away. Duke and Ellis were immune. They stayed while it blizzarded around the camp, the fever whipping through the men as fast as the snow hurled past the barracks. It tore those strong men down, their fevers rising, pus oozing from their skin. They all caught it at the same time, from blankets or shirts sent in.

So the stronger ones lugged in the cased dynamite, and the tin kegs of kerosene. They told Duke and Ellis to leave. They cried and clung to their uncle's leg until he cuffed and kicked them out into the snow, barring the door behind him, leaving them nothing that would carry the disease. No food, no blankets.

By the time Duke and Ellis reached the lake they could see flames rise above the tree line licking winter air and heard the dynamite thumping as it exploded uncapped in the wooden crates.

᭟   ᭟

We visited in the church basement at night until the ice broke, eating potatoes baked on a broad lip of tin. Then, when the ice turned black in March and the few pelts being turned in were getting thinner, shedding their winter skin, Duke and Ellis secured a place at the operation north of town and they quit the church. They returned there only once, staying a month, suffering themselves to wear the white-and-red smocks of altar boys. By then I was in Iowa.

After they left and summer broke open dusty and dry, my mother couldn't walk anymore and could barely speak. So I gave her the mink she had moaned about, then cut it from my scalp, leaving everything behind except for the quilt. I walked to the camp.

It wasn't very far, just along the lake to the river and across.

Four miles. The landmarks were gone, the trees gone, and the roll of the land crushed flat by oxen and pushed up by dynamite. The men who were just returning from the war, who came back to a place that had turned into a desert, said that our mud looked the same as French mud. Some of them jumped and shouted when the charges went off, others just bent in closer to look at the rim of a tin cup or the hard leather of their boot toes. Steadying themselves against shapes that didn't move or spurt blood.

Duke and Ellis were at the camp already. They dressed me up like a boy and got me a job peeling sticks, peeling the popple they railed to Minneapolis for the paper mills. We peeled the bark off those logs until our arms ached and our fingers were blistered from the dull rasps they gave us to work. We pulled the bark from the aspen they used as pulp wood, and the wood oozed. It sweated as we uncovered the logs layer by layer, ripping until it was pale and smooth; able to be nicked with a fingernail. It slimed our hands and made our clothes sticky with the sap and the blood from our broken blisters.

Raw and hungry, we stayed at the lumber camp. The foreman let us sleep in the saw shed, where they stored the big two-man saws and the one hydraulic power saw that was always breaking down. We curled up in a couple of blankets because it got cold at night and I always pulled closer to Duke and Ellis because I dreamed of teeth. The teeth on the two-man saws came off the metal bands and floated around the shed, whirling like bats or moths around a lamp. They were always filed sharp in the mornings, and at night in my dreams they caressed the wool blanket, sticking in the fabric, trying to pull it off. Duke always slept sound, not really snoring but wheezing. Ellis would wake up when he felt me move closer, shivering. When he saw me he curled around me.

Even though Ellis fought them, the teeth won. The priest came up with some women from Davenport. Women in long brown dresses that were the same color as the beaten, oiled saw blades. Women who wore their gray hair in buns and had the longest, whitest fingers I had ever seen. They talked with the foreman and he pointed to where we were stripping the logs. I was ankle-deep in shavings and the women looked over to me, nodding and smiling.

The priest came. He had seen me from church and recognized me in my trousers and cut hair. He took my hand and ruffled Duke and Ellis's hair, they stood motionless, dangling their rasps. He peeled the knife I was using from my hand, and it tore my blisters because the mixture of sap and blood had cemented my hand to the handle. The women handed the foreman some money and pushed me to where their buggy was waiting. As I sat on the seat of the buggy I knew it had springs and teeth. I had never been in a buggy. We usually walked, and if we had any luck, we ran and jumped on the back of a wagon, dangling our feet over the edge. The wagon rides were always bumpy and rough, but the buggy shot me smooth and pure over the ruts of the path leading to town, and far away from Duke and Ellis.

The springs creaked and whined, the sound the saws made as they cut through the pine. They got hot and swelled in the trunks and the huge Swedes who cut them had to pull harder and harder. The blades got dull and screamed through the trees. It sounded just like the buggy springs. So even though I didn't know where we were going, I knew it was bad, because of the teeth.

The teeth took me past town, farther and farther south. Then, on a train, I saw the trees go by. No one was cutting them. Duke and Ellis weren't there to strip them. Maybe they had been stripped before. And then there were no more trees. Fields went by empty.

There weren't any trees in Iowa, where the women took me. At least not any real trees, ones you could show yourself to, and it would be four years before I stood in our woods again, four years of Iowa and fake trees.

On the bluff over the Mississippi where their huge house stood, there were oaks. Scraggly things, they never grew close together, never stretched a straight line. It was like they didn't trust each other, content to lift up from that rich soil, stunted and alone. There were apple trees too, red and crab, along the back edge of the garden. These belonged to the house. What belonged to the house was considered work, and since I belonged to the women I belonged to the work. Picking apples, digging potatoes, white-washing the fence, spading the garden, weeding the cracks in the bricked walk that ran the length of the front lawn and then looped behind the house to circle the garden and the flag-stoned patio. I was a saved Indian girl. Belonged.

To the hat-and-shoe ladies who looked out from under the laced eaves of their straw sun hats, I was a charge.

As I weeded, watered, scrubbed, as I worked in the sun, they called out to me. Made me repeat in English what they said. They read poetry, and would get lost or stuck, sometimes carried someplace completely else by the words. Then it wasn't so hard. On the patio with ice gently clinking in their lemonades, sur-rounded by the sparrows that flitted close to the scattered crumbs from the crust thrown to them, the hat-and-shoe ladies let themselves read on.

With my feet in the black dirt I continued my work, their recitation a dull hum in the background, dusty words flowing end-lessly out of a wrinkled mouth. I tried to think of my work in our language, in Ojibwe. Digging, dandelions, worm, gentian. I had forgotten so many of them, even though I had been in Davenport for only three months. Still, now, there are words we no longer use, phrases that used to anchor us to our trees and our river that we don't speak anymore. Maybe that's what this is here, because words get lonely like people do, get hungry like we hunger. They get jealous, they scheme. Maybe this is the words struggling to break the surface of the rippled long stretch of calm. We, Duke and Ellis and me, we all three were cut away from our parents, but we were cut loose from our words too. Though we were never boarding-schooled, never mission-educated, we were cut adrift and unmoored from our words, those beautiful, sweet, tricky, and twisted words.

There were other trees, too, besides the oaks and the apples, but these were city trees, planted by city people, trapped between the lanes and the avenues, the sidewalks and the houses. There were rows of elm and silver maple. Straight and thick, they crossed and bordered, were planted there on purpose, and had no life of their own. They were pruned when people thought they should be pruned, cut down when people thought they should be cut down, admired only for doing what they were told to do.

Once every two weeks during the summer and fall I would go with the shoe lady to town for groceries: salt, pork, beef, yeast, flour, sugar, thread, cloth. Sometimes we needed none of these, sometimes we needed everything, but regardless of material need the shoe lady, having hundreds of shoes, needed an occasion to show them off.

It all depended on her shoes, the route we took, when we left, the clothes she wore. Everyone wore their dresses long with so many undergarments it looked like they were wearing three or four dresses instead of just one. Everyone except for me, who wore a simple one, cotton, with loose arms so that I wouldn't rip it while scrubbing or raking the lawn free of branches and leaves. Despite these fashions, if the shoe lady was wearing a particularly high pair of laced boots with a high heel, her dress extended only to the very top of her boots in order for everyone to admire them.

In town, while walking, she waved and smiled, gestured with her straight black cane and always passersby looked first at her, then at me with distrust or pity, and last they looked at her shoes glowing conspicuously underneath the rumpled frill of her dress and petticoat. Her, me, her shoes, a triangle of envy; a perfect outfit.

We walked into town and at the mercantile store we bought flour, and salt; then to the fabric store next door, where we bought what fabric the shoe lady thought necessary, though it was never based on the weather or the season, or the type of fabric and how easy or hard it was to sew, but on the color and pattern only. Last of all we walked to the butcher's, which was closest to the house on the bluff, so that the meat we bought wouldn't spoil before I carried it, along with twenty pounds of flour, five pounds of salt, and an always varying amount of fabric, carried up the hills home.

I liked the butcher shop, the smell of sausage, of pepper and garlic. I liked the weight of sausage, of beef roast. There were cuts of meat that I know I had seen in living form, because I had seen living cows and pigs, but to see the slices, the cuts: beef-knuckle, T-bone steak, these wonderful sections with weight, water, and marbling of fat. I had never seen those. Once, at the butcher shop, Kryschk set out a roast, grayer than beef, darker than pork. I didn't know what it was. Kryschk carefully set it out, his long, skinny fingers wrapped around the meat like it was precious, a piece of marble, gold maybe. He set it in the glass case by the counter carefully as if it were valuable but not fragile.

Kryschk, the butcher, was about six and a half feet tall, and skinny. Since he spent most of his time over the stoves, smoking the sausage, frying up blood sausage, singeing the pinfeathers off of chickens, he had taken on a reddish color, the veins under his eyes and on his nose pushed out against his skin. Even his hands were red, from cooking, cutting the meat, and from continually washing them so he could attend to customers without getting grease all over the outside of their packages and on their money.

Disobeying the standing order from the shoe lady, which was to do what I was told, listen, and not ask questions, I pointed at the roll of meat he had just placed in the case. I asked him what it was.

Leg of lamb, he said.

I repeated it to myself. I had just learned what a sheep was, being constantly reminded in poems about flocks and shepherds, of the rolling hills and fleece. It had recently been explained to me that a shepherd was the first one to know of Jesus. The angels had let him in on the secret.

Leg of lamb. It sounded so sweet, not sweet the way most people think of lambs, soft and fluffy, bleating out, scared. It sounded sweet the way plums are sweet; firm and tender at the same time.

I looked up at the shoe lady. She had moved away from me and stood with both hands on her cane, one leg outstretched so that the curve of her extended foot followed the curved sole, from the arched heel to the carefully pointed toe. She was pursing her lips, looking from her foot to the cuts of beef and back to her foot.

I asked her. Ma'am. Do you see that? Pointing to the leg of lamb with my finger.

Yes, she said. I see the lamb.

She always took great care to reply in full, so I would learn English faster. I see the lamb, each word stopped short, her mouth making a complete revolution around each word, the fat jiggling under her cheeks.

Can we get it?

Another rule broken. I wasn't supposed to ask questions, especially in public where I might embarrass her, but the stakes were high. I wanted that leg of lamb.

She looked down at me, tapping her cane against the scratched floor. She was wrestling. Maybe she was wondering if she should teach me a lesson about asking by not getting it, or get it because she really wanted it for herself, or because Mr. Kryschk might think her uncharitable.

It is not such a good leg of lamb. She bent next to the glass to inspect it.

I butchered it last night, said Mr. Kryschk.

You probably fed it hay, said the shoe lady.

Grain and alfalfa only, Mr. Kryschk said.

I knew it. *I* knew. It was perfection.

Please.

She paused and opened her purse, looked at the list of things we needed to buy. She pretended to count her money. She nodded and asked for Mr. Kryschk to package it up. Tightly.

I was in heaven. I had no idea how it would taste, even how to cook it. But if shepherds were good enough for God, then they must be doing something worthwhile.

He handed the package over and the shoe lady motioned that he should hand it to me. He set it in my hands, and it felt full. Some things, when you pick them up or touch them, feel empty, light. A bag of tea, mealy apples.

I hefted it in one hand, the rest of the groceries in a bag that I had thrown over my shoulder. We turned to go and trailing behind the shoe lady I lifted the leg of lamb up to my nose so that I could smell it, to see if any of the magic would leak out of the white wrapping paper, so I could have a head start on ecstasy.

Then, disaster. The worst possible thing happened. I lifted it to my face, closed my eyes and sniffed. I didn't notice that the shoe lady had stopped, had turned to say good-bye with her leg outstretched, and I walked directly into her. My dusty dirty foot stepped squarely on her shining boot.

Her eyebrows jumped together, the fat wiggled on her face. Despite the white powder she'd applied, her face turned bright red. Whirling, she smashed my knee with her cane. I fell, dropping the leg of lamb, and coming down on her other foot with my knee. I tried to roll out of the way, but she cracked me with her cane across the back of my neck.

I scrambled out of the way and stood with my back against the wall. My knee throbbed and my neck was as tight as a rusted tin lid. Tears ran down my face. Not from my knee or my neck, but from giving the shoe lady a way to shame me in public.

She smoothed her dress with her hands. I could see them shake. Bending down she inspected her boots, pretending pain, though I didn't come down on them with my full weight.

They are *so* hard to train, she said to Kryschk.

He nodded.

The shoe lady told me to pick up the groceries, and with a small wave, tense with rage, she walked out of the butcher shop, not waiting for me to catch up, a stiff figure dressed in gray walking between the silver maple on her way up to the hill.

That night I sat in my room surrounded by 117 pairs of shoes, three cans of Kiwi shoe polish (blue, brown, and black), and a stack of flannel rags high enough to sew two quilts with.

As soon as we got back to the house the shoe lady told me to put the leg of lamb in the icebox, peel six cloves of garlic, slice a lemon, and to go to my room. I was told not to leave.

I waited, listening to the kitchen sounds coming through the floor of my room. I heard the cupboard doors opening and closing, the clash of pans and the rattle of pie tins.

I knew that neither of the women had a clue where anything was in the kitchen. They discovered frying pans below the flour bin on the baker's table when they were looking for the broiling pan, and found the meat grinder when they looked for the gravy boat.

The hat lady must have taken over the search for cooking things because the pitch of clanging and slamming wound down to quiet, rhythmic thunking and I could hear her whistling "My Bonnie Lies over the Ocean" out of tune. I hadn't figured out the different ways you could use the word *lie* yet so I thought the song was about a tremendous liar.

> *My Bonnie lies over the ocean,*
> *My Bonnie lies over the sea,*

Lies and more lies.

I heard a tapping, the high-laced boots were walking the hall to my room.

The glass doorknob turned and the shoe lady swung into my room on her heel. I looked up.

She sat in my desk chair with both feet stretched out in front of her. Turning her head to the side she told me to take off her boots.

I picked at the knots. They were cinched into wooden loops by her tense stride and her bad mood. I picked at them, but my fingernails were too weak to loosen them. She sighed. Her toes began to wiggle. I bent down, my face next to the leather strings, trying to figure out the line of the lace.

I got one and managed to pull the lace from the first three eyelets. I pulled the lace loose and grabbed the heel. It came off, wheezing like an old man walking up a hill.

Then the other.

You'll save these for last, she said.

I didn't know what she meant. I raised my eyebrows.

English, she snapped. Ask in English.

What do you mean?

You will clean and shine all of my shoes. Save these for last.

I was surrounded by hundreds of shoes, the flannel, and the polish. The shoes were black, brown, blue, and green. All the different colors a bruise can take.

My hand began to cramp after the first ten pairs. There was a twitch in my back after twenty. My eyes burned from the polish, my hands looked gangrened in the lamplight. Then a smell began to whisper into the room.

At first the polish clouded everything else, the wet smell of leather, the faint wisp of marigold pollen on her gardening shoes, the mold of oak leaves on her walking boots. Clay, cut grass.

These smells passed by, silently. The wax and dyes in the polish swept everything else from the room. But then underneath, sneaking around the corner of polish smell, came something else.

It was thick like sage smoke and sharp like cedar. Fat dripping, but clean, like rendered bear fat.

It was the leg of lamb. The kitchen right below my room sent the smell through the floorboards and in the walls. I think it even forced its way through solid wood.

No wonder Jesus loved the shepherds. No wonder. It was the most beautiful smell.

I shined the shoes harder, exacting a glow from the leather, making them whole. I expected to be called down. Ten more pairs and they'll call me.

The smell grew stronger. I could taste salt in the air, greasy smoke. Every time I took a breath it grew stronger, the shoe polish retreating distantly into the corners of the room.

Another ten and they'll come up with a plate. With bread to soak up the grease.

I was wrong. Twenty pairs of shoes later I could smell the garlic, the sharp of lemon, and the lamb, all fused together like the voices in the church choir. The church we went to in Davenport was huge. All brick and carved limestone. There were rows and rows of stained glass that you could look at no matter which pew you sat in. When you walked in the pre-service hush made the echo of your footsteps bounce along the stone floor. The swish of skirts and the snap of closing umbrellas at the double doors could be heard all the way up front.

Later I would go to school there, at the church, but only in the winter when there were fewer chores to do. I left the house at 4:30 A.M. because the priest who tutored me wanted me there at 5:00.

In the pre-dawn I would walk along the iced path to the road, rutted from hooves, tires, and carriage wheels. Gray and cold, I always walked alone: the hat-and-shoe ladies were still tucked under flannel sheets and feather beds as thick and soft as fresh-baked bread. I walked alone and loved it. It was when it all, the bluffs, the river sluggish with ice and cold, the misplaced and misled trees, when it all seemed the most human.

The road, water frozen into ridges and long jagged lines, stretched on before me. There were tracks frozen into the ice, horses and people, with no carriages, cars, or people in sight. See here? Someone fell. The hoof marks pointing down; a horse had been startled.

The trees stood for what they were, without the protection of leaves or even of choice because they had only one option: either grow where they had been told to grow or die where they had been planted to grow. Sometimes, even in winter, there was barge traffic on the river. Hedged between the shallows and the eaves of crusted ice the barges inched the channel. I couldn't hear them from where I walked along the hills into town. But a light, dim in the winter dark, shone from the cold water. Sometimes I saw a figure moving on the flat, checking ropes and peering up- or downriver for dangers. But not very often. Even when the barges crept into my view they became part of it because, like the trees in town, they only had one choice: they could go up or down, the river never allowed them to stay in one place.

The priest would greet me at the side door, under the weak electric light that he never failed to point out to me. The marvel of electricity, he said, gesturing from inside his coat, the fat under his chin jiggling.

Taking me inside he would sit with me in the back room, teaching me English by lantern light. Thrift only allowed limited doses of the marvel of electricity. English, writing: he made me do it all and would report to the hat-and-shoe ladies when we all came for the Sunday service. I've never instructed her kind before he would say, rocking up on his toes, his thick hands clasped behind his back. But she learns well despite what God has withheld.

During the service I mumbled my prayers, kicking my feet against the Bible racks screwed into the backs of the pews. It was only when the choir sang that I came awake. Listening for the echo floating high in the rafters. I would crane my neck around so that I could see the choir in the balcony and try to pull the voices apart, match the sounds with the open mouths.

The way the music dipped and looped, floated down to us and then picked up speed to shoot out ahead, was like the lamb roasting in the kitchen below me. High, medium, and low, the smells of the roast lamb, garlic, and lemon were a harmony where all three smells took turns singing, the other two retreating, pushing from underneath or hovering up high. I was starving. My mouth watered. I could hear my stomach.

Two more hours went by. I couldn't smell the shoe polish anymore, only the leg of lamb. Still they didn't call me. My arm, shoulder, and back were numb. But I refused to cry, refused that defeat. Instead I cleared my throat and spat into each of the boots I was working on. I sucked through my nose as hard as I could to get all the mucus, the green shards of phlegm.

I spat into fifty pairs of shoes. By the time I did twelve pairs my mouth was dry and the sides of my nose stuck together. I couldn't smell anything except dust. The shoe lady would never know, by the time she slipped her shoes over her withered fish-white feet the spit would be long invisible and dry.

When I finally finished with the tall boots I fell asleep surrounded in a room crowded with feet glowing in the low light, a sea of feet shining in the sputtering lantern glow.

So when they gave me an orange that summer day when I broke the china and I looked up to see Duke and Ellis on the other side of the screen door, I knew there would be no more shoes, no polish, no lamb. When they took me and we walked back north at night, sleeping during the days, it was quiet. There was no buggy, there was no train, no hats, no poetry.

They led me by the hands, too numb to speak or cry out. We cut down by the river after we got out of town because there would be fewer eyes watching. Those who could watch from the river, whether they drove the barges or steamers, paid us little mind. We were just more bugs in a place where the blackflies stuck to your skin until you wiped them away like angry, buzzing little crumbs. When the night came we pushed our way into what we thought was the thickest brush along the bank. Duke went on about how they most likely had dogs, great big German shepherds who could smell you a mile away. So we burrowed deeper into the brambles, great twisted walls of hazel brush and blackberry.

If we kept close to the ground, where the clotted fingers of the brush didn't bend and trap we could see ahead a ways, where there was an opening in what looked like endless tangles. Duke was in front clearing sticks out of the way, looking like a little porcupine waddling along the ground. I came next clutching my orange in my hand, half-eaten. It slowed me down because I couldn't pull myself along with the branches and roots. Ellis was behind and he touched my leg as I clambered forward, not wanting to let go of my orange.

"Jeannette."

He said my name not like a question, or a command, or even wistfully, or angrily. It was just my name, pure. It was just my name, and nothing else.

"Jeannette."

I started to cry. Because there by the Mississippi, under what seemed like miles of twisted wood and thorns, I finally knew what it meant. I looked at my orange, which was now covered with broken leaves and twigs, caked with dirt. I had been squeezing it and the juice covered my hand so it had a layer of dirt and bark over what once had been fresh. I opened it and pried the half-eaten orange from my palm. It sat on the ground in the roots and tangles. I grabbed a branch ahead of me and pulled myself forward. When I looked back I couldn't see that orange anymore and then we broke into the clearing.

For some reason the brush didn't grow close to the ground and the space formed a small circle. The branches arched overhead, met, and wove into each other so that we had a roof, with just a little bit of sunlight creeping through. The ground was blanketed with so many layers of leaves it was hard to tell where they left off and the ground began. We lay in the center on our backs, Duke and Ellis on either side of me. The last thing I remember as I went to sleep is Duke spreading the blanket over us and both of them bending in to cover me with their bodies.

We walked from Iowa. We walked the whole way, and the earth was silent. We were so small that we made no noise. When we pulled away from the river because it bent too far to the east, and took to the fields, the grass bent under our feet. At night when we walked, stopping only to pick sweet corn and squash from people's gardens, the grass was slick with dew, so no matter how dry it was there was no rustle and no cracking. Some nights, when there were no clouds, the northern lights pointed our way across the sea of soy and corn. They arched overhead, and shimmered and danced. We walked lighter because of them. After we crossed the fields they still guided us, prodding the three of us along, even though we had blisters on our feet and our stomachs contracted at the thought of solid food, until we reached our river. Behind a hill, suddenly, it came sneaking from the north, and we followed it upstream. We followed its bank along the old paths our parents had shown us, that their parents had shown them, which we all thought had been buried under ten feet of moving water, but which had actually been waiting for us. Once we were back in the woods, there was only the whisper of branches, the touch of waist-high grass.

Now, after I gave up my indecisive view from the nursing home for the regularity of the accidents of child life, of watching the mistakes and broken bones, I know they have to know more than we did, to play that way. After I walked from the nursing home along the highway, a feat they didn't think me capable of, I sit in Poverty and my view is certain. I walked the highway back to this tract, to Poverty. I walked it and the secret of my feat is that underneath the broken asphalt, the crumbling tar, and the frost-heaved dips, underneath the gravel bed and the leveled ditches there used to run a path. This wasn't a river path. It was a woods one, a quiet one, and we remembered each other as I placed my foot on the shoulder of the highway. We recognized one another, and that is the secret of what carried me home to Poverty, to where Duke and Ellis waited for me with my pregnant daughter.

Iowa
1966

The farmhouse, along with the barn and silo, squatted belliger-
ently on the soil. As if it couldn't decide whether it should claim
its space or let the wind eat it away, it fence-sat, as it had since it
had been built. Because of this it needed at the least the outward
appearances of solidity, it needed to front against the ocean of
fields outside and the tide of lives that moved within its walls, so
it pushed everyone away. Independent. But soon the earth and
the sides of the house would be the same color, and maybe in that
moment they would become equals. Until then, however, the
boards on the house had the shiny gray color of beaten cedar
even though they were cheap pine. The knotted siding had an
uneven toughness to it, as though it had been beaten with ham-
mers against anvils of cold iron with a strong arm and a palsied
hand. Even though it showed this strength — to stand caught
between the burning sun (which it hated) and the people who
tried to offer it protection (whom it hated as well) — the paint
left in favor of the wind and fields that crossed miles of land that
used to be covered with aspen and oak. Once the wind took the
white chips from the boards they were ground into thousands,
millions of pieces of dirt. The house knew this, and knew also
that its inability to commit would cause its own death.

Until then, however, the house stubbornly and continually
resisted the carefully applied coats of paint, oil and latex, just as
it resisted the dirt and earth. It balanced between them, cornered

in its own efforts to turn into something that could never be anything more than a defense.

It was a house with all the outward appearances and inward products of guilt. The fields, corn and soybean, that flourished out of sight of the yard and barn, grew gradually smaller and thinner, withering finally until they merged with the circle of dust around the house. The sometime great ordered rows of corn and wheat knew that they didn't belong in that pathetic circle of humans, that theirs was a different life, a much different cycle. The men who planted the fields sensed this, but they planted there anyway in an effort to reconcile the different places in which they sat and worried, or out of habit or incompetence or the instinct not to waste the ground on which they owed back taxes.

The house knew it didn't belong there, that it was truly alone and had been constructed and then abandoned like a child left on a busy city-street corner. The house was being eaten by the land on the outside and by the people who ate the land on the inside, and no one could feel what it felt: its foundations badgered by the frost, its shingles ruffled and torn by the wind, its carpets and interior walls worn down constantly with the consistent insensitivity of its inhabitants.

The house guarded itself against the uncertainty of farm life, against the fields and the way one could never tell whether the harvest was going to be good or bad. This made it like an indisposed child. One could never tell when the combine would break, or if the oldest son would trip and fall under the rake. Sometimes the arm springs would break on the reaper just before harvest and, during the wait for a new one, the rain would come, rotting the crops where they stood. One could never tell whether all the children would decide to move to the city or, even worse, there would be no sons born to that family. Catastrophes on that farm never had the grace of premonition, and so one could never tell who would own the farm the next year, or the year after that.

It was in this way that the house grew into maturity with a profound distrust for anyone living inside it, stunted, short of faith as a result of its fear. Frightened of being left behind to sit empty, it lashed out at its inhabitants with squeaks and leaking

roofs, collapsing gutters, and drafts from the cellar. It didn't
bring misfortune upon itself because it had no control over the
fields or the people. It did draw attention to itself, testing those
who lived there, asking them to prove themselves. It gave out
trust in small doses and hoarded its favors because deep down it
knew that it didn't belong.

Uncertain as it was, it knew that it hadn't been there forever
and that what was there before was best not talked about. It knew
that the planks that made up its bones and the wallpaper and
shingles that constituted its skin had no history on the swells of
earth and arcs of sky; it knew its very fabric had been imported
from somewhere else, everywhere else. Its pipes and plumbing
didn't belong to the soil the same way that the water that coursed
through them did, so they rusted and stopped up. And it had no
irony with which to combat the blame that was heaped upon it for
its apparent failure. Its timber attracted wasps and carpenter
ants and hadn't the history or right to fight them off, and it was
blamed again for that. Not even the stones of its foundation came
from the surrounding land; the fieldstones had been carted in
from Illinois.

Generations of Europeans and their descendants traded off
and on. Germans, then Swedes, and then Irish came and left,
until the cycle repeated itself so many times that the similarity
of leaving overrode all the differences. The people always looked
the same. Some were tall with wide shoulders and had no problem carrying two bales of hay at once, throwing them up into
the mow in clean arcs. Some were short, requiring a hammer to
bang the wrench around the first three rotations, until the bolt
on the hitch was loose enough to use their arms. The house saw
different meals. Sometimes it was stew and sometimes apple
strudel with raisins.

Despite these differences in build their eyes always *looked* out
beyond the curtained windows the same way. Every morning at
five-thirty — first light in the summer and the pitch black of
winter — the curtain was teased from its place before the cows
had to be milked. If there were no cows to milk, the lace curtains
were pulled back a little later, but the eyes always looked out at
the day and saw their future in the rain or the dust, which swirled

into the columns of numbers that the farmers often couldn't read. They couldn't read the numbers but they didn't need them when they saw that the silo was half empty, or that the cows had stopped lactating because of poor feed.

Since there was no difference in their eyes, the house knew of their betrayal before the owners did. The knickknacks, porcelain cat figurines, needlepoint Christmas scenes, and antique bottles never rested on shelves and windowsills with ease; instead they sat dangerously contemplating the floor. So it was with the people. They also were balanced precariously in the house, excusing themselves from it whenever possible. The residents, whoever they were, would go out just one more time to see if the corral gate had been fastened or to look in at the calf that had fallen sick; anything to get outside. For this they were unforgiven. The house yearned for a little disorder, so it was kept spotlessly clean.

A family descended from Germans lived there and the father's eyes were always turned to the fields. The mother paged through the Sears catalog, the *Farmer's Almanac,* and the Bible equally, with unreasonable absorption. The twelve-year-old boy never scuffed his feet, but lifted them and set them carefully. He opened things and never shut them. His clothes spread across the floor and his mother, instead of calling him away from the radio, picked them up for him.

He opened things but never found enjoyment in the things inside. The red-haired twelve-year-old boy loved the wrappings of all things, candy, boxes, and fruits. It came that he would secret away the tightly wrapped pieces of hard candies from his aunt's purse, the kind his mother would never allow in the house except for guests or at Christmas. In his loneliness he would concentrate on the membrane and he would try to peel the foil from the candies. The shiny paper, which couldn't have been wrapped carefully, or even consciously, as it was processed by machine, defied his fingers, white, fat and short. The paper never gave way in one piece. The tinfoil ripped and came away in flimsy pieces that could never be used for anything. If only he could come away with a whole piece, only then would the candy taste good. Only then would the taste make any sense.

His mother did not have any feeling for the need of complete wrappers, or a perfect square of tinfoil. The boy never asked this but he sensed it, in his mother's cooking, and in the way she ordered only the most conservative items from the Sears catalog, and only when his father was out of the house. To order anything that wasn't a necessity or to have a sweet tooth was to go to weed, as his father put it. Whenever the subject of Paul's cousins came up, or his aunt got a little too drunk at a Christmas party, his father would say they've gone to weed. People are like fields and if neither are tended well, they go to weed, which means going to waste. It's nothing less than throwing away God's gifts. But the taste of sugar confused the boy. It too was one of God's creations and the way in which it was used shamed his mother's pies. There was never quite enough sugar in the apple pie. It hit his tongue too hard, the apples came off mealy, and the crust had a doughy taste. The rhubarb pies didn't have any taste either; the tart had been boiled out and too little sugar added to give it any character. The boy wondered at this, and decided that it was a result of the unwrapping. The apples were never pared to his satisfaction, even when he was forced to do it himself.

As with the pies, it wasn't the slaughtering of cows, pigs, or even chickens that bothered him. It was the way that his mother cooked them. They were always prepared perfectly. The beef steaks or roasts were always neat, the fat trimmed off. His mother never left the steaks unattended to scorch on one side. The roasts were never dry or too watery, but existed in harmony with uncommonly rich gravy. The fat iridesced on top of the meat broth, and when his mother added milk, butter, and cornstarch they were always in perfect agreement, so that the gravy poured, and didn't stick to the bowl or ladle. The hams were salted just enough; it was never necessary to boil the excess off before they were baked with spears of sweet potato surrounding them, pressed into a string mesh. The sweet potatoes, too, were perfect, roasting in the bottom of the cast-iron Dutch oven, soaking up the melted fat of the ham.

The cooking defied the way in which the animals were killed; all sticky mess. The same curve-bladed knife was used on cows and pigs. It had a smooth wooden handle with brass rivets that were covered up with hair and blood. He wondered at the ability of the knife to kill so many animals with so little sharpening. The cows were led, farting and clomping the shit from their hooves, from the pasture to the side of the barn near where they parked the tractor. They shuffled along and chewed what remaining grass was in their mouths with determination. They died the same way; silently, stubborn, still chewing while their blood slopped in the pan. The pigs screamed and kicked, churning the dusty air. The cows, after the knife had punctured their necks, just stood there while the blood gushed out. They kept their eyes on the ground where the blood fell into the wide pan, the way dogs look when confronted with an alien command. Soon they dropped to their knees, shit dripping out their cavernous bung-holes, and they died quietly.

Paul didn't know how to avoid the killings. The farm was only so big, and the fields of soy and sweet corn spilled in all directions, clinging to the Iowa topsoil. Once he went up in the biplane that came twice each summer to dust the crops. Seeing the farm from the air confirmed his worst fears: it was a smudge of brown that kept its head up in the expanse of green. The only thing he could think of, seeing the alternating patches of corn and the closer-growing soybeans, was the carpet in the living room. The carpet was a thin, stubbly thing, with a plusher throw rug in front of the couch. The living room wasn't shabby: the couch was mended where torn and the table to the side was always orderly, the Bible and Sears catalog side by side. But the difference in texture between the carpet and rug startled him into the habit of wearing shoes or socks when he was in the house. The throw rug was as plain a color as the carpet, placed on the floor to stop the cold from seeping through the pine boards from the storm cellar. The gray rug didn't fit under the couch, which was flush with the floor, and Paul's legs were just long enough so that his toes touched the border, where the rug and carpet met.

Seeing the textured crops swing by below made him think of the rug and carpet and he saw that there was truly nowhere to go, and he actually felt the fields glide under the distended belly of the biplane. When it dipped low for a run over the crops he winced and curled his feet up in his boots. A shiver passed over him and he clenched his teeth, only to cringe again as if he had clamped down on a bit of crumpled tinfoil.

With no escape from his feet or his mouth, he knew that there was no way to avoid the killings. There was no pattern either, at least none that he could fathom. Sometimes spring, fall, anytime. The only forewarning he received occurred five minutes before each slaughter when his father called out to him.

Paul, get the pan.

There was no question, nor did his father wait for an answer as he walked straight-shouldered and bowlegged down the slight slope to the barn. Paul went into the pantry in the kitchen and took the stainless steel bowl from the floor where it rested in the corner under shelving that held hundreds of shiny, frosted Ball jars. On his way to the barn he would look down at his legs and he wondered if they were bowlegged like his father's. Paul's feet looked too big to fit on his skinny ankles, great flats of floppy flesh. His work boots, standard farm Red Wings, weren't broken in like his father's — covered in tractor grease, cow shit, blood, neatsfoot oil, and paint — so that the original fawn skin color was a muddy black. Paul's boots kept their new look and they only shined where the leather rubbed against itself, creasing by the ankle. The soles never wore down, except for the heels, which he dragged in the dust and gravel semicircle that spread out from the front porch. So his boots never looked old or felt very comfortable, except when he wore them in the house. They made his feet look big and he stumbled in the freshly mowed grass as he neared the barn with the metal basin.

Paul was always made to kneel on the ground with the basin, by the front hooves of the cow. He was supposed to catch the blood from the jugular so that his mother could make blood sausage and so that the blood-soaked ground wouldn't attract skunks. Paul wobbled with the slopping basin up to the house. It spilled on his legs, making long rusty stains on his jeans, but it never ever spilled onto his boots. His mother took the blood and fried it on the stove and the bloody syrup soon became a rubbery and smooth custard.

After the sausage was fried in grease Paul took the pan outside to the washhouse. He filled it with water from the pump and swished it. It rolled around in the metal pan until the deep red became pink and he threw it from the door into the yard where it sank into the sand. There in the yard he scraped off the crusted blood with a kitchen knife and the bloody water just disappeared into the ground, marked only by the presence of flies and yard wasps.

≈ ≈

It was after they had dammed up the falls at St. Anthony, a hundred years to be exact, that Paul came to Minneapolis. The gurgling mass of the Mississippi as it fell past the rocks — the last rapids before the river became wide, deep, and muddy — was silent for years before he came from Iowa with one cardboard suitcase and a Bible. He came when the Mississippi was low from the drought that lasted all summer, shrinking the river until it exposed the dead stumps and rusted bodies of Dodge pickups that had fallen through the ice in the winter when they had been driven down along the edges to cut it into blocks that were then packed into sheds filled with moldering straw. He came long after the water had turned muddy, the topsoil washing in from the banks as the water rose and rose, after the cement and steel blocked the water back. The river stretched thick and dirty past where it met up with the Minnesota River. The bluffs too, had been eroding and sliding into the river, because all the stone had been taken to build the capitol building, the post office, and Foshay Tower. He came from Iowa long after the wheat had ceased to be sent by train from Iowa, Nebraska, and Kansas in long steel rows where it was bleached and ground at the Pillsbury plant by the river. The tracks were rusted and the only line that still ran was the Northern Pacific from Duluth, which carried the poor-grade taconite and ore from the Mesabi Range. The good minerals, clean, undiluted, which used to make the best steel in the country, were all gone. The range had been sucked dry to build Chicago and Milwaukee. Now the rusted boxcars — those that still worked — carried ore not much better than dirt. Sometimes whole families from the range stole aboard the cars to get to Minneapolis where they lived on the South Side, along with the blacks and Indians. Those who used to be employed by the mines, now found jobs as mechanics or carpenters whose only jobs were to fix things that were there and already broken, decrepit, and rusted through, because nothing new was being built. Sometimes when the people couldn't stay up north any longer they tried to leave by train in the winter, and their bodies were found frozen to the metal sides of the boxcars, huddled in old woolen blankets that had frosted to their cheeks and hands. It was during these times that he came from Iowa to go to school and to the seminary in 1966.

He came when the South Side was growing and growing, black families moved from the south, the poor white farmers and rangers came from the north, and Indians came from all over, their reservations having been terminated by Eisenhower. They took over the South Side. The bankers and businessmen who used to live there, along the river, moved when the property values fell on account of all the colored moving into shacks and cramming into the condemned houses. They crowded into houses that used to belong to the old-money families who got rich off the lumber, until that too had folded, and they had moved to the suburbs. The northern poor were stacked in rows during the winters because there was no money for coal, and every tree within walking distance had been cut down. Even the brush, sparse and beaten by the wind, had been burned in old furnaces and then set on fire in the middle of the living-room floor for maximum heat. The old flooring, oak and pine boards fitted and sanded smooth, had been torn up to burn, along with all of the trim and the two-by-four studs under the plaster interior walls. Entire houses had been gutted for fuel and when it was gone, three or four families would crowd together into single rooms. Side by side they stacked themselves so that they could get what heat they could from each other.

This was far away, on the south side of Minneapolis; it was only across the bridge and down Lake Street that they found houses full of poor whites, blacks, and Indians frozen solidly into blocks of ten to twenty bodies that were stuck together until they were thawed loose at the morgue. On the other side, in St. Paul, where the lawyers and doctors from the university hospital lived, the houses were spacious, and even the children had their own rooms with warm wallpaper, plaids and floral patterns that had been pasted up by the whole family one summer day. The glue, a mixture of Elmer's and flour, had been splattered over everyone and they'd all had a good laugh. They had taken long breaks, and had drunk fresh-squeezed lemonade. They even let the littlest one put up some of the wallpaper. It had gone on crookedly, and the mother or father had inevitably straightened it when the child was out of the room.

The downtown was full of offices and shops. The accountants' and lawyers' offices had large plate-glass windows with the firms' names lettered in gold letters and old-fashioned script in long arcs. The stores sold coffees and antiques. Old oak desks, and shelves, cases, and tables were crowded into small boutiques with plank flooring covered with Oriental rugs. There were all shapes of kerosene lamps and butter churns, bread boxes, and cedar hope chests, all of which had been purchased at auctions in the surrounding states. The dispossessed farmers and transients who lived on the South Side never came to the downtown. If they had, they might have seen their old table in one of the store windows. The farmer's very own table that had been sanded and oiled every spring so there were no water marks or cigarette burns on the smooth surface. They might have collapsed while they stared in the windows at the tables that they had cut, pegged, and finished, even adding a little groove with a chisel around the edge, because their wives had wanted a nice touch. They had sat around the tables during the winter with pages and notes, receipts and bills piled high, while they figured out their taxes for the year. While the kerosene lamp burned lower and lower and they knew that they would never be able to pay the taxes the government required; not with the new tractors and the rakes that had to be repaired, and the doctor's bills for when the little girl, no more than six, who had been playing in the haymow when the rotten boards of the barn had broken under her slight weight. Or the boy who had lost his finger in the mower hitch, or the slow one who had been born that way. It was the third year that these farmers had owed taxes and the IRS farm representatives couldn't give them another extension. The auction houses from the city had made bids and bought out the farms. The tables and chairs were perfect for antique stores. They could be tagged as handmade, vintage farmhouse, and were sold to stores in Minneapolis and Chicago. The families used the auction money to pay the remaining doctor's fees and then moved to Minneapolis where the mothers worked in the cafeteria and the university, or as night bakers, until they were fired for stealing flour and lard for their families.

They might have raised a fuss on the sidewalk, looking in as a rich housewife from Edina strolled around the table, comparing its price with others she had written on a yellow pad of paper after she had visited other shops that afternoon. They might have hollered and tried to enter the store, only to be met at the door by the owner who told them firmly that they weren't allowed in unless they were buying. They might have, but they were too cold and too hungry, and if they had walked as far as St. Paul to find a job they would have to start the walk home to Lake or Hennepin if they were going to be inside before dark, when the wind picked up and the temperature dropped.

All the shops closed at five sharp because there were families waiting at home, with dinners of ham and oven-browned potatoes. As the shops pulled the blinds across the front windows and the proprietors stepped out of front doors with long woolen coats tightly belted and scarves tucked in, they turned their keys and locked all the doors. They climbed into their cars and handed dimes to the clerks who had run out half an hour earlier to start them.

If it was a holiday, the bells from Macalester didn't ring and the sons and daughters of St. Paul's businessmen were picked up by car and driven home where they ate turkey or goose and entertained the family with stories of college life. They sat back and drank wine with their parents, which gave them license to confide that they had gotten drunk on beer one weekend. Their parents shook their heads, but the fathers remembered their wild days when they grabbed milk bottles from front steps and smashed them on cement walks before they ran away in the night. The better-off families sent their children to Carleton in Northfield, or to Princeton on the East Coast. The more religious though no less established families sent their children to the Catholic school St. Thomas to learn and be practiced in the correct manner of living, to instill within them the work ethic that they had received before they moved from Boston, or Elmira, New York. They argued over which school they should attend because it was crucial that they get into law or medical school, or work in the state legislature, continuing the good family name in an ocean of Protestants.

The Twin Cities. Cities of shops and solid brick buildings and brownstone that Paul came to from Iowa. The wide streets, not so wide as to be gaping and not so small that they seemed to be closed in or dark, opened to him as he stepped off the Burlington train from Cedar Rapids. His parents had borrowed the neighbor's car and driven him to Cedar Rapids. The roads through the fields and pasture were full of gravel and the car lurched and bumped on its springs. Once they gave way to tar he was glad, and felt no nostalgia or anticipation of longing for the land he grew up in. He was impatient, and his father, too accustomed to driving tractors, drove so slowly that Paul was irritable and ready to get on the train. They got to the station just before his train left, so he didn't have to deal with a long good-bye from his mother. His father's gruff handshake was so painfully obvious that he didn't even feel compelled to take one final look back below him as he stepped up the three steps to his car. All he could think about, no matter how many books he had read with tearful chapters about saying good-bye at the train station, was that the steps were worn and dirty, and the floor of the car was scuffed black by boots and slippery with tobacco juice. Paul sat on his wooden seat and looked around at the other passengers, his neck chafing against the starched collar of his new shirt. He tried not to turn his head in the direction of the window because he knew he would see his parents standing, looking up into the car, trying to spot him among the other people who boarded the train.

He tried to doze in his seat, the way you were supposed to do on the train, and the quiet conversations going on around him, conversations in hushed, even voices about the price of wheat, or feed corn, only reminded him of where he was coming from, and were too familiar to excite him. When he looked out at the scenery passing the windows it was the same old fields of wheat and corn that he had looked out at from the window in his room back home. Even his view from home interested him more: the peeling paint on the window frame, the light curtains, had given him a feeling that he was miles away from the fields that began by the barn and ran for miles in every direction. The farm sounds, the wind in particular, created a distance between him and the earth, while he spent his time in his small attic room. The wheat made little noise in the winds but the corn stalks clacked against one another and the sound created the illusion of movement. Trees would have served that purpose better, but the only trees for miles around had been the elms planted as a windbreak. Not good trees for a windbreak, these had been cut down because of Dutch elm disease. So these trees, the only possible structures of distance and natural history, were merely a double row of blackened and hacked stumps bordering the driveway: two rows of short, rotting sentinels. But these at least had a peculiarity, a difference from the rest of Paul's surroundings, even in their state of rigid, worm- and ant-eaten death. The train, with its bumpy ride and the sound of the wheels, told him that even though he was moving away, his family was only one of thousands stuck out in that brown ocean. The old coal-burning engines had been replaced by electric ones so that he didn't even have the adventure of smoke or cinders flying in the windows. He had wanted his ride to be memorable, a stuffy coach, with cinders whisking in the openings, but the windows were closed, because even though it was early fall, the night air was cool.

He turned every way in his seat, but the wood cut into his legs and his back ached. His shirt burned his neck and he wished his mother hadn't ordered him a new suit. She felt that he should have a new suit to go to the big city and this was the only thing he and his mother had agreed upon. However, it felt stiff and the fabric didn't fold in the right places so even the backs of his knees and the waist, cinched with his old belt, felt abused. It was a brown suit, made of wool, like the city folk were supposed to wear, but it was a rough cut and he longed for his work jeans, which were packed, just in case, deep in his brown cardboard suitcase.

His mother had wanted to fix him a meal to take with him on the train, so she roasted a ham, sliced it, and made him three sandwiches. He hadn't wanted them and the thought of cold greasy ham made his stomach turn. So they too sat next to him, just in case.

The "just in cases" and the constant whispering voices discussing crops and the number of combining outfits added a harmony to the dull turn of the wheels. There was a constant blur; the mixture of the familiar and the alien. It confused Paul and he yearned for either one or the other; anything but the muddling of both.

If Paul looked out as far as he could look, the fields trickled by, floating diligently but with dragging feet. It made his neck itch. He could pick out the individual stalks of corn, the rows of beets, in uncomfortable detail. They were too much that way. The brown, dusty, rusted places crept past. Farmhouses showed their missing shingles and the tractors with their tires bald from grinding against the sand, sagged in the yards. They were great piles of iron and rubber that pulled along the same field every day, every week, dogs too old and tired to want to go anywhere ever.

If he turned his head and concentrated inside the car he was caught in the slow drawl of prices, or the repetition about taxes and seed. But if he stared down at the edge of the tracks it was different. The ties blurred into a brown streak and only when he craned his neck and gazed down to the wheels did it seem that he was getting anywhere.

It occurred to him then, that the tracks didn't stop at his father's farm or even in the Twin Cities. They traveled and carried, supported all sorts of people, not just farmers, well beyond any place he had ever been. Past Winnipeg, past Saskatchewan. As the ties blurred past his window he wondered if they led straight up to the ocean. Paul was used to thinking of the ocean as something that was either east or west. But as he sped toward the Twin Cities he knew that there was the sea straight north of him, and even thousands of miles to the south. So when the farmers spat their tobacco and calculated prices in their heads he was content, because he knew they were surrounded. Paul felt better when he knew that they weren't just lost in a sea of wheat or corn, but caught and snared by a real sea. Salty and deep, it comforted him even though he had never seen it. There was more. It was deeper and wider than any of the people around him knew, or even dared to guess. So at last he was able to fall asleep.

The drought that propelled Paul toward the Twin Cities lasted only a short while. The dust that lifted from the streets and walked into the air, a fact that everyone knew was bad and that should be hated with Lutheran restraint, was welcomed. In whispers. The dust that should have coated everyone's car, carpeted the front porches, and sheened lacquered tables and piano tops was secretly loved for its beauty. It was the kind of weather that the wealthy could afford to love. Because despite the drought, the groundwater levels were as high as usual, and even though the river was low, scraping between the rocks below the dam, it meandered and courted the irregular banks lined with oak in a way that was pleasing to the eye.

Even though the heat blistered the Midwest, everything was as it should be in the Cities. When the bells pealed at noon the sun, which was usually pale and weak, the result of being cowed by the latitude and the strength of the winters, beat back the clouds and danced with the haze of dust in the air. It didn't simmer or make one's vision crazy with lines of heat as it did elsewhere out in the countryside. Instead, it drew people from their homes with wicker baskets full of summer apples, iced tea, and ham sandwiches with lettuce and mustard on fresh-baked bread.

At homes and offices, shirtsleeves went up and windows were left open. The lawns that should have been left cracked and brittle by the sun and dust had a life of their own. They grew so green and thick that when they were cut it was a pleasure just to lie back and feel the mat of blades supporting your weight, only inches above the soil.

The sun that had been visible for weeks on end drew women from inside to the backyards so they could enjoy it on their shoulders and on their arms while they scrubbed the laundry. As they rubbed Fels Naptha into the wet garments, sudsing the water cupped in enameled tubs, they smiled. They smiled into their shoulders both inwardly and outright in front of everyone, at the peculiarity of it all. And they dared to do it in their bare feet. They dared because it was summer in the Cities and the air held it longer, drew it out. It was selfless. It gave whatever their mood commanded and even so, it begged no attention to itself.

Those who lived along the lakes even had enough water for tulips and daffodils, and the spindly potentilla bloomed beyond reason. Some people even had the nerve to plant lilies-of-the-valley, which under any other circumstances would have withered on the spot. Those who planted these delicate plants under eaves and bordering walks dared the sun to prove them foolish, taunted the generosity, and won. Most of the lilies-of-the-valley held and bloomed and no one could remember when it had smelled sweeter. The nectar floated almost visibly to where families dined out on their front porches, or on patios with no screens because even the insects had granted everyone a reprieve. The aroma of those adventurous flower gardens prompted homeowners to put out not one, but two fruit baskets, one in the kitchen and one in the living room. The adults were so pleased that they allowed their children and their friends from next door to take a plum or a peach and eat it between meals while sitting on the sofa, something never before allowed. The scent of lilies-of-the-valley was so full that even the violets seemed to give off a sweet smell, though these were meant for the eye.

When dinner was served, normally heavy meals such as steak or roast together with the thick tender smell of the lilies created a perfect counterpoint that hovered just out of memory, evoking only a feeling or an emotion that, when remembered years later, wasn't so much an event as an aura that suffused every recollection of that summer.

The drought that constricted the fields and farms outside of the Cities, that crumpled ripe corn, that shriveled beets still in the soil, that withered the wheat into patchy stretches of low-grade fiber, barely reached the people living among the wide streets, sleeping on soft mattresses dreaming of full flower beds and the smell of lilies-of-the-valley. There was always enough to eat for them, and the bakeries were stocked with so much bread that the only difficulty lay in the choosing.

While farms folded and combines stood still, becoming more

scenery than machines of utility, the Cities carried on their business as if separated by some divide, some chasm of chance,
linked only by railroads, highways, and newspapers.

Couples picnicked above the dam near the university where
they could watch the warehouses during the day, where the working men sweated and heaved. At night they lay on their backs
and searched the sky for northern lights, softly laughing out
their naiveté, the lights of the Cities outshining anything that
could come from the sky. This was just as well, because this summer, at least, the northern lights saved themselves for the people
up north. Not that the picnickers noticed, they were too involved
in their fortunes of well-packed sandwiches and warm nights under which they lay on the grass.

They stretched out on their lawns and on the grass by the
river, things that previously had been impossible. This summer
the mosquitoes were nowhere to be found in the Cities, and the
dew that used to soak anyone crazy enough to brave the insects
outside never seemed to settle, but hovered somewhere between
sky and earth. It misted the air, but dared not break the spell
holding the Cities in a comforting hug.

Everything was as it should be in the Cities, and Paul hated it.
He hated the streets of St. Paul because of their spaciousness,
their order. Even though they weren't planned that way. Their
turns and dead ends, circles and one-ways were benevolent, always turning those who were lost and confused back on their
paths.

The riots that were beginning to grow in every city south,
east, and west of Minnesota had the good grace not to touch
their hand to the Cities, and once Paul learned of the blessing, he
secretly cursed that too. Perhaps the streets were too wide to
hold anything that could be raucous or teeming, or the buildings
were too short to command a human feeling of entrapment.

For whatever reason, the streets remained empty of anger
and outrage, and of most feelings altogether. Paul even disliked
crossing them. The sidewalks had been constructed so that they
were too wide, and they made Paul feel as though he was simply
walking down another lane, this one cobbled and marked with

storefronts. He imagined cars and buses careening down the expanse of stone and cement that was separated from the streets by a thin row of widely spaced elm, chosen for their straight height and reach.

The walks brought out no emotion nor strong reaction, none that Paul could see. They evoked no intensity from couples or friends. Joys were reduced from exuberance to secret smiles and nudges; a hand on the shoulder of a print sundress, the run of a finger down a white forearm unused to work, veins hidden deep within the flesh. Arguments never rose above frowns or everyday speech marked by distanced eyes and uncadenced delivery.

The streets never invited laughter nor anger. Rough, hard young men, who in the movies lounged around corners and drugstores, never showed themselves in the city. The homes, old and new, big and small, were where the bruises of city living were manifest.

So during his stay in the Cities, Paul was forced to guess behind windows, curtained and lighted, but closed. He was compelled to wonder at the slamming of doors, or was it simply the wind? Smiles between people, whether young or old, made him want to expose the lie. He pondered the success of one Christmas party against the shame of failed others. The torn clothes — an elbow of a mohair suit, the patched shoulder of worn flannel — infuriated him because the rips never spoke to him of intent, and the mended fabric seamed on the inside could never be ciphered, whether they were pulled together by familiar hands or mended by a tailor.

When a tree was downed he was never allowed to know whether it was cherished or simply an obstruction of a dead view, because there was no real view in the Cities. Whatever one wanted to see there had to be invented.

When the winter came, when the flowers were mere memories or crisp impressions from having been flattened between the pages of a heavy dictionary, it took Paul in. The winter sheltered him, warmed him, and was the inevitable price paid for that delicious summer.

It snowed before Halloween and when the children went door-to-door the snow was too dry, the wind too strong, and it was too cold for it to stick to their feet.

The wind caught the crops unaware and the corn, which hardly had the chance to break down and crumple into jagged stalks, had frozen in its place, iced solid. Then one day around sunrise, the wind blew so strongly that all of the stalks crashed down at once. Those who got up at dawn, whether to milk the cows, or to indulge an impulse they themselves could not name, counted themselves as unlucky. They saw, in the collapse of brittle stalks and in the orchestrated harmony of malice — the cold and the wind — omens not only for the coming spring, but for everything unthinkable and thinkable alike that happened thereafter. They could see that the winters had taken final possession of what was theirs. These people had seen hard winters before, they had been frozen, touched. They counted and recounted times when the oil had frozen in its pan, and the tires on automobiles and tractors alike had frozen so solid that they were flat on the bottom, slapping rhythms against the frozen gravel until they reluctantly warmed up. They had seen blizzards when perhaps they had needed to tie ropes from barn to house so they wouldn't lose their way, though it was only a matter of yards from the barn to the front step.

But the simple and final crashing of stalks, which didn't so much as make a sound, spoke of other things, and different hardships yet to be endured; endured even though winter always gives way to something else, as a specific pain transforms into another equally devastating debility, a broken ankle becomes a hurt back, a cut begets infection. The silence of the catastrophe was the true mark of misfortune, just as the suddenness of the transformation was hinted at the end of all things. The farmers who saw the stalks disappear against the iced dirt were forced to consider themselves unfortunate because even though the rows would have eventually decayed if they hadn't been turned under already, they were receiving a sign, if only whispered, of what was yet to come.

Paul knew the signs already, he knew them as sure as he knew the sound of pigs being slaughtered. He knew whispers too, because cows, unlike pigs, never made a sound. So when the winter came, expectedly, inevitably, he was relieved. He could predict the snow and the wind, and the way in which windows were even beginning to shatter against the gusts that had the audacity to enter the Cities.

The winds came from the north, spoke of no compromise, and brought no snow. The drought that had blessed the Cities throughout the summer was vicious when the temperature dropped. The streets were frozen, and even though the city spread salt and sand along them it did little good because there was no snow to melt, there was no ice to scrape or chip off the walks. But even so the cement, the bricks, the marble had a crystalline appearance. They were hard and brittle and people sensed this so they stepped gingerly along the sidewalks, and slammed no doors. They opened faucets slowly and deliberately, just as they walked stairs one step at a time. While striding halls they spoke, and even felt compelled to cajole others to speak, in whispers.

Five hours to the north, beyond the tall buildings on the horizon, and therefore out of reach of the sidewalk imagination of the city people, a priest named Father Gundesohn was being drowned in his church by the people he had wronged. Paul didn't know this, and he never would know why the priest had died. So he would never know why he was to be sent into the north at such a young age that the chill of the wind still buffed his cheeks into a rosy red.

II

Don't do no good to kill a dead Indian

Donovan
1976

It was summer when Jeannette collected us, Little, Jackie, and me, and led us upriver to the dam for the first time.

It was past May. May had rolled over, the lilacs had wilted and dropped off, and I had been released from fourth grade. There hours were not marked by the movement of clock hands red and black, but by the rhythm of scuffles and sighs, and the gentle whirl of chalk dust in the May light. The caragana and the raspberries grew up to the edge of the schoolhouse. They grew up to the warped boards, which had been replaced in spots with painted sheet metal, and topped just below the frost-buckled wooden sills. So, staring out we saw a bed of yellow brands, and beyond that the red pine that grew through town, and beyond that we knew the highway ran, and beyond that, the river. When the half-time janitor clipped the caragana, even pulled it up by the roots, it came back bringing wasps, yellow jackets, bumble-bees, and butterflies. They danced for us, through the warped panes, through the schoolroom dust, the marks of chairs scraped over the varnished wood floors. They danced through the drawl of chalk and the sniffles that marked colds and fevers that had held since February, which no amount of fry bread or commodity cheese could cure.

It was after this that Jeannette relieved us of the games we picked at; games like "assault" — tactics that Stan had learned in the marines — and acting out the egg scene from *Cool Hand*

Luke that we saw on late-night TV. Jackie demanded that she get to be Paul Newman and so she ate the hard-boiled eggs. We did it in her house while Violet was out somewhere; it was a weekend. Jackie started eating, and after the first one asked for salt and pepper and water, but that was against the rules, so she ate them dry. She only got six down before she threw up on the Formica counter and over half the linoleum in the kitchen.

Jeannette collected us from this after the dance of the but-terflies against the sagging glass had ended. Those butterflies, brown- and rust-colored, the ones that graced the caragana also settled on piles of shit or fish guts. We called these small butter-flies "Shiteaters." They had no real color, other than that of shit and dried blood. They lighted on top of the caragana and sat, with their wings moving together and out, together and out. It looked like they breathed with their wings. Slowly, patiently, with no mind as to where they settled, they breathed to us stuck in that room. They danced against the bubbled surface of the windows, and would have joined us in the room if not for the paper-wasps that fed along the yellow arcs of caragana too. Because of the thick-bodied wasps and their indiscrimination about who or what they punctured, the windows always stayed shut. We had to be content dangling our sneakered feet from the rungs of our metal desks, rolling the sand and grit over the pine floors with worn toes.

So it was always beestings that marked our release from the single room of dust and mute insects. When we were let go to get stung and to run barefoot wherever we wanted, slicing the soles of our feet on broken beer bottles, we knew it was summer. When we got scabs on our elbows and let the front door swing open so that the flies battled with the glue strips hanging in the kitchen, when we could spend hours hunting them with rolled-up newspaper, and when Jeannette paid us a nickel for each white moth we could catch and kill because they ate holes through her pea plants and her string beans. When these times came we knew it was summer and it was then that Jeannette rescued us from our games to bring us fishing at the dam.

It must have been June. The lilacs had melted away from the spindly clusters of waxy leaves, and the pile of rotting suckers, left or forgotten since spearing season in an old leaky washtub, had been burned. Duke and Ellis had smelled the rot from their car and when they found the source of the stench they poured a gallon of kerosene into the galvanized tin basin, stood back, and tossed in a blue-tipped farmer's match. They stood back and listened to the maggots crackle like popcorn.

It was after this. After Stan took us aside from our scuffing in the yard dust, away from where he was trying with one hand to shim the sagging front steps, and taught us how to assail a position the way he was taught to do in the marines.

He gave us sticks, broken from the lower trunks of the jack pine that grew behind our house. He put the chipped-bark machine guns in our hands, and gave us each a pop can for a grenade. He knelt on the ground next to the tilted and rotting front step. And we circled around him.

"Do it like this: You gotta find your objective. Your goal. Then you move up on it. Safe though, you've got to keep each other safe. When one of you is moving, the others stay still, behind cover. But looking out. See."

He pretended to duck and peek out from behind something. A stump maybe.

"You gotta aim at the same time, while you're hiding. You can't be looking around, spacing out, looking at the birds, or picking your ass. Because if you fuck around, like talking or smoking, you're going to get it. All right?

"So when one of you's moving, then the others stay under cover until the one in front finds some cover of his own. When they're in good cover then they'll wave the person in back to start going. Then the next person. You keep leapfrogging until you get close enough to shoot, or throw one of your pop cans. Okay?"

I nodded. Jackie flexed her hands and said, "Yep."

Little jiggled in place and offered his one word. You.

Stan ignored it, but put his arms around us, his stump resting on my shoulder.

He leaned in close and whispered.

"Give it a go on the Catalina."

He nodded over to Duke and Ellis's car, where they were playing the radio and smoking. We could see Duke's feet sticking out of the open car window.

We broke up and the three of us headed toward the car. We spread out across the yard, slinking through the weeds, brown-eyed Susans, and the hoary alyssum. We bent our backs low to the ground, and moved around the junk in the yard. It reminded me of the grass-dancers we saw at the Fourth of July Powwow the summer before, with their fringes touching the ground and with painted faces, doing the sneak-up dance, tracking the game while tracking the women at the same time, teasing them where they stood on the edge of the dance grounds.

We crouched. Jackie whispered toward me.

"Cover me."

Little and I hunkered down and aimed our sticks at the rust-riddled Catalina as Jackie sprinted over the open yard and threw herself behind the woodpile. She settled and waved me forward from behind the broken lawn chair that I had chosen.

I jumped up. Ran. Moved my arms and passed the woodpile and Jackie to the sagging and broken fridge, about halfway there. I checked my gun, peered over to the Catalina. I still had my pop can. My gun was still in my hands, my sneakers were tied.

I peered over the top of the blue Frigidaire that lay on its side.

Duke and Ellis hadn't moved. Cigarette smoke trailed out of the windows. I could see horseflies and deerflies zooming in and out of the car. It was Little's turn.

I looked back to where he waited. He was still down by the front step. Stan was squatting next to him, smoking a Camel. Little's hands, his fused and deformed fingers, looked like they were glued to the dead branch.

Jackie hadn't moved an inch, she stared ahead at our objective.

I held the stick-gun in my left hand and waved back to Little. Stan gave him a nudge.

Little jumped up and started running. His legs pumped and his shaggy hair got swept back by the wind. His dirty T-shirt was pressed against his front and he shut his lips together though he was smiling and laughing at the same time.

He blew by Jackie and I turned to face the Catalina so I could cover him. The next thing I knew he had whipped past me. And he kept on running.

Through the grass, past the turned-over Frigidaire, past the burn barrel. He sped beyond all cover out in the open and headed straight for the car.

He was supposed to stop, to let all of us set it up. Stan had said so.

I looked back at Jackie. She shrugged her shoulders and raised an eyebrow. We both stood up and starting running after Little toward the car.

We were about fifty feet behind him and he was still going. He was shouting as he ran.

"You! You! You!"

"Little. Shut up."

We were catching up.

"You! You! You! You!"

Jackie was muttering to herself under her breath, "Jesus Christ."

She sounded just like Jeannette.

Little came up close to the car and, still shouting, dove through the window headfirst onto Duke's lap.

"Holy shit!!" we heard Duke yell and saw a tumble of bodies and clothes in the front seat. Jackie and I ran up to the car door. We saw Duke wrestling Little down in the front seat. The back was empty.

Jackie and I felt something against our backs.

"Got you. And I got you." We knew it was Ellis, so we turned and saw him grinning with his index fingers pointed into our spines.

"Jesus Christ," Jackie said again.

Duke's hand found the door handle and he and Little fell out into the yard dust and grass.

Duke stood up and shook Little off like he was a dog slacking off water.

"We got all of you so good!" He turned in slow circles with his head tilted back and his arms raised high above him. Like Pelé in the end of the movie *Victory.*

"Yes! Yes!"

He was crowing.

"You guys had no idea. No idea. We knew it all along. Knew it!"

I think he was so excited that he was forgetting to complete his sentences.

"You all were dead meat!"

Ellis was laughing behind us, stroking his smooth chin, shaking his head.

"Yep," Ellis said. "Absolutely no idea."

I looked back and saw Stan doubled over, laughing so hard he had to support himself with his stump on the rickety front step.

Jackie and I didn't know what to do. So we just stood there. Jackie cracked a smile and pulled her hair, which had been sticking in her mouth, and tucked it behind her ear.

Little jumped up off the ground and ran around to where Ellis stood behind Jackie and me. He ran up and latched on, hugging Ellis's legs.

Duke was still so excited that he had to light a cigarette just to calm down.

We were standing there, knocking our sticks against our feet, and smiling to ourselves because Duke was beginning to rub off on everyone, when we heard Jeannette yell from the kitchen window of our house, our lilac-and-orange-painted house.

"Christ. Can't you keep it quiet out there? How's an old woman supposed to take a nap?"

Duke took a drag on his cigarette, and spoke up.

"Come on Jeannette. It couldn't have been *that* loud."

"Bullshit."

She leaned her arms against the sill. She was just getting started.

"I may live in a house painted like a gypsy wagon. A house you drunks painted. But that doesn't mean that it's got to be as loud as one."

"Well why don't you try sleeping at night like other normal people?" offered Duke.

"I would," she spat. She was beginning to huff. "If Stan and my daughter weren't so loud."

She leaned further out of the window. There was no screen

and both of her hands were on the sill, her head sticking out into the summer sun.

"I'm shocked," said Duke, still puffing on his cigarette.

He jumped up onto the front hood, his booted heels bouncing against the tire. "I didn't think Stan could last long enough to keep anyone awake."

Ellis busted out and Stan, who was just getting his air back, choked on his Camel, blushed, and sat back down again on the rotten steps.

"Duke." Jeannette sighed his name out. "You wouldn't know what long was any way you cut it. Even on a good day."

Ellis was still holding Little, who was trying to squirm free. Ellis was jiggling because he was laughing so hard.

"Jeannette," he said. "I didn't know you could feel the difference."

Jeannette's hands gripped the peeling sill.

"First you all teach these kids some useless, stupid game. Then. Then you go and talk smut around them. Can't we talk respectable? Can't we teach these kids something useful?"

Jackie and I scuffed pebbles and bottle caps with our feet.

Ellis muttered under his breath, "Well *she* started it anyway."

Jackie and I felt Jeannette sizing us up and down. We stared at the hubcaps on the Catalina.

And finally, softer now, she said, "Come on, I'll take you up to the dam."

We squinted up at her through the sun.

"I'll take you to the dam to catch some fish."

We walked through the cedars.

After the butterflies breathed their wings for us, after the lilacs gave off their final, ripest scent, which Celia and Jeannette skimmed off cups of water set on the sills, and after we learned how to attack the position of old identical twins in their rusted-out car, Jeannette rescued us and brought us to the dam. A place we visited for years, when the summer drew long, and the black-flies were too much to bear, and when we knew the river was finally ours. Though by that time it was just Jackie and me. Little had died.

Saying that we should learn something useful, Jeannette collected Jackie and me from where we stood on the outside of a joke, from where Little danced around it, and walked us upriver to the dam. She walked us in the light of the river. It was afternoon, and we walked underneath the drooping branches of the smooth-barked cedars that cut a smell so good that it was everywhere: hovering just behind the trunks, in the air ahead and above, and it cloaked us from sight along the old path we never knew existed before.

We never knew, Little, Jackie and me, though we had been to the river so many times before. We never knew of the path, could never have known what to look for; the creased trunks, the mat of roots, the saw grass and red willow, all of which hid and protected that path that courted the river, and that Jeannette said was "really old-time."

We couldn't have guessed behind the fringed gentian and the joe-pye weed, sometimes "old-time" things. But not forgotten, like a scar or a favorite shirt left at a cousin's house during deer season. When we find these things again they come back, we are visited again by how the mark found its way onto our skin forever, and are reminded of the people we met, the meals we had in that shirt. So that's why . . . or so this is where it is. No cry or outburst. So our journey down the trail at the river's edge was marked by silence on our part, and the careful feet of Jeannette remembering over the twisted roots and over the dips and bends. At times the trail looked like nothing; the weeds and marsh grass sprang up among the smooth sweet-smelling trunks and I thought it was done, that Jeannette had forgotten or lost the way. But she pushed through, while the river flowed on our right. She pushed through gently, gently remembering through.

It was like when Little's intestines got stopped up. He couldn't shit and he screamed with it. I thought he was going to die because this wasn't like him; he couldn't open up, and it was torturing him. He clawed with his deformed hands, and screamed and sweated in Celia's bed. Jeannette sat by him and pushed through his stomach, kneaded the skin and sang some "old-time" song until he fell asleep. I had been confused at what was going on in the first place. I asked and they said it was his "track." I thought they said "Tract," that his Tract wouldn't move, and that meant us. They said they needed the Tract to move, and confusing Little's bowels with our group of houses I tried to help the best I could by packing all of my stuff into garbage bags, which I set by the front door.

Pushing like that, away from the Tract, along the path heading to the dam, Jeannette remembered her way along the river. It wasn't until years later, until Duke and Ellis left, that I knew her passion for that river, and for them.

When we rounded the bend and walked off the path where it ended, where it had been bulldozed smooth to make the approaches to the bridge, we saw the dam.

Of course we had seen it from the road, through car windows, from the backs of pickup trucks, but up close we had never seen the great slabs of concrete, the rusted metal railings, the surrounding chain-link fence. These we had never seen up close or walked among, like we do now.

From our level it sat above us as we picked our way along the bank, over the rocks they had dumped there in some crude excuse for rip-rapping. We worked our away along the boulders and the scrub pine that grew among them, until we came up against the chain-link fence. There we stopped and looked to Jeannette; we didn't know where to go except through.

The fence, chain-linked and strung with barbed wire along the top, traveled down to the edge of the river and extended a good three feet past the bank. The water was dark with depth and current so we didn't dare cling to the mesh and work our way around. Back tows and undercurrents, Jeannette said, would suck us down and hold us at the bottom for weeks until suddenly a current or underwater eddy would free us up and we would float to the surface dead and covered with leeches. That's what Jeannette said anyway. And as we looked across the deep channel over to the shallows below the let-down, we knew that it was too far to cast across, especially with the old battered open-face spinning rod that we had borrowed from Duke and Ellis. Who knows where *they* got it. Anyway, it was too far to the other side, and we didn't know what to do. We looked up to Jeannette again.

"Well, you gonna stand there all day?" she asked.

We shrugged in unison.

"Under. Under. Pull up the fence and crawl under."

We searched the fence down by our feet and saw that the bottom of the fence had been pulled loose from the twisted-wire couplings and bent in so that it would be harder to snag clothing and skin on the rough cuts of the metal. The dirt and rocks had been scraped away too so that there was a hollow.

"I'll go first," Jackie volunteered.

She tucked in her T-shirt and bent down next to the ground. Headfirst, she eased her way in. She arched her back, and once her arms were through, pulled herself forward with her hands. It looked like she was doing the limbo, only in reverse. But that was only natural because Violet said that *she* was the best limbo dancer on the reservation, the limbo queen. Violet claimed that she could go under a broomstick a foot off the ground without even touching her hair to the floor. Jackie was giving her mother a run for her money by squirming under the fence.

Once she was through she stood up and brushed the pebbles, broken clam shells, and dirt from the front of her blue T-shirt and her faded jeans. Then, flipping her hair over her shoulder she stooped and grabbed the bottom of the fence with her hands and pulled. A bigger space opened and I turned to Little.

"Little, go on. It's your turn."

He walked up to the fence, and tensing his legs like he was going to do the standing long jump he jumped up, and latched on to the fence. He started climbing the wobbly, poorly strung chain link.

"No, Little! No. Go under the fence!"

He kept climbing, lifting his crooked, deformed hands and reaching higher.

"Get down, fool! You'll cut yourself up," snapped Jeannette.

Little kept climbing up until he reached the barbed wire. Then he vaulted one leg over at a time, and pushed away with his arms and landed on the other side. Smiling. Without a scratch.

He grinned at me.

"You."

I shook my head.

"No way. I ain't no Bruce Jenner," I mumbled.

"Hurry before my arms fall off," called Jackie. She was still bent over, hoisting on the fence.

I bent and crawled through. Even Jeannette stooped, lay down, and pulled herself through, though she was going to turn seventy in August.

"Higher," she said. "Pull it higher. I don't want to rip my dress."

I helped Jackie strain on the fence. Once Jeannette was through she stood straight, grabbed the front of her cotton print dress, and shook it free of dust and bits of broken glass.

"Let's go," she said. She took the lead and we walked along the bank reinforced with concrete that rose above the river. We approached the body of the dam.

The channel of water from the turbines was on our side, the right bank, and Jeannette led us across the narrow plank walkway that ran above the channel. I looked down and it was dark, fast-moving water. We had no idea how deep it was.

Sweat was beginning to drip down my neck.

The sun was still high, but hidden by the bulk of the dam to our left. The surface of the water coursing from the chute was rippled, but not like waves, nor like the pictures of sand dunes I looked at once. It was all tight swirls and dents. Like fat or muscle, the river water was puckered into dimples and ridges, and it looked so deep and thick. I hurried along the pressure-treated planks that held me above it.

The causeway ended on a cement platform about twenty feet square, ten feet above the water level. On the other side of the platform the let-down sloped at a forty-five-degree angle from the top of the dam to four feet above the water. A thin sheet of water slipped down over the top and smoothed over the concrete that had been worn slick, and tumbled gently over the ledge onto the rocks below.

We stood on the platform while we wondered where to fish.

I took the tackle that we had collected from toolboxes and back seats from where I had stuck it in my back pocket, wrapped in a paper towel. All we had were a few hooks, a chipped Lazy-Ike that swam crooked, and a bent red-and-white Dare Devil with the paint flaking off the metal spoon-shaped lure.

I took them from my back pocket and separated them from where they had dug in and torn the paper towels, and then placed them carefully down on the cement.

Jeannette looked at them disdainfully.

"You expect to catch fish with those?"

I tried to explain what Duke and Ellis had told me: that the Lazy-Ike was supposed to look like a minnow and that it even swam like one when you pulled it through the water the right way.

"Donovan, it's painted orange. And I don't think I've *ever* seen an orange minnow."

I told her what else Duke and Ellis had said: they had said that fish were color-blind.

She threw her hands up in the air, gesturing the whole expanse of the river.

"Then why don't I just drag my house behind a canoe? I'm sure I'd catch a whole mess of fish then. Donovan, who told you this stuff?"

Jackie backed me up, "Duke and Ellis did."

"Oh God," she rolled her eyes. "I should've known. Come on, we'll catch some bait."

None of us really knew what she meant, but we followed her as she walked to the edge of the platform next to the let-down. We saw that it had been crumbling and eroding with the constant moisture, and that it sloped down to the water's edge.

By grabbing the wild rose and the small river willow that grew into the cracks in the cement, we were able to lower ourselves down onto the rocks below the let-down. I looked around. No bait. It was shallow below the let-down, and the field and river stone that had been piled there to stop the erosion stuck up out of the water. We could move from rock to rock without getting our feet wet. The water wasn't more than six inches at its deepest parts in its slow course between the stone.

Jackie, Little, and I started moving downstream.

"Not there," Jeannette called out.

She hadn't moved from where she stood next to the let-down, and the spray was beading in her hair. Her hands were on her hips, and she balanced with her feet on two separate rocks. As we rock-hopped over to where she was, she bent down and started unlacing her canvas high-tops. She carefully pulled the laces from the eyelets of her Chuck Taylor's, and tied the laces together in a bow knot. She swore that they were the best shoes on the market.

We untied our shoes too, and knotted them and slung them over our shoulders, with both shoes bumping our chests so that they wouldn't fall off when we bent over.

Following Jeannette we walked in the water with the let-down at our left side, the water spraying our backs, which were already getting hot in the June sun. Jeannette crouched down as she picked her way slowly forward.

"Look in the rocks," she instructed, speaking over her shoulder as she peered at the rough seam of cement and river stone.

We bent our heads close to the river and squinting against the patter of water thrown up from the rocks we searched for whatever Jeannette thought was there.

The sun escaped above the let-down and it pushed against our backs as we swung and balanced our weight from foot to foot along the stones slicked with algae and wet moss. The light played off the splashing water and hit the tops of the wet rocks. Deep down we could hear the low hum of the turbines rounding in the dam.

There was the smell of the water, an algae smell, a growing smell. It wasn't rotten or moldy, it was patient, it was calm. It was with these smells, and with the small sound of the splashing water, and with the kingfishers swooping and crying over the shallows, that our eyes grew used to the wet rocks and running water so we finally saw what Jeannette had known was there all along.

By the edge of the cement let-down, pushed between the boulders and the concrete, we saw them. Minnows. They must have been swept over the top of the let-down and killed by the drop onto the rocks. They had been killed and kept there by the rocks and the slow current, tucked back and kept cool by the continuously falling water. They were big and there were all kinds of them: chubs, shiners, red-horse and sucker minnows, fish too small or too young to avoid the suck of the dam and the pull of the current.

Jackie and I gasped at the same time, and even though I couldn't see her face I knew she was smiling just like me. We began reaching for them.

"Told you so," said Jeannette.

We grabbed them with our open hands, skin gone puckered by water against the fitted scales as smooth as wet plastic. We closed our fingers over them but they were soon full and the bright silver-speckled fish slipped back into the water where they floated sideways a bit until they sank and shimmered under the current. I took off my T-shirt and we used it as a bag, gathering the edges together with my fist. We filled it with the dead minnows. Once we had enough, twenty or thirty, we turned and felt our feet along the rocks back to the bottom of the platform. We clambered up to the top, coating our feet with dust, rose thorns sticking in our hands. We climbed to the top to where we had left the hooks and the battered rod that Jackie had left next to them, that Jackie had insisted on carrying from Poverty.

We caught our breath and scanned the breadth of the river, from the dimpled channel over to the rocky shallows. We looked for the right spot to fish, *the* spot, though we knew without Jeannette's having to tell us that the only real place to fish would be the drop-off. That was right below the platform.

Jackie pulled the only bobber we found back at Poverty from the fraying front pocket of her jeans and set it down next to the bait, the hooks, and the rod. We had scoured the closets, looked below kitchen sinks, had searched under the front steps and in Stan's toolbox, and finally found one, only one, among the clothes and scattered tools (a screwdriver, an unopened package of Champion spark plugs, a crow's foot pry bar) on the floor in the back seat of the Catalina.

It was the red-and-white plastic kind, red on the bottom and white on the top. Like a buoy. There had been a small hole cracked in the side that we had patched with a small square of duct tape, and we hoped that it would float well enough.

Jackie, Little, and I squatted down next to each other around

Jeannette and the hooks and rod, to watch her tie the hook.

She snipped off the kinked end of the line with her teeth, and wetting the plastic line out of sewing habit, she threaded it through the eye of the rusted hook.

"Twist it five times," she said, holding the doubled line between her thumb and her index finger, while she stuck her other pointing finger through the loop and whirled it around the way you would spin a ring from the cap of a plastic milk jug during breakfast, or whirl a key chain.

"Then bring it back through the loop."

Pushing it past the clear line she let the end go and, wrapping the line about the hook around her left hand, she hooked her pinkie on the curve of the hook and pulled it all tight.

After we put the bobber on four feet from the hook we stuck on a minnow, a fat shiner. Slipping the barb through the tiny frozen "O" of its mouth and then up through its spine. Our fishing rig was complete.

After brushing her hands off on her skirt, she picked up the rod and handed it to me.

"Put it over the drop-off."

I knew this, but I didn't say a word as I pressed the line against the fiberglass rod and flipped the bail open with my thumb.

I had to hold the rod above my head so the dead shiner bait wouldn't drag on the ground, and rotating it around once, like I was lassoing in slow motion, I let my finger off the line. The bobber and the baited hook sailed out over the water. It landed perfectly; twenty feet out from the platform right over the drop-off.

"Cool," said Jackie.

Little didn't say anything.

We sat and dangled our feet off the platform while we watched the bobber travel back and forth between the conflicting currents of the channel and the water from the let-down. It was caught in an eddy and it idled there in the sun.

Ahead, over the surface of the river, the kingfishers swooped down from the branches of the spruce and cedars, picking at the surface for fish that we couldn't see. They either couldn't fly straight, or they didn't want to. They cut at the air, knifed it with their wings, fought with it, like when you stick your hand out a car window while doing eighty and it gets pushed up or down, just by the movement of your pinkie.

We liked them, the kingfishers; they were never still with their flicks and sudden loops and low passes over the water. We admired them like we admired hoop-dancers we didn't know; they were all grace and skill, but sometimes they took themselves too seriously.

The sun had arced beyond the top of the dam and parted between the taller trees on the far bank. It gilded the surface of the river downstream, highlighted by the pollen and fluff from the weeds along the bank, taken up by the down from dead cattails. Like fat on broth, it was broken only by the ripples of fish lipping dead dragonflies off the surface.

The hooked bait hung somewhere below surface, hidden by the shadow of the dam and the murky water. The bobber lazed on the surface until we didn't pay it much attention.

We leaned back, passed the rod from hand to hand, and kicked the cement with our heels. We picked at the grass that grew in the cracked cement where the seeds had been blown into the fissures and the soil broken from the solid form of the cement platform.

Jeannette told us of the river, what it was like in Davenport, that it was a mile across at least and muddy top to bottom with topsoil and barge traffic. She said that there weren't any pike down there, instead there were catfish. She had to explain that they looked like bullheads, but that they grew to one hundred pounds.

We couldn't imagine it then, couldn't see it. A mile across? Our river that big? And with monster bullheads to boot.

We laughed at the thought of flat-nosed barges butting their way up the river, much less any boat with a motor trying to navigate the river, a river that was for us so shallow in most places that you were hard pressed to a find a sinkhole or an undercut bank deep enough to wet your head without lying down. We believed that our relationship with the Mississippi River was untroubled.

The rod came back to me. I wondered if the shiner had been

nibbled or had fallen off the hook. I started to reel it in to see if we had to put another one on.

"It's still there," Jeannette assured me. "What's it gonna do, swim off the hook?"

I peered down, trying to part the waters with my eyes so I could tell for sure that the hook was still baited.

"Jig it, Donovan," said Jeannette.

I bounced the tip of the rod up and down. I only did it a few times.

Then the bobber disappeared.

"Good going, dork," said Jackie. "It fell off."

She was getting bored.

I craned my neck and looked to see if the hole in the side of the bobber had caused it to sink. I looked down and saw the red-and-white bobber angling away toward the deep part of the channel; not floating or sinking, but cutting a straight line to the deep water.

Jeannette jumped to her feet and started shouting.

"Set it! Set it! Set the hook!"

I jerked up hard on the rod, and somewhere below the surface, below the bobber, somewhere *down there*, something jerked back harder.

"Holy shit, we got one!" I was shouting.

Everyone was on their feet.

Little was jumping up and down. Jackie had moved next to my shoulder. Jeannette was leaning over the water with her hands on her knees, trying to get a better look.

"Don't give it any slack, it'll snap the line!"

I think it was Jeannette who was shouting orders.

The drag was screeching and line was whipping off the spool. But the surface of the river hadn't changed.

"Don't let it get in the rocks, it'll break the line off on them."

Jeannette never gave good advice when you had the opportunity to listen to it.

I took the crank in my right hand and, easing the rod up, I turned it around once as I let the tip go down again. The drag was quieter; the fish must have stopped its straight run, it must have been trying to zig-zag. I was able to take up more line; pull up, dip and crank, pull up, dip and crank. I was taking in line turn by turn. It was like climbing up a steep hill of mud: slip and pull, gain ground and lose a hold. It was like slowly mounting a muddy slope but with the adrenaline rush of being one number away from bingo.

However, you never sit for long on the edge of your seat at the bingo hall with a dabber in one hand and a cigarette in the other. Well, not for as long as I sweated the big fish jerking and slicing through the water below the dam.

My hands were sweating, and I could taste salt on the ledge of my upper lip. My forearms ached and shook, they were cramping and trembling as the tip of the rod beat a pattern through the air in front of me. Even though there was struggle — my shaking arms and the quivering rod, the fish thrashing below — the surface was perfect calm.

There was no wind, the kingfishers had settled in the trees while the motes of pollen, the dandelion spores, and the tufted filaments of dead cattails dipped lazily down the river. The surface of the water rushing in the channel didn't make much sound. The low hum of the turbines was dim and constant.

I didn't have much time before the fish broke loose. There were so many points in the system connecting me and the fish, and the balance of these points, their symmetry, could dissolve or break easily. There was the hook itself, lodged somewhere in the fish. It could have pierced a cartilaginous lip, or fixed solidly through pink gills, or even driven through the eyeball and socket up through the top of the skull. There was also the knot that Jeannette had tied. Her old hands could have cinched it tight while the line was twisted so that the pressure would cause it to snap, or the rusted eye of the hook could fray the line. And then there was the entire distance of monofilament line, fifty feet or more of clear plastic, which at any point along its length could have the smallest nick or scrape. The smallest damages that were impossible for us to spot could snap the line like dry spaghetti noodles if there was enough weight on the end; and there was.

This system of catches and knots, catches and tensions, extended up to the rod itself, which was made from cheap fiberglass and rusty, brittle metal eyelets that guided the line into the clanking reel. The reel itself was untrustable and after our fight with the northern pike it was put out of commission forever. It wasn't the reel that broke, and we didn't know it was a pike until right before all hell broke loose.

We saw a flash below the surface, almost like when we shot bottle-rockets into the lake and they exploded underwater. We saw a flash less than ten feet out in front of us, while the top of the water remained calm. We knew it was a pike because nothing else turns its side, nothing else has such a long stretch of belly colored like thick cream.

I kept pulling and it flashed again closer to the surface. The water boiled up where we had seen the second streak of white, and instead of diving again it jumped into the air.

It was huge; the body arced into the air and even through its water spray we could all see that it was at least three feet long. The fish slammed back down into the water. I took in line so it couldn't dive again. The northern thrashed against the surface, pulled against the line, but I had cranked it too short for it to go anywhere.

As it was about to jump again, the tip of the rod, which had been bent almost double, snapped off and hung by shreds of fiberglass.

The line was going to break. But Little stepped up to the edge of the platform and without a noise, he jumped into the channel on top of the fish, and they both disappeared below the surface.

Jackie and I screamed his name.

We were bent over the edge of the platform yelling for him until Jeannette cuffed us both upside the head.

"We gotta get down there."

I dropped the rod onto the cement and we ran over the slope of crumbling concrete and gravel next to the let-down and slid to the water's edge. We waded the shallows toward the drop-off, toward the muscled waters of the channel. Past our ankles and over our shins, dragging at the fabric of our jeans, the water got deeper. The current was getting stronger but we forced our way further into the water, up to our thighs, and then to our waists. We reached the edge where the bottom dropped away to the channel. It looked different the closer our eyes came to meeting the water — the pace seemed faster than it had above. Rippling and flexing, it pulsed out from the open mouth of the dam. Once we were in it we knew it was stronger than we were.

The sunlight that caressed the surface of the river downstream was blocked by the height of the dam, shut out by the cement platform on which we had been standing. We stood in the water frantically looking for Little. The tea-colored water and the tight current curtained the river bottom from our gaze, but we fought with it. In front and below us we saw Little's form on the bottom of the river in more than seven feet of water.

There was no way we could reach him; the current would carry us away and we didn't have anything long enough or with enough strength to fish him out.

We were running out of time.

Jeannette had no advice for us, and we didn't know what Little would do underwater; whether he would drink it in, hold his breath, or just lie there on the bottom.

I looked around my feet for something that would help. Nothing but rocks, flat, round, small, large, all sizes.

I bent down and started loading them into the pockets of my jeans. The pants were loose, and I began cramming handfuls of them in every pocket I could.

"Donovan. What the hell are you doing!" Jeannette yelled.

"Rocks," I said.

"What?" asked Jeannette and Jackie together. They must have thought I was going insane.

Once all of my pockets were full I bent down and heaved the largest stone I could. Then, holding it with both hands, I stepped forward to the drop-off. My head disappeared under the water.

I was in the shadow, the shadow of the dam and the shadow of the water; tannic-acid brown and fast. The current pulled at my legs, tugged at my torso, but the rocks held my feet on the bottom, anchored me as I took another step forward to where I could see Little's shape on the river bottom below me.

The current snatched at me, jamming against my bare chest. It twirled my hair with stubby claws.

I took another step. Another. Little's body became clearer and I saw that he had latched onto something; he had his legs and arms wrapped around the northern pike, and he wouldn't let go.

I stepped again, the current was pulling the strength out of my legs. My lungs hurt, I wanted to open my mouth. My hands were slipping from the stone, my fingers felt like they were being bent back by the water. If I let go of it I knew I would shoot to the surface.

Another step. I was close to Little now. The deeper I got the harder it was to keep myself on the bottom. I was leaning to my right against the force of the current. Little was just ahead of me on his back. He didn't seem to have any problem with staying down there.

He was on his back with his legs scissored around the pike, which was almost as long as he was. He hugged his arms around the pike's head and his crooked hands were folded underneath his arms, by the fish's head somewhere.

I was running out of air. My head felt light. My arms were shaking. And the water was cold, banging into my ears, jetting up my nose.

Another step. Almost there.

Another step. Closer.

He was two feet away.

The rock in my arms was slipping.

It fell from my arms and I bent down and made a grab for his shirt.

I missed and my hands scrambled for any part of him I could hold.

I made a grab and landed a fistful of hair. Bending my knees, I jumped for the surface. I shot upward but Little's weight stopped me short.

Heaving, I curled my arm into my body, pulling Little up close to me.

We broke surface downriver twenty yards into the sun and the kingfishers, the cattail plumes.

The depth of water was still over our heads but I pulled Little's face out of the water. I couldn't tell if he was breathing.

We floated downstream and I tasted the air. There was nothing to stop us from being carried by the river. I tried to turn my head so I could see where Jeannette and Jackie were, but with

Little plastered to me I couldn't move. I was dizzy and it was all I could do just to stick my head out of the water.

Suddenly I felt a hand on my neck; it moved around to under my chin and I felt myself being pulled over to the shallows.

"I got you, Don. It's okay."

It was Jackie, and although she wasn't strong or tall enough to lift us out she held on and we swung away from the faster current until I kicked my legs and felt gravel under my feet. I stood up and pulled Little by his hair along into shallower water. I laid him down and knelt close. I looked into his face.

"Hey, Little."

He looked around, and smiled at me. He was alive, but he hadn't disentangled himself from the pike.

I pulled his legs loose and pried his arms apart. There was blood running down his left arm. I grabbed the fish and tried to wrest it away from him, from where it almost stuck to his body. Pulling the fish away I saw that he had crammed his right hand up into the gills of the pike.

The fish was dead.

I took his arm and jerked it free of the pike. The gills ripped out and his wrist and the back of his hand were cut jagged from the rough edges. Later, we filled a cup with iodine and dunked his whole hand in. It was cut bad.

We all lay in the shallows, breathing hard and listening to the water coursing around us, cooling as the sun went down. The light was fading and the swallows were beginning to dart at the dragonflies that hovered over the water, snatching at fish-flies and mosquitoes.

Jeannette sighed, not an impatient sigh, more like a tired sound.

"I gotta be the grandmother of the two stupidest kids on the reservation, maybe the whole state of Minnesota."

I turned my face away from her. Little was still in my arms, sleeping.

We stood up and waded down the edge of the river to the bridge. I knew Jeannette didn't mean it, and as we walked she rubbed my head and pulled Little close, holding his hand. Jackie carried the fish, which we later found out weighed over twenty pounds, and she shifted it from her arms to over her shoulder and back again until she was coated with slime.

It was dark by the time we made it onto the "old-time" path. The cedars shrouded us and even though the river was only a few feet to our left, it was hard to hear. There wasn't any moonlight to be seen between the trunks. No reflections off the river's surface were visible. It was like the river was cowed by our rescue of Little and by his theft of the fish. The river hushed itself and slunk along next to us.

So without sound and without light we made our way along the path. The cedar boughs shut out the stars and replaced the view with the smell of sap, sweet and sharp at the same time.

All we had was a twenty-pound pike and ourselves as we walked back to Poverty. Even though none of us could see a thing, Jeannette led us all the way without faltering once.

Stan

It didn't matter whether we went down the trail (a night march) or stayed camped where we were. It was still raining; we were still in Vietnam and we were still cold, sober, unshaven, and hungry. My hands were still scarred, puckered from rain, cut from brush, stones, and needles. My fingertips were still blackened from trying to smoke the last shreds of a single joint passed among five men.

Not that the war was all that bad. How Pick and I stuck together from the reservation clear to Vietnam busts me, but we were together. He and I had just been talking that day, about how comfortable we were there, in the jungle.

"It's just like home." Pick was from the same reservation, though he didn't live at the housing tract we called Poverty. He lived with his brothers on the other side of town. I think we were cousins. He had a long face, puckered and bumpy, scars from too much fry bread. I asked him once if someone had tried to put out a fire on his face with an ice pick. I only asked once, cause he busted up my jaw. We had been drinking, and there was this girl he was trying to pick up, so he had to make a show. After he hit me I tried to tell him that he shouldn't fuck her anyway since she was his cousin. 'Course my jaw didn't work so well so I didn't say anything. His arms were so damn long. He stood a good six-two. From then on I just called him Pick. He looked like a tooth-pick and he always had one in his teeth too. He said it kept him from smoking.

116

"It's just like home," he was saying around his grubby tooth-pick, "We get all our food in cans, and we get checks from the government!" he laughed and damn if his teeth weren't bright. White, they looked like horse teeth.

"Yeah, and we're always ducking cause some asshole's trying to fuck us up."

"Here, they got every reason to want our asses on a pole. The best thing is that we get to kill 'em back. Your dad would've loved it here."

"The only reason he would've liked it here is he could kick your ass without having to go over to your house to do it." He just smiled his horse smile at me, his toothpick clamped between his teeth. Pick had wrestled my little sister down, to steal a kiss. Violet was six and Pick was ten. After he left, my dad went over to his house and slapped him dry.

"Where do you get all your toothpicks anyway?" asked Roy. He was a little white boy.

"They don't grow 'em here." Pick leaned closer, taking the wood out of his mouth.

"I whittle them. From ammo boxes." We all started laughing. Roy shook his head: he was a bible boy from Ohio. His mouse-brown hair was slicked black from the rain. When he shook his head, he reminded me of a dog, shaking, wanting to be let in. We just called him Bible, cause he carried one right in his backpack. He was always reading it until his face paint and mosquito repellent soaked into it in the rain. All the ink ran together so every page was just a streak of black. The only thing that you could read was the title page, The Holy Bible, published in New York. He went out to buy a new one but the only one he could find was in Vietnamese. He couldn't read it, but when we asked him if we could use the pages to start a fire in the rain one day he said that the word of God was the same in all languages. Yeah, Pick had said, and our asses are freezing in all languages too. Pick ripped out some pages for the fire.

"A bullet is gonna come flying, looking for the box it come from and it's gonna jump in your mouth. It's gonna jump in and root around your brain," John-Two gestured with both his hands around the barrel of his gun. We had two Johns in our squad. We

called them John-One and John-Two so we wouldn't get them
confused. They were both from Alabama, but John-One was
white as a paycheck, and John-Two was black as oil.

It had been our first week in the bush when we started calling
them One and Two. When we started calling them that, Two
went up to One and said that he knew why he had been called
Two. One just stood there, looking at his hands. It was dusty and
there was a haze in the air that stuck to the sweat on our arms
and necks, creating rings of filth.

"So you're One. And I'm Two, huh?"

"Look John, I didn't start that shit. I'll call you John. Just
fuck it, okay?" He kept on staring at his hands, picking some
mud off the barrel of his M-16.

"Now One, why do you think they call me Two?"

"Don't know man. Jesus, you were fuckin' born John, I was
fuckin' born with the same fuckin' name." Sweat dripped into his
eyes along with the dust and grime on his forehead. "Jesus fucking Christ."

"Maybe you should call me Two. Maybe it'll help remind
you."

"Come on John." One turned to walk away.

"Hey One. You ever treat me like my name and I'll bust you
up." One nodded as he walked away. He talked over his shoulder.

   "One thing, Two. We're both here. Both our asses are all the
way over here."

"Now ain't that the truth of it all."

One just kept on walking away.

Up ahead, MC raised his hand in the brown air. We kept our
pace until we reached where he had stopped with Roy, who had the
honor of carrying the radio. They picked the runt of the squad to
carry it; that piece-of-shit talk-box must have weighed forty
pounds. The trail we were following ran right beside a stream, and
up ahead I could see the village's rice paddy fan out in the distance. The stalks were brown and stuck up in clumps. They only
stuck out of the water about a foot and they grew in rows, but I
just wanted a mouthful of some wild rice from back home. Just a
mouthful of lake wild rice. Or maybe a bowl of it with some milk

and sugar over it. Anything but the shit we got. The only time we ate right was when we stole a pig from a farmer near the base the first week we got over. The pig was small but we fried it up over a fire and we ate the pieces hot right off the sticks. The fat dripped down our chins and our faces were all shiny and slick.

"Okay boys!" MC shouted. That fuckin' Anglo was always hollering in our ears. Maybe that's why we were losing; in World War II most people fighting were white so it didn't matter if they were loud or not, but in Nam it was mostly white against mostly dark, and whites just can't seem to keep their mouths shut. He put the radio up on Roy's pack. He held the coordinate map in one hand and his gun in the other with the butt resting on the toe of his boot. Two stood next to me and leaned in close to my ear.

"I fuckin' hate bein' called 'boy,'" It was Two who started calling our Sergeant MC. His last name was Connolly. The "M" stood for Master. We told him it meant Mister.

"All right, shut up Two," MC glanced around the whole squad. "Second Company fucked up this place yesterday. Really fucked it up. We got the papers taking pictures all over so keep it cool. Keep it really cool. We're just stopping to get some food, so don't mess around."

It was the first village we had seen. The village was dry, cracked all around the edges. The dogs were all skinny and the dirt was packed into their greasy fur as they nosed around the doorways and outside the open windows where the old women sometimes threw a spoiled bone through the gaping hole where there wasn't even a woven bamboo shutter to keep out the flies. The flies were everywhere around the place. They flew inside all the huts and gathered in small groups on the dogs. They rubbed and chewed the dogs' ears until it was a wonder they had any ears at all, because they bled continually. Some of the villagers had been hit the day before and the flies swarmed around the cuts, scrapes, and burns. There wasn't any food in the whole village. At least that we could find. MC ordered us to look through the houses. The people just sat and watched. Some stared right at us. Others gazed straight through. Pick and I split from the others and went up to the first shack. An old woman sat in the doorway and we had to step over her if we wanted to get inside. She had gray hair that hung in rags down her back and her blue-gray dress was mottled with blood and dust. Pick squatted next to her.

"Hey, we gotta get some food." She didn't say anything, clasping her hands together patiently.

"We need to get inside," I said. I made a motion with my hand to the rear of her hut. She blinked her eyes as a fly landed on her nose. She held them shut against the sun and the grit in the air.

"I can't do this shit, Stan." Pick stood up and paced next to me.

"MC told us, man. He told us to get the food."

Pick turned. "Look at her, man. Look at her. Can't do it." He stood up and we walked back to where the others waited in the center of the village. No one got any food but the dust that stuck in our throats. Since then I always welcome the rain.

Now it was four months later and Pick was pointing to his helmet, and there were dozens and dozens of toothpicks he had whittled, stuck in the band of his camouflage helmet cover.

"Two, if a bullet wants to come and root around my brain it can try. Those bullets can come and try. Come on now, you guys should know that shooting out my brain wouldn't do no good anyway. Every government agent knows that Injuns don't got brains. You think we'd live on the rez if we knew better?" His voice got real quiet. "You want to kill an Indian?" He leaned in close to us all again, looking around as if to guard his secret.

"The only way to kill an Indian is to kill his horse first. Do you see any horses around here?" Pick sat back with his arms behind his head, one leg crossed up on the other.

"I'm safer than anyone else out here."

"Oh yeah," said Two. "Well I can't die neither."

"You got a horse hid on you somewhere, Two?" Pick started opening Two's pockets, nosing around his pack.

"Get off, man. That's the problem with you Indians. You're all communists." We all busted out laughing.

"That's right. You're the reason we're over here. That domino theory's correct. The next commie country ain't gonna be in Asia. Shit, it's goin' to be right in the middle of fuckin' America." He winked at me and I nudged Pick.

"Yo, Comrade Injun brother. Let's take over this here black comrade and show him that he's a capitalist pig." Sitting there, we lit up some of Two's cigarettes.

It had been dry when we were marching around earlier that day, but later on it began to rain. Mist, then harder, then a steady patter dripping off the rim of my helmet and soaking into all our clothes. We'd thrown away our rain gear before, it made too much noise. Besides, there was one guy who was with us and who was shot when he was wearing it. It was the first day out and he was the only one wearing his gear, and they could see him 'cause the moon shone off it. It was raining hard, the moon peeked through a hole in the clouds and, bam, John was dead. He got sniped. He was called John too, now we call him JFK (as in John-'Fore-Now). Someone suggested that we call him LBJ because for one, Kennedy is dead, and "*now*" isn't spelled with a *K*. Roy said that LBJ could mean Long-Back-with-John, or Lucky-Bitch-got-Jacked. But JFK stuck. We didn't really use time, months, days, hours. Our time was deaths, surprise attacks, and paychecks.

So by that night we were soaked and MC was radioing to the tents 5Ks back up the trail askin' some fuck lieutenant what we should do. He must have said get a good position and stay the night, 'cause MC shut off the radio and told us to start hoofing it down the trail. He turned to me.

"Stan. Indians are supposed to be good scouts. So hike your ass down and be point man, you too Pick. And John-Two, get your skinny ass along with theirs, we need a good nose down there."

We moved off down the trail. John-Two shook his head.

"We should be running around killing fuckers like that, not VC." He was walking behind Pick and me, the third in line. We were moving down the trail. The hills narrowed in and the mud was about six inches deep. If the dirt wasn't so thick it would be a small stream, but it just stayed, squishing around our boots.

"Easy, Two," Pick said over his shoulder, his voice hushed by the rain. "Just cool down. If you don't kill him, and you get out of here, you can do that all you want. Besides, maybe you need to learn how to fight better. Just think of this as practice. You want to be a marine, don't you, son." He said the last bit in a deep voice while he puffed out his chest like the marine recruiter we saw in Minneapolis.

We had been down to the Cities with some friends from the rez. We took Pick's brother's Thunderbird, parked it on Hennepin and Lake, and walked. We were all tired from the four-hour ride down from the reservation so we didn't pick any fights. Besides, Lyle, Pick's littlest brother, was with us. He was only fourteen; I didn't want him to see the inside of any jails until he was at least as old as me, twenty-one. We were broke too, so we had trouble getting drunk. We were just standing in the bars wondering what we should do. Sooner or later we'd get bored or kicked out. At closing time we were at Moby's. We'd lost the rest of the gang from our reservation, so we didn't know what to do next, and this girl walked up to us. She couldn't have been more than eighteen.

"Hunter. My name's Hunter."

"Stan," I said. I gestured with my thumb to Pick who was staring at the ceiling, a toothpick in his mouth. "That's Pick. Guy next to him is his little bro, Lyle. Where you from?"

"Pine Ridge. What tribe you from?"

"Chippewa."

"Chippewa. I should have known any Indian with any sense wouldn't just be hanging around here like you." She winked, and her long black hair swayed. Her white T-shirt was tight. I laughed when she said that.

"I should have known that any Indian girl as rude as you had to be Sioux, and had to be from Pine Ridge." I winked back. She smiled.

"You got a car?" I shook my head no. Pick and Lyle kept on looking up at the ceiling, or tipping to see how full the spittoons were.

"Let's go to the river. It's pretty at night. Besides, the owner gives me some of the unfinished bottles," she said.

So all of us trooped along with her to her car and drove down to the warehouse district. All the way to her car and while we were driving she talked. She talked about Pine Ridge, about her parents, cousins, high school, music, the Cities. She talked more than any Indian I ever met. We drove past the Pillsbury grain elevator and factory, and under the Third Avenue Bridge and parked right on the river, below the dam. We could hear the water rolling off the cement let-down and it gurgled toward us. The lights reflected off the water and the car horns and traffic sounded far off in the distance.

We all got out of the car and stood at the river's edge. We stared down into the blackness that was rushing by. Us guys were waiting for Hunter to say something. It was like we were waiting for a priest to bless the food at a church feed, before we dug into the beans, the ham sandwiches, and downed the Kool-Aid. She stood with her hands on her hips, her hair trailed over her white T-shirt.

"It's so beautiful here." All of us nodded, our hands stuffed into our pockets. Someone pulled the bottle of vodka from a coat pocket and we passed it back and forth. We were all lying on our backs on the cement, looking up at the stars and an occasional satellite. Lyle was quiet, while Pick bitched about their mother for a while until the vodka made his insides and outsides the same temperature. Hunter missed her little sister. I just lay there thinking that I liked us four Indians by our river. It was our river, the Mississippi. It flowed by Poverty. It stretched clear from our reservation down to the Cities and kept on going. And we lay by it. Not worrying about our cars, or our houses. Not thinking about how some white cop was going to rough us up, calling us dirty Indians. Calling us timber niggers. We weren't worrying about getting enough food or finding work. The river was just flowing by us. Hunter mumbled that she and her sister used to swim in the river near her house. Lyle said his ass was numb. Pick said he could feel the stars coming closer, then jumping even farther away to the beat of his heart. Me? I felt the river. I felt us just lying there. I felt tight.

After a while, everyone quit talking and fell asleep. Everyone except me slept, while I stared at the stars trying to get them to come in and out with my heartbeat. I couldn't do it. I looked over at Hunter; she was stretched full out, thin. Pretty. Lyle was right next to her, just as skinny but almost a foot longer. They looked a lot alike. Both of them had real long black hair. Black like the river, it ran down their shoulders as their chests rose and fell. Hers went up and down faster than his. His beat like a bear, really slow, his ribs pushing way out. I imagined them full of stars, pushing up and down. Pushing in and out against their T-shirts.

If Pick and I stayed it might have messed up their balance, the stars would leave. The river might turn bright. They might wake up. I felt real tight on the outside but my insides were tender and I felt like I might just slip into the river and float. I would float clear down into the ocean and keep on going. The ocean scares me. It's too big. It's too deep. The river kept pulling me there, tugging at my heart, my feet, and the stars.

"You're real pretty," I whispered to them. I nudged Pick and we stood up, walking quietly away through the early morning. The Mississippi kept on. It kept on flowing by, the water spilling over the dam rasping in the background. By ten o'clock, we were uptown and we walked straight into the recruiting office. We signed up that morning.

➴ ➶

"Real pretty," John-Two was saying. "This spot ain't a real pretty place to camp." The hills had come up more sharply on either side, the rain was coming down even harder. It was pitch black and I could barely see the others. "Let's go back up and tell them we should stay up there."

"Why don't we just wait, they'll be coming down here any minute anyway. Let the white cat figure it all out. Let's just hang here, better yet, let's smoke." Pick pulled a pack of cigarettes out of his jacket pocket.

"Fuck it." Two spat in the rain. "They're going to be wet."

"Not these. Hard pack, brand new."

"Shit," I said.

"I lifted them off MC. They're Camels, let's smoke."

"Now I can smoke that shit." We held out our hands as Pick gave us each a cigarette. I lit mine first, and only smoked one lungful. Just as I was exhaling, savoring the American smoke, Pick's head emptied itself onto my face. I didn't hear anything. I didn't even see anyone, but Pick was standing so close one second, our shoulders touching, then in the light of my lit cigarette, the left side of his head got blown clean off, bits of it sticking to my helmet and face. The back of my right hand as I held the cigarette in my mouth. The VC sniper must have seen the glow of my cigarette. He compensated for the length of the cigarette and, thinking it was me, blew away Pick. Just by chance. Dumb luck. If he had been leaning the other direction, or standing a few more inches away.

I ran down the hill. By now I could hear shots all around. I ran and dove into the brush at the side of the trail just where it got a little wider. I dove with my right hand first, and the earth ate it away. I felt a shock. It shoved straight through my bones and smashed me headfirst into the hill. I tried to push myself up with my right hand, but my body collapsed, mashing me further in the mud. I picked up my right arm. Something was not right. Something was definitely fucked up. My whole right hand had been blown off. All I could see was a small bit of the flesh of my palm, dangling from my pulped wrist. Between the mud, and the dirt, and the blood that covered my body I couldn't see shit. There was a ringing in my ears. Rifle shots, thuds, rain. I needed to quit bleeding. Dog tags, dog tags. I took off my tags and wrapped them around my wrist. They slipped off. There was nothing to hold them there. I wrapped them around my elbow, twisted the chain and metal best I could, then passed out.

"Did you get it, Dad?" The deer jumped across the ditch and over the road.

"Let's get it, Stan, get it before it's too far off the rez." Dad shouldered his gun. His giveaway gun never missed. It had been Uncle Earl's favorite gun, and Dad got it at his giveaway. Uncle Earl had been hit by a car along the highway after he had been drinking. They gave all his stuff away at his funeral. Dad got his gun. There was some blood dropped on the highway, so we crossed and walked through the ditch. Dad was in front of me, staring at the ground. It was summer, but we could hunt on the rez year round. The jack pine grew close together on the other side of the ditch and we could hear the deer cracking the pine branches as it broke through and headed up to the tracks. The railroad used to go through but it went broke and they ripped up the rails and ties so the tracks were a dirt road that

stretched straight across the reservation. The dirt was fine and the dust lay quietly on top of the loose sand. We could see the red on the trees where the buck had brushed off the crisp black bark. We broke through the trees and headed up the ditch to the tracks. A forest green pickup was on the tracks. The blue sky, hard and clear rose up behind it. The sun was setting behind us.

Dad pulled up short, then we walked up to the truck.

"Lincoln," the man said, "what are you doing hunting on this side of the road?"

"Well, Marshall Marshall. I ain't hunting here, I'm tracking. Stan and I got it on the reservation and it run this way." Dad leaned his arm against the truck.

"You sure?"

"Yep, shot it back a half mile from my place." It was just Jeannette's shack and ours, there in the woods. Poverty hadn't been built, didn't exist yet.

"I been watching the whole thing. I saw it shot on this side."

"Come on Mike. Its blood goes right across the highway."

"Sure it does, it got shot on this side, run across the road, and looped back." He gestured with his chin down the tracks in front of the forestry truck. The deer lay dead in the dust twenty feet up the tracks in front of the truck.

"You haven't even stepped out of your forestry truck to take a look. Besides you're so fat you probably couldn't even bend over to read the blood. It's my deer, Marshall."

"If it's yours, then you was poaching. Maybe I shot it, 'cause it was hit by a car and I put it out of its misery. You weren't poaching, were you?"

"Mike, you shouldn't be talking to no one about poaching." Michael Marshall was the reservation's most practiced poacher. He took everything out of season. He trapped fox, wolf, coyote, ermine, muskrat, fisher. He netted walleye pike in their spawning beds and shot bear by the garbage dumps. Only no one could catch him. Finally the department of natural resources just made him a game marshall so he would have to quit poaching.

"Well I'm Marshall now. And Lincoln, I don't think you can afford a poaching fine of five hundred dollars, can you? 'Course, we'd have to confiscate your gun too."

"Yeah, you're Marshall Marshall, the last man standing between the state and all the lawless, savage Chippewas from Grand Portage to Mille Lacs. Mike, I can't afford no fine. Can't afford to pay the prices your brother charges at his store either." His brother, Doug Marshall, owned the only grocery store on the reservation.

"Say, isn't that Earl's old gun there? He brought that back from Japan, huh? Seven point seven, old sniper rifle. You got that at his giveaway? That's a nice gun there."

"It's my deer. You know we shot it on the reservation."

"Yep. And you better get back there 'cause the deer's off the reservation now."

We just stood there, numb, and watched as he got out of his truck and walked over to the deer. He stooped down, grasped the deer by the front legs, and dragged it over to the truck. Grunting, he heaved it in the back. He got back in the cab, and started the engine.

"Lincoln, you'd best get back." We stood on the tracks as he drove off. Slowly we walked back across the highway and to our car.

Ma fried the dough in melted lard and we ate the fry bread with butter and honey that night. She always cooked the best bread, just a little brown on the outside and white, puffy, in the center. She melted the butter and honey together over the woodstove and it dripped onto our fingers as we tore the bread into pieces, waiting for it to cool just a little bit. It was a smooth sky that night. I couldn't see any clouds but the stars were muted as we sat at the dinner table. The Kool-Aid left us with raspberry mustaches and the house was hot from the fire in the stove.

My legs were scratched and tired from pushing through the trees and hazel brush. My arms were heavy from carrying my dad's old twelve gauge. With the fry bread a warm bundle in my stomach I went to bed.

Later, after my mother woke me up and told me Dad was gone, she said to go and wake my sister and get her dressed. It had gotten colder outside. The August day had been warm, but after my dad and I came home and after supper the wind picked up. It tossed the tops of the red pine back and forth in front of our house and the dust from the road swirled all around. The sky was hard and thick now, the clouds had turned gray like the calluses on the bottoms of my grandfather's feet.

After my mother woke me up and told me to wake my sister and get her dressed in her red coat, not the blue one, I could hear her talking to my uncle Rick in the kitchen. He had driven over from the tribal police headquarters. He had driven over to pick us up in his police car.

"It ain't possible, Rick. That just ain't possible."

"I got him right there. They saw him do it."

"My man ain't no criminal." I heard her opening the cupboards, lighting a fire in the stove.

"Come on, Rose. We don't got time for that."

"We got time. He's got time for some of my bread. I got to make him bread." Uncle Rick sighed and sat down heavily in one of the chairs.

Before my mother woke me up and told me my daddy was in jail I was having a dream.

I went over to my sister's bed and shook her awake.

"Come on Violet." I shook her again, but she just mumbled. "Come on Vee. Get up." She sat up and looked around.

"You ain't Daddy." She looked again to make sure.

" 'Course I ain't. We got to go see him. We got to get to him, okay?" She nodded and I helped her slip on her cotton dress and lace up her shoes. We walked out into the kitchen. Uncle Rick was sitting in one of the wooden chairs. The legs bent under his weight and his gun was almost hidden by his stomach, which flowed out from underneath his belt. His meaty hands wrapped themselves around a cup of coffee and he was talking quietly to my mother who stood behind him by the wood cook stove. She took a gob of dough and dropped it in the melted lard in the cast-iron skillet on the stove.

"Stillwater," Uncle Rick was saying. "They're taking him down to Stillwater in the morning."

"He didn't do it, Ricky, you gotta know that."

"Damn it, Rose, they saw it. Hear? Marshall's own kids saw it." Rick had turned around and was searching my mother's eyes, but she had her eyes on the fry bread as she forked it out of the hot grease and wrapped it in tinfoil. Rick looked back and saw us standing in the doorway of our little room off to the side of the kitchen. He was my father's brother, but he was as fat as Dad was lean.

"Come here," he said leaning back in his chair. I walked over to

him and he pulled another chair around the small table, his arms reached clear across. He was taller than he looked, but I always pictured him as a bear, big and thick.

"Rose, would you get this man some coffee." I sat down next to him.

"Ricky, he's ten. There's only one man in this house." He looked down at his hands.

"Stan here is the man now. Stan here is the only man in this house now." Ma poured the coffee in an old tin mug and set it in front of me.

"Stan, you know where we're going?"

"To see my dad."

"That's right. You know where he's at?"

"He's at the jail ain't he?" I never had coffee before. I took a sip and set my cup back down.

"That's right. You gonna take care of your little sister? You gonna take care of Violet?" I nodded. "You gonna help your ma out and listen to everything she says?" I nodded again.

"Stan, they gonna need you bad. Your ma says you're only ten, but you gotta be the man." I took a longer pull of coffee. Uncle Rick was looking down at his hands again. I stared over the rim of the mug, out the window. A rain had started. It hit the panes softly and slid down, dripping off the wood sills. It fell straight down from the sky in long gray strings, slipping quietly into the dirt of our driveway. The drops parted and ran down the brown hood of the police car.

"We'd best get on," Uncle Rick stood and I went and picked up Violet's hand where she was still standing in the doorway.

"You ain't Daddy," she said to me. "You ain't my daddy." Her black hair hung in her face and her skin was still blotched from sleep. I took her hand in mine and we walked to where Ma and Uncle Ricky stood by the front door. Ma had her sweater on, one of Dad's old flannel shirts over the top of that.

"Uncle Rick. The rain's coming down." And it was. All the way to the jail and back Violet kept on saying: You ain't my daddy, you ain't my daddy, you ain't daddy, daddy, daddy, daddy.

Getting my hand blown off saved my life. I heard voices, far off. They were speaking my language. Some were telling me to get up and start walking; others more hushed said, "Stay. Stay. Don't move. Don't move." Dad? "You'd best get on Stan. You been an Indian longer than you been a marine. You'd best get on." Soon the voices were mixed with a language I didn't get. Was it Sioux? Was it Hunter's mother? Grandmother? I couldn't hear any of my people speaking anymore, and my ears buzzed with the other sounds. I felt my blood oozing into the mud and leaves next to me. It soaked through the top and into the sand where it ran with Pick's blood. I tried to stop it. I couldn't hold onto it before it was emptied into the ocean. The great salt water took it away from me, separating it until the ocean was blue green again.

It was VC and they were standing above me. I was on my back in the mud and my stump lay bloodied, thrown to one side. They walked away then, down the trail, their voices pinging and sliding away from me. I think it was noon. Flies had started to buzz around my ears and land on my eyelids. They crawled over my stump.

Do you know why they didn't get me, why they left me for dead? Dog tags. It was 'cause my tags were missing. They know that whenever we're killed and a good guy gets to us first, they take our tags. Mine were gone, or at least had got covered in mud, grass, blood, and leaves so they figured they already got to me.

That's what John-Two says. He made it up the trail, but he got blasted in the leg. That next day they carried us by chopper to the hospital. On the chopper, John (we didn't need to call him Two anymore 'cause One took a bullet in the back of the neck) told me about my tags. He looked at me real hard.

"What about Pick?"

I just looked at him.

"He's gone, huh?"

I turned away, facing out the chopper door. The tree tops skimmed by dusty and cracked.

"What happened to his horse, man? What happened to his horse? They get his horse too?"

"Shut up, John. We ain't horse Injuns. Us Chippewa weren't ever horse Indians. We live in the woods. Sioux are horse Injuns."

I looked at my right forearm. It was wrapped in white cloth. Some of my sweat was soaking through the edges. I was numb with codeine, wishing I was numb with heroin. John lay next to me as we flew up and over the jungle. His leg was wrapped and he smoked a cigarette.

"I'm getting back, Stan. I'm getting back to Alabama."

"That was our kill, John. That was our deer. You tell Marshall that was our deer."

"What?"

"I said it's ours."

"You want a cigarette? They're army, but they still smoke."

I just looked away. The tops of the trees looked so soft. I could just lay myself down right on top of them. I could just lay myself down and sleep.

"You come to Alabama. Stan, you can come with me."

We live in the woods, I thought. We live like rabbits. We live at the tracks, at the bar, detox. We live in the woods. We live in Chevy Novas when we're too drunk to drive home. We live walking, dragging Lyle home from some party, stinking, too young to stink like he does. We live getting beat, beating up, going home to jail. Don't do no good to beat a dead horse, Pick would say. Just fuck 'em. We might mess them up, they fuck us up worse. Better to be shit on and missed than shot at and hit. Don't do no good to beat a dead horse. Don't do no good to kill a dead Indian.

Celia

Stan came back in June, 1969. It was after the war, and after the veterans hospital in New York. He came back with one hand and a radio, which he gave to me. After Duke and Ellis had found Donovan that winter. He came back without Pick, and without us knowing what happened. He came back to find that not only wasn't there a letter to tell us, but to find out that Lyle had run off, no one knew where to. At first he stayed put with his sister Violet and his mother, helping them take care of Violet's newborn baby girl. Jackie. No one needed to tell him that she was Lyle's child. Since Stan didn't work or anything he came over from across the way with the radio tucked under one arm. He would come over and we'd plug in the radio in the kitchen and sit drinking iced tea. The only stations we ever got were country, but that was okay with me. We never had one that worked good enough to pick up more than one station before, so all summer we flipped stations and drank tall glasses while it got hotter and hotter. I propped open the front door but it didn't do much good, and the flies flew right through the holes in the screen. The flypaper that we strung up in the kitchen over the sink and above the table caught most of them, and when the music was on we couldn't even hear their wings flapping against the ooze.

I asked him where he got it, and all he said was that he'd made a trade. I didn't get it, so he held up his arm and his shirtsleeve hung loose down his arm. His stump was all closed up, and it

132

looked like the end of a sock tucked in on itself. Or a belly button. I nodded and he left the radio there in the kitchen that day, said he was sick of lugging it across the way all the time. But he didn't live more than fifty yards away, so I just let it drop. He came every day, standing by the screen door, never coming in until I held it open or yelled at him from the back room, or where I was at the oven with hot pans.

Lines. I thought of lines and Stan saw them clear as if they were painted on everything around him. That gave me a good feeling. He was softlike, but hard because of the lines. With me, and with Donovan, he was real good and so I drew the lines around us big and fat. Wavy. I let them bend and include. I kept on thinking of the words to most of the country songs we listened to on the radio. He didn't fit on any of them lines either and so my feeling was right. He didn't own a dog, or drive a pickup, and he never cried into his beer. He never even drank beer, but sometimes he brought over a bottle of Southern Comfort and we added it to our tea, after Ma and Donovan had gone to bed. And once in a while when it was warm, the days all humid, which made it cool at night 'cause of the fog, we went out with the pitcher and the bottle and sat on the hood of Duke and Ellis's car. He was mostly quiet then. Duke and Ellis went on and on, talking war. They would start in and ask questions about Vietnam.

"Was it hot?" They asked because when Stan had been over there they drove their car under the radio tower in Grand Rapids and listened. They figured they might hear about Stan or Pick doing something brave, or receiving an award from the president. Stan would just say "yeah," or "I guess." But Duke went on about the president and the war.

"We listened for you, but they never said a word over that station from the Cities. I figured that times being what they are, they might have, but nothin' much has changed. I mean, Ira Hayes, he was Navajo right? He fought his way clear across Iwo Jima and raised that flag right alongside those other guys. Did they give him anything? Hell no. He was Indian. They didn't give him nothin'. Some skins get down on you guys who go off and fight. Those AIM guys yellin' about fighting for something we don't even got. What they mean is rights and all that shit. But don't listen to them, Stan. The way I figure, we'd all be in deep shit if those Vietcong got over here in America. Just the same as the whites.

"Same goes for the War. Hitler woulda treated us a hell of a lot worse than Roosevelt did, that's for sure. But it seems killing's got all different now. Like they don't think that soldiers should die when they're fighting. What the hell are we supposed to do when we get hit with a bullet? Laugh? Dance around and holler? It seems pretty stupid now, the way everyone's all concerned with killing."

Ellis who mostly didn't say much would chime in.

"Killing ain't what it used to be."

"Hell no!" Duke would shout, when we were about half a pitcher empty.

"That's for sure, things ain't the way they was. Back when we were fighting those dogeaters, them Sioux, we had it all different then."

By the time we got to "the way they was," Stan and I just lay there on the hood, looking up at the stars. Duke kept going, but his voice got real far away and I held Stan's hand. He would shiver a little and squeeze my hand.

"Don't they feel close, but not at the same time?" I told him sure, they sure do. The pitcher was empty and Duke and Ellis were asleep inside the car, one on each seat. Stan and me? We just lay there some more, trying to find the brightest stars, but never really agreeing on which one was brightest.

"Too close," Stan said. I asked him what, but all he could say was too close, they're too close. His breath got real short and I looped my hand around his neck. Feeling the skin on the back of his neck. He smelled warm and the lines he drew brought in the smell of gasoline, oil, and Southern Comfort, mixed with sweat. Right then I thought that I would never forget that smell. It was good.

"Rivers," he said, not looking away from the sky. I mumbled into his neck, asking what he meant.

"I mean rivers. Don't they look like rivers, only real slow?"

"Sure they do." I tried to feel them like he talked, but his smell kept me too close. He shivered some more and he couldn't look away from the stars, kind of like when you're listening to the radio and some song comes on. Some song that you should know, but you can't remember the name. You get all frustrated but keep on listening, because you might understand in a few bars. You might just know the answers. He kept looking, to see if he knew. I think that's why he was shivering. It wasn't cold or nothin' but maybe he was afraid he would know.

So I took his hand and led him off the car, into the house. I kept the radio off and we lay on the couch. I felt all the lines, and the whiskey made them bend and dance. I knew I had to get Stan's mind off the lines. It was like looking at telephone wires reflected on the river. You knew the river was going, but the wires looked real straight. Then something would happen; a beer bottle was thrown in or a fish jumped and they disappeared, it was only a long time later that you could see them again. But they always looked different to me.

Stan lay under me. He couldn't support his weight on his one hand so I swayed above him, just moving a little and he closed his eyes. I saw him, and even though he was inside me, he wasn't pushing. I wanted to tell him that there weren't any lines inside, there couldn't be any straight things anymore. He just breathed in and out, sucking in air. I couldn't tell if he was far away or not, and I wanted to tell him that it wasn't him. It couldn't have been him before. I got this caved-in feeling. Like everything that happened before wouldn't let him be there. I cried and cried. Even though that's something I never do. The tears soaked into his shirt and with his sweat I didn't think he noticed. But he whispered to me.

"Does it hurt?"

It couldn't hurt, and that was the hardest thing about it all. I couldn't regret it, and that's why I wanted to take it all back. The radio, the whiskey, Pick, Duke. But the thing was that I was making a trade too.

And all the time I was still moving. Rocking above him, where no lines could go at all.

After he came, strong, deep, because he didn't have a choice, we lay there. He still didn't say anything, even when his hand traced my stomach and felt its roundness. He traced an alphabet on my stomach, spelling things I couldn't make out. His fingers didn't leave any trace at all, and they felt far, far away. Maybe he was spelling the stars, close but not at the same time.

Even the times after that, while my stomach got bigger and bigger, he spelled. And while he began to spell, he whispered down to my skin, stretching tighter and tighter. He spelled and whispered past the outside, past my flesh and deeper.

"You're mine. You're mine. It's all mine."

He is now.

And the whispers were in rhythm with my breathing, with his breathing, and with the lines that had begun to disappear.

I figured it was like the river and the lines. Even though they straightened out after a while they never *were* the same. For the longest time I figured it was me but after a while I knew. Every reflection, even after they settle, is on different water. Because the current never stops, it keeps going and going, only we can never tell that. All the lines keep showing up, looking the same, but they are different, every second, every minute. And five months later Little came to us. Count them and know. Six fingers and five months, but the numbers don't stay put and we can change them. We did.

He is now.

Paul
1969

The house that Paul, the new priest with Iowa memories, moved into on the reservation, across from the peeling white church, the house the regional diocese had sarcastically called the rectory, was painted pink. Easter pink. Styrofoam-egg-carton pink.

Father Offstahd, the wheezing priest from the next town over (the town off the reservation) had picked Paul up from St. Thomas in an aging 1958 Chrysler whose springs thumped over the frost-heaved highway. Its wheels groaned along the split and crumbling asphalt muffled only by the chugging motor that to Paul's ear was missing at least one cylinder, and the watery, phlegmy sighs of the fat priest behind the wheel. Sweat beaded across Father Offstahd's upper lip even though the March air was heavy and cold, the snow dirty, and the sky a thick lead. Between sighs and over the constant drone of words that spilled out of his mouth, he would stick his middle finger under his collar and scratch the bulging skin irritated to a bright rosy pink from his fingernail and the starched white collar.

He spoke on and on, never dislodging the sweat that perched on his clammy hairless lip, never wiping it away or even licking it off. Paul had to look away.

He gazed out of the window past the chipped door lock that showed the cheap metal through the black plastic veneer. Paul's eyes searched past the cracked stripping around the window edge that was so loose it flapped in the wind. He stared into the fields

137

given over to grass, rusted irrigation trolleys, and scattered windbreaks half-dead from blister-rust and neglect. Years later he
would leave thinking that the reason he was never allowed to be
owned by the land or its people was that he was too aware of the
broken-downness of things, that he had an eye for it; for wells
that had gone dry or the water too hard with rusty minerals, for
rains that didn't come or that came too early, for family tragedy,
for taxes, for death. He never admitted to himself that the real
reason was that he had come too long after everything had
already been set in motion; after the priest whose pulpit he was
filling had drowned inside his own church, after the departures
for Vietnam, after the lies of right and fatherhood had been
sown, and after everyone up there believed that it couldn't get
any worse and then soon realized that it could and did. As the son
of a farmer, Paul should have known that it could always get
worse. If he hadn't been there to see it, to be part of the beginning, he should've known that he could pass through unnoticed
and untouched. Because, as the only son of a farmer, Paul had
always been forced to see. He had seen the bull's thick penis pen-
etrate the heifer, he had thrown the afterbirth out in the grass for
the skunks, and later he had to kneel underneath the same cow
with a polished steel basin between his freckled arms as his father
sliced the neck with a dirty knife. Paul should have known. He
had to carry the slopping basin of steaming blood through the
dust up to the kitchen where it was fried solid. Paul should have
known that he needed to be there from the beginning in order to
belong to anything. But as he looked past the battered and
scratched glass and the aged rubber stripping, he didn't realize
that the fields that tore past the clanking wheezing Chrysler were
empty spaces on which ancient forests used to stand, and what he
was seeing wasn't decrepitude but rather the slow march back to
the way things used to be.

Once Paul and Father Offstahd cut over to the smaller highways
past St. Cloud — the ones with no shoulders and with cracks running crossways and for yards down the broken travel of asphalt
— the trees grew closer to the road, the ditches were small or
nonexistent, and the small towns appeared less frequently. From

around a bend or unexpectedly stuck in the middle of a straight-away, there seemed to Paul no reason for the placement of those towns nor for the few remaining occupants who still lived there although they couldn't have jobs or any other support that would allow them to live any sort of comfortable life. There were no factories and no plants. Within the barbed-wire boundaries of the scattered farms the soil didn't look as though it were worked diligently or with any success. Even though the snow still clung to the dips and bottoms in the irregular fields, Paul could tell that all of the nutrients had been sucked out of the soil by overplanting and poor crop rotation. The sagging barns, half-shingled and with trusses rotting from swallow nests and swallow shit, hadn't seen a full loft of hay or straw in years. Paul could tell, because if they had, the weight would have collapsed the rickety structures in seconds.

What kept them? What made those farmers stay? What paid for the snowmobiles on which they packed the ditches and careened over the frozen lakes?

Father Offstahd was explaining to Paul the mysterious circumstances of Father Gundesohn's death by drowning in the baptismal urn, but Paul didn't hear. He didn't latch onto how strange it was that a priest had drowned in a shallow bowl no bigger than the one in which he caught steaming cow blood. He didn't realize the absurdity of a death by drowning in holy water any more than he understood or listened to what his responsibilities as the new priest were to be. Paul couldn't connect because he had no idea, no clear vision of the rectory in which he was going to live, so he was unable to hear of what had come before and of what he was expected to do. With the dirty snow outside the window and the blubbering priest next to him, he couldn't imagine what the church looked like, whether it had a balcony with an organ, whether it had a steeple with bells or a steeple with speakers that blared out recordings of bells. He didn't know if the lectern was a big affair of oak stained to a deep hue, or a skeleton of cheap pine. Paul didn't know whether there were any stained-glass windows, or simply old glass, bubbled, tall and narrow. And Paul certainly did not know that the house in which he was to live was painted pink.

Since Paul had no way to imagine where he was going, Father
Offstahd's wet voice blended even more with the one-cylinder-
short engine that needed an overhaul. The wet slap of the bald-
ing tires over the crumbling asphalt gurgled along with Father
Offstahd's voice to such an extent that Paul missed the story of
Father Gundesohn's death. Paul failed to hear that the priest had
choked on the holy water, stumbled back, and smashed his head.
No one was in the church when it happened, but the story that
Father Offstahd related with relish was the combined best guess
of the sheriff's department and the coroner, who had the misfortune and displeasure of having to travel forty miles from the
county seat to the small reservation town they both believed was
populated with nothing but drunks. It was a Friday night and
they had both been at the first home game of the local high-
school hockey team. The fluorescent lights had been bright inside
the arena, and although the plastic seats were cold, the sheriff
and the coroner had whiskey in their thermoses of hot chocolate.
Although their team always lost, and the one year they had made
it to the state championships, in 1961, they lost to a rich city
team in the first round, even so, the sheriff and the coroner were
excited beyond expectation by this year's team. There was a new
player. He played left wing and he was from the rich suburb of
Edina whose team had made the state championships as far back
as anyone could remember. He was a rich city kid and everyone in
the town knew that the only reason his family had moved up to
northern Minnesota was that his doctor father had been slapped
with a malpractice suit. Part of his fine obligated him to work at
the reservation clinic for two years if he wanted to keep his lucra-
tive practice in Minneapolis. Even though the left wing was a rich
city kid, and the local whites usually carried with them a reserved hate for both rich people and Indians, they exempted him
because of his skating and his ability to handle a puck. He was a
good two hundred and thirty pounds and as fast as an arrow. His
slap shot would travel so fast as to be nearly invisible, at least
that's what was said by those who had gone to the afternoon
practices. They had him for only two years. Since the last three
seasons had seen their team consistently place last in the region
both the coroner and the sheriff were pissed off at having to

drive forty miles to look at a dead priest they both knew to be as drunk as they believed his whole congregation of Indians to be, and who was certain to remain as dead as his flock was to remain drunk. The coroner (a thin man who once dreamed of being a professional bowler) and the sheriff (who subscribed to *Road & Track* and who loved bass fishing almost as much as his wife loved to screw the deputy) were doubly pissed off at having to climb into their cars and drive forty miles in the early December dark because their cars were carried out of radio distance in the last thirty seconds of the game, which at that point was tied three to three. Their team was even battling a power play because the left wing from Edina with a slap shot that sounded like thunder was in the penalty box on a bad call.

So upon arriving at the icy cold church they quickly decided it was an accidental drowning, put the body in the back of the coroner's hearse, and with the sheriff's lights and sirens going they raced at one hundred and ten miles per hour back into radio reception to find out the score.

Father Offstahd told Paul all of this with obvious relish, even though he knew Paul wasn't listening. He relished the story not because he had known Father Gundesohn and had never liked him. He *hadn't* liked him because of his neatly trimmed side-burns and his black wing tips, the tops of which were always in need of a dusting and a shine. Father Offstahd also disliked him because Father Gundesohn's summer youth league softball team always beat his even though Father Gundesohn's team was all Indian and he was drunk on J&B scotch every single game. It wasn't that Father Offstahd had an inordinate love for softball. On the contrary, he hated it because the dust and the goldenrod that grew around the diamond set off some of his worst asthma attacks. Moreover, the church officials set a lot of stock in soft-ball as a way to make the church appear less intimidating and the priests more friendly. Father Offstahd's continual losses to the now-dead Father Gundesohn, and to everyone else for that mat-ter, did little to endear him to his congregation and earned his team the epithet of "The Jobs." But this wasn't why he really enjoyed telling the story of Father Gundesohn's death so much. The real reason for the fat priest's pleasure in the telling was that nothing exciting had ever happened to him in his entire, asthmatic, overweight life. Never, ever had there been anything out of the ordinary during his time as a priest or before it. The routine of Ash Wednesdays and Palm Sundays, Christmas, confession, and the weekly sermons he didn't even get to make up himself had instilled in Father Offstahd an absolute and unshakable boredom. It had gotten so bad that he secretly envied the Lutherans because at least they got to decide what they wanted to talk about, what they wanted to say. The only time Father Offstahd got to do that was when he had to eulogize some poor broken-down old farmer, or his wife, or their child. More often than not he couldn't even remember who they were; he couldn't connect the tear-and-mascara-streaked face with the pasty, made-up face of the dead husband, or the gray, lined face of the husband with the dead wife who was to be buried in her favorite blouse even though it was red with purple lilies. Most likely they had only been to mass once or twice, perhaps once a year at Christmas, so it wasn't really Father Offstahd's fault that he couldn't remember. Since these were the only times he could choose the themes, the scriptures, and his words with absolute freedom, he delivered the most beautiful, the most heart-wrenching, and the most articulate funeral speeches, sometimes becoming so excited that the excitement induced one of his more severe asthma attacks. But these funerals were too few and far between for Father Offstahd to be completely satisfied, and a funeral in and of itself was nothing special; every small-town priest could claim them, just as every human could claim to have one pain or another, or even claim to have two eyes and one heart.

A dead priest. Well, that was something different, something extraordinary. There were so many things to attend to. The autopsy. Actually Father Offstahd had missed the autopsy. He had been at the hockey game as well and since he left later and had to drive slowly because his Chrysler was getting on in years, Father Offstahd had arrived there after the coroner and the sheriff had sped off with the body. But Father Offstahd had been able to speak in soothing tones to the crowd of ten to twelve people who had gathered on the cement steps of the church so as to console them in their grief. He didn't know that they hadn't assembled in the cold wind that swept past the church to mourn the priest; rather they stayed on the crooked chipped cement to make sure that the coroner and the sheriff weren't coming for a family member or a friend and to see whether they were in some way implicated.

In addition to the autopsy, the church authorities needed to be notified and the funeral planned. All of these things were highly out of the ordinary in Father Offstahd's highly ordinary life, a catastrophe distant from Father Offstahd's daily routine. And even though the coroner declared it death by accidental drowning, Father Offstahd had a different opinion: he believed Father Gundesohn had been murdered. This may or may not have been true, but regardless of the reality of the situation Father Offstahd's firm belief in homicide gave him the space in which to cherish the circumstances and the facts as other people cherished children for years and years and years. He watched his carefully nurtured facts grow up and gain weight and he gave them a life of their own, which is why he relished telling them to Paul; this was the beginning of Father Offstahd's relationship with the story and the culmination of his direct involvement with the murder. Father Offstahd's last official duty concerning Father Gundesohn's death was to bring Paul up from St. Paul and get him situated in the pink rectory. Years later, when his asthma kept Father Offstahd in the house and diabetes had claimed his left leg, he sat in his armchair and religiously watched the *Father Dowling Mysteries*, which he got from his satellite dish. He saw himself as Father Dowling, played by Tom Bosley, whose character on *Happy Days* Father Offstahd never did like.

It was late afternoon by the time Paul and Father Offstahd turned off the highway onto the still-frozen dirt road that *was* town. Paul knew that he had arrived, not because of the five buildings (a gas station, a hardware store, a community center, a nursing home, and a church) that lined the dirt road nor because of the rotting log cabins and tar-paper shacks in which the townspeople lived, but because the timbre of the whine coming from the '58 Chrysler engine and from Father Offstahd's voice changed to a different pitch. Once the car turned left onto the frozen dirt there was no sound at all from the rusty car springs or from the pinched sweaty lips of Father Offstahd.

Paul looked away from the side of the road. The black Chrysler came to a stop in front of a one-story pink house with an attached one-car garage painted mint green.

"The Rectory." Father Offstahd announced it portentously. Father Offstahd took great satisfaction in being chosen to bring the new priest to perhaps the most ridiculous structure to ever be associated with the Catholic church. He didn't mind that Paul didn't seem to notice or care and hadn't listened to a word Father Offstahd had uttered during the entire ride from St. Paul. Father Offstahd was used to being ignored, it was another facet of his interminable boredom. He was used to being ignored by his congregation on a biweekly basis. He was portentous in his pronouncement because the small church and its pink rectory were perhaps the smallest and most unattractive location in all of Minnesota in which to live and preach, and being able to say "The Rectory" made Father Offstahd feel just a little bit nasty because he liked to bring bad news. It was a temporary cure for his boredom. The priest beside him was young and soft. His skin was milky smooth and there were no calluses on his hands, which were spattered with small gold freckles. Father Offstahd didn't mind not being listened to by this soft young priest with his shock of red hair because Father Offstahd knew the boy now had to preach somewhere no one else would. Father Offstahd liked that by saying "The Rectory" while staring at a decrepit pink house he was giving Paul what was worse news than the circumstances that brought Paul there in the first place: the death of the priest. Father Offstahd thought that living and preaching in that community was worse than death, not because the town and congregation were mostly Indians (after all, weren't Indians God's children too?) but because it would last and last. The reason it was a fate worse than death was that it was a life with which Father Offstahd was too well acquainted; boredom like a long shallow lake that was never deep enough to pass midthigh, but worse because it was hard to understand and justify one's presence in *that* lake of souls. Father Offstahd hoped that the full import of Paul's situation would unfold in the slow drag of years (if Paul lasted that long) so that Father Offstahd could counsel and console the young priest in the hardship that he would certainly face in the time to come. Father Offstahd was certain that Paul didn't know what he was getting himself into, and although Father Offstahd wasn't quite sure either, he surmised that it would be dull and boring. Quite worse than death.

Paul opened the door to the '58 Chrysler and it made a soft slow groan as he stepped out into the late afternoon air. Straightening his black polyester slacks, which had crept uncomfortably up his legs during the four-and-a-half-hour drive from St. Paul, he stood straight and looked around. Across the packed dirt road he could see the church. Narrow and not very tall, its face was square with the road. Paul could see that the cement steps leading up to the double doors were cracked and tilting slightly to the left and that the wind had battered the paint off the wooden siding so that it hung in the deepening twilight like flaps of dead skin. There were no windows on the front. Glancing up, Paul saw that the belfry was devoid of either bells or loudspeakers.

Father Offstahd had with much difficulty lifted Paul's suitcase from the trunk and walked to Paul's side of the car. Wedged in between the car and Father Offstahd's bulk, Paul had no choice but to turn and walk with the huffing priest up to the front steps of the rectory. Father Offstahd opened the door with a brass Schlage key on a ring of other keys. He pushed the door open with the end of the suitcase and dropped the key ring into Paul's hand. These were all the keys that Paul would need for his house and for the church. They walked through the kitchen into the living room where Father Offstahd set down the suitcase with a thump on the brown carpet and ambled over to the thermostat to turn up the heat. Father Offstahd looked about the room, empty except for a large chair and an overstuffed plaid couch, mumbled another long string of advice to Paul that he didn't hear, and walked out of the pink rectory closing both the front door and the rattling screen door behind him. Paul heard the aging Chrysler wheeze to life and Father Offstahd pulled out of the yard. This was to be the last winter for the '58 Chrysler; it would never run again.

Paul put his suitcase in the bedroom next to the Formica-veneered dresser that stood opposite the bed, which had been made up for him already. He didn't know who had tucked in the sheets, fluffed the pillows, and folded down the comforter over them; he simply couldn't imagine that it had been Father Offs-tahd, though there was no way for him to know that the wheezing priest prided himself on his hospital corners. Paul couldn't picture Father Offstahd's triple chin holding the foam pillows to his bulging neck while his stubby fingers eased the white linen cases over the cheap pillows. Paul *didn't* want to know whether the sheets and blankets themselves had belonged to the dead priest, so leaving the bedroom he walked to the kitchen, not that there was much else to see in the small rectory. There were only four rooms — the bedroom, living room, bathroom, and kitchen — but since the house was unexceptional and very midwestern in its construction, the kitchen served to focus all of the house's scant attention. Like a magnet, or some dungeon crossroads, three doors opened into the kitchen: the front door, a door to the bathroom through which one could reach the bedroom as well, and a door to the living room that opened to both the bedroom and the breezeway to the garage. Since the kitchen seemed to be the place that negotiated all the house's other spaces, Paul entered it with great expectations through the living room with its puffy couch and brown carpet. Standing in the doorway, he had to search for a minute in order to find the light switch, which, because of poor planning, was located behind the refrigerator. Although Paul had entered the house through the front door (also pink) and therefore had walked through the kitchen before, he hadn't been able to get a good look at it since the winter light was fading and because he was anxious for Father Offstahd to bumble his way back into his awful car. Finally, after having found the light switch nestled behind the slightly humming GE refrigerator, Paul clicked it on and saw the kitchen for the first time. The sight almost blinded him: everything was white.

The linoleum was sparkling white with clusters of small blue flowers in neat rows and intersections like the kind on Corning Ware pots. The wooden cupboards had all been painted white too. It looked like one fresh unbroken coat but it was actually the twenty-first time they had been painted. The previous coats had been sanded meticulously so as not to show edge or flake at all. First with sandpaper, then with steel wool, and finally wiped free of grit with a damp cloth. The aging wood was smooth and unbroken underneath a score of applications, the last of which was a dewy white.

The refrigerator was white inside and out, marked only by the chrome handle and the metal racks inside. There were no smells or stains, no scrapes, no marks. It was empty except for an open can of condensed milk.

The four chairs that surrounded the Formica table were wooden, and they looked to Paul as if they had been painted at the same time as the cupboards. White, of course.

The table had chrome legs and the Formica top was white. There were no burns on its entire smooth surface. It was smooth and level with gold flecks embedded in the Formica, scattered over the entire surface. The gold-speckled Formica was to annoy Paul for years to come because no matter how many times he sponged it clean it always looked as if an even spattering of bread crumbs had been thrown across it.

Paul pulled out one of the white chairs and sat facing the kitchen window, but the light was too bright. It banged and careened off of everything in the kitchen; nothing seemed willing to take it in; not the tabletop, not the counters, not the refrigerator, not even the white-paneled ceiling. Nothing would budge from its desire to push away the light although the light's color matched that of everything in the room. The sickly light cast by a single bulb would not be accommodated so it scampered to the window and fled through the glass into the yard and out into the street. Paul stood up and switched it off. It was too much for him after the long ride and it made his eyes water. As he stood next to the refrigerator with his freckled hand thrust behind it, his other hand on the doorjamb that surrounded the door leading to the living room, he looked through the picture window. The view crept into the kitchen.

There were only three lights on the street of dirt from the highway, one of which stood in front of the church directly across the road. This light, a huge flood on top of a telephone

pole, hung back; it was reluctant to enter the pink rectory
through the kitchen window. It was as if the outside light was shy
or wouldn't deign to enter the sad little house coated in cheery
paint. In place of the outside light that hovered just beyond
Paul's front yard, movement and motion entered without hesita-
tion. The rustle of living things and of the dead never touched the
interior walls of Paul's new home. Instead, the low hedge of wild
rose crawled into the room. Nothing more than a line of spindly
and crooked wild rose bushes, transplanted from some back field
somewhere, they scratched and clawed, daring each other to go
first, to crawl over the small front yard and through the window.
You first. No you. The jack pine on the corner swayed and the
lower branches lifted jerkily in the March wind, which brought
neither snow nor warmth, just icy air that sucked at all that had
made it that far through the harsh winter. The huge white pine
that grew near the street light danced in front of the light's spray
so that the shadow wound its way across the packed and frozen
dirt into the small space of Paul's new yard.

Paul needed something to stay the balance, to mediate the
extremes of his kitchen and the bare moving growth beyond the
window. He felt that if he had something to hold between the
real flesh of his pale hands, something whose weight and motion
he could control; he could then deal with the movement that
crept and crawled along the edges of his white kitchen.

Keeping the kitchen light off, Paul opened the refrigerator
door and in its bare light he lifted the can of condensed milk to
his nose. He sniffed it to make sure it hadn't turned sour. He left
the refrigerator door open and placed the open can directly on
one of the electric coil burners and turned it on. Soon he could
smell the sugar heating up. Picking up the can, using his shirt
cuff as a hot pad, he poured it into a coffee mug with an equal
part of tap water. Leaving the refrigerator door open, he moved
to the table with his warm milk, and with the comfortable glow
of the fridge light behind him he was at last able to sit and look
out the window.

The pink rectory was situated on the only real corner in the
small town, unless one counted the turn from the highway or the
dirt trails and worn ruts that linked the shacks and cabins

together as roads. Paul's new house occupied the corner, though it
didn't sit square with the road; rather, it was positioned at an
angle so the kitchen window faced a triangle of grass bordered by
a row of wild rose. Paul didn't know it then, but in the spring,
when all the bushes and trees grew fuzzier and fuzzier until the
buds opened into leaves, the rose bushes had scattered pink blossoms. When the leaves unfurled on the poplars in the most
vibrant of light greens and the tamarack needles grew back waxy
and soft, the gnarled and twisted rose bushes pushed out inter-
mittent blossoms, pink tinged with red. With only four, sometimes even as few as three petals, they were pathetic and made
Paul feel lonely and battered by what was happening around him,
all of which he was forced to guess at because no one told him
anything. Though the wild rose gave off no scent and to call the
thin pale flowers "blooms" was a joke, Paul missed their real sig-
nificance. Long after the first spring flowers had died, the roses
bloomed on. Up north there were no crocuses, no tulips, no daffodils. There were no hanging vines, no creeping flowers. There
were certainly no bougainvillea and no magnolia trees. Everything that did grow looked at first glance to have an economy of
architecture, but on closer inspection there appeared the most
amazing intricacies in the most common of flowers. Indian paint-
brush and fringed gentian, which graced the ditches and empty
fields, looked plain from a distance, but the petals from both
extend in a slow fan from the tough stem. The growth places of
these flowers also mark the best strawberry patches, whether in
ditches or bordering swamps. But the wild rose surpassed these
flowers. They bloomed long after others had wilted in the heat of
July, and kept going until late August. They hung on. They were
tough. But Paul couldn't see this. He would never notice that
more than blossoms the wild rose grew rose hips. As hard as
acorns or marbles, they grew twenty to thirty a bush, so that even
in the winter one could walk outside and pick some for tea, to cure
a cold, or to make a room just a little bit more livable until the
thaw came, until the frogs and turtles disengaged themselves
from river mud and lake bottoms. But Paul didn't know this. So in
the March cold, in the month when winter had its last chance to
give all it had, Paul twisted in a white wooden chair in northern

Minnesota. He twisted in his chair and peered left down the frozen
road that intersected the one from the highway. It was dark. The
wash of the floodlight outside the church traveled only a short
distance down the side road. Paul could see one, perhaps two
lights in the darkness. They were yellow, feel-good lights from
kerosene lamps and candles. Paul had no idea where the road
went. Out of town it traveled, between the arches of tall pine.
Even later in the summer he never really could figure it out.
Everyone he asked told him that it was an old logging road, that
it turned and looped back in the woods, skirted a couple of lakes,
and then turned back on itself. Paul tried to walk it once. It
seemed to go on and on. It ran through the thick of a tamarack
swamp. The trees shot up straight; their branches hung low to the
ground, and Paul could see no great distance among them. On and
on, the woods surrounded the logging road. The tamaracks and
swamp spruce crowded Paul in a rush, silent and drooping. Their
slow death into stagnant swamp water nurtured another life that
poised on the surface of stilled waters. Growing things, delicate
flowers and insects lived on the edge of the world between the rise
of brown trunks and the depths of muddy water. Paul turned
back that time having walked only two miles at most. The vacant
sandy road made him feel lost in a place in which even the trees
seemed to know where they were going.

Paul took a sip from the coffee mug of warm milk and turned
to his right, trying to look down a more knowable view. His eyes
searched the short distance of road from his new house to the
highway, illuminated by three street lights and the lights from
the gas station and the bar.

The gas station sat along the highway, and from the warped
boards that made up both its frame and its siding, it looked like a
cheap summer cabin that had been moved from its first home,
along one of the many lakes somewhere, and carted to the edge
of the highway. It had been. Paul didn't know it yet, but it doubled as a grocery and as a bait shop in the summer.

The other buildings staggered on either side of the road were
all made from cinder blocks. RJ's Hardware store was on the left,
the lights were off, and the glass door locked tight. No matter
what the season, the weather or even the holiday, it was a strict
nine-to-five establishment. The community center was straight

across from the Six Mile Bar. The front light was on even though the plastic sign that had *Pabst Blue Ribbon* scripted at the top and *The Six Mile* across the bottom had been smashed through with stones and no longer worked.

Right next to the pink rectory stood the nursing home. Sometimes, during the coming winters, they invited Paul over to talk to the people incarcerated within its white walls. He would come on Monday afternoons, bingo afternoons. It seemed to Paul that all of the Christians on the reservation lived in that building, though none of them ever seemed to make it across the way to the church on Sundays.

Taking another sip from his milk, which was losing heat almost as rapidly as Paul was running out of view, he settled back to contemplate the church. The place he was to work. The reason for his travel to the far north of America.

Tomorrow, he thought. Tomorrow. Paul liked the idea of strolling down the street the next morning to buy some food for his kitchen, maybe even some new towels if he could find them. He thought he would really stroll, leisurely like. He would nod to those he saw, tilting his head and lifting his hand as if he wore a brimmed felt hat. They'll wave back he thought. Then again, they would catch themselves and ask each other, Who was that new face? Is that the new priest? Little did he know that the wind would turn bitter overnight, a vicious wind full of spite. A last-chance March wind would whip his leisurely stroll into a brisk walk. He would see no one on foot on the street. Those who looked from behind curtained windows would see him tilting into the wind with his hands thrust deep in his polyester pockets. They already knew who he was, having seen him through the rectory window or having heard from someone who did. When Paul entered the gas station the first person he would meet was actually two people who looked exactly alike. They would size him up and down and finally one of them would speak.

"You know Halloween was over five months ago, and this here attendant don't give out no handouts just for looking weird."

Duke was remarking on Paul's clothes, on his frock, on his black pants and black shoes. Upon meeting the first person from his new parish Paul would blush scarlet up to his hairline.

However, as he sat in his empty white kitchen, Paul had no

idea that this was going to happen. He had no inkling of the wind, the already knowing eyes, the jibes of his first acquaintance. He didn't know this was going to happen so he locked his fingers together and stretched his arms high above his head, a self-consciously confident gesture that no one saw through the window. Paul was satisfied with his vision of the coming day.

Gazing through the dark over to the church across the road he noted the obvious affinity between the white church and his white kitchen. He thought it quaint, poetic, and done on purpose. Since they were linked in color Paul thought of how people would gather in his kitchen to discuss personal matters with him as they would gather across the street to discuss personal matters with God. He imagined how they would "drop by" and "see how he was getting along." He imagined they might come with loaves of zucchini bread and bits of gossip, safe church gossip. But in the years ahead no one would ever enter his kitchen of their own volition. No one would enter because they wanted to. Only once did any people step across the sill into his house even against their wills. Three of them at once.

But Paul didn't know. There was so much he didn't. Draining his mug of now-cold milk into the sink and closing the refrigerator door he walked through the bathroom door and into his new bedroom. Looking about the room made him a little sad and excited at the same time. It was bereft of any personal touch. Paul didn't know whether this was because the priest before him hadn't had any photos or a favorite picture, or if they had been cleared out after his death. Paul looked for light squares on the walls where pictures might have hung, but he found none, nor did he find any dust or lint at all in the room. Single, bare, empty. It was a sad thing. But it excited him the way hotel rooms excite some people with whispers of anonymity.

On Paul's first night on the reservation he swam into a deep sleep between the slip and whisper of white sheets under a blue comforter that didn't belong to him, whose previous owner he would never know because he had drowned inside a lonely little white church, surrounded by miles and miles of swaying, scratching trees.

III

Mourning Doves

Donovan
1978

It's time.

Stan woke me up the morning of my first hunt while the
house was closed, locked tight. Not the doors or the windows,
which were never latched. It was the light, the house sounds of
the day, the mentholated smoke, the slip and scratch of Jeannette's red Hoyle playing cards. The snap of someone silently
announcing "Gin" or the rustle of counting when the last hand of
hearts had been played out. Out and down. These sounds were
gone, had slunk away as the cold came up through the floor after
the coals in the barrel stove had been banked.

Stan squeaked open the door to the hallway closet where I
slept curled around myself in the cold on a bed of boots and a
wool blanket. The rustle and drift of drying jackets giving off
the smell of wood smoke, cigarettes, and fish from where Stan
had a job at the fishery as an egg counter. They hung over my
head and creaked on metal hangers, swayed from wooden pegs,
or penny nails sagging through the thin drywall.

It's time.

The sounds had died down except for the radio in Celia and
Stan's room that usually played until late. In the summer it
played longer, but was harder to hear. Maybe it was the winter, or
the songs themselves that carried better in between the walls,
and it was always country that leaked late into the night. Con-
way Twitty's "Tight Fittin' Jeans" along with Celia's sharp

155

laugh crawled among the coats, courted the sleeves, the rips and careful mends, the smell of pine sap.

The door squeaked and its tap against the small of my back set me awake.

It's time. Donovan, it's time.

Light was now in a band from the kitchen where I heard Stan strike a match along the rough iron edging of the range to light the burner and his first cigarette of the day. Light was now tripping over the sill into my nest, but thin enough so I could move my head away from it, thinking as kids do that it was the light that was forcing me to wake. I didn't want to leave the tossed boots and the smell that always brought me sleep. During those winters the only time I was conscious of warmth was when I curled up by the stove while the grown-ups played cards with whiskey in their coffee, if Duke and Ellis were lucky enough to steal any, or Stan remembered to get it on the day of his paycheck or his disability from the army. Sleep always came long before any feeling of heat did, so the light made me move my head, inch it from the smoke and light, the sound of Stan working the bolt on his gun, oiling against the frost. There wasn't any snow.

It must have been early yet. Celia hadn't moved from her bed and Little hadn't even stirred, or started thumping his deformed hands against the arm of the couch across from the stove; an old oil drum cut open on the end with a metal plate for a door, set on cinder blocks away from the wooden floor. Jeannette wasn't grumping her way out of bed. Those were morning sounds not yet started, and the night sounds had ended. It was that in-between time, before sunrise, when Ellis said the sun came up to the horizon and dipped down only to rise again. Before the sun. There was the light from the kitchen and the slide of metal on metal, the bolt sleeve caressing the chamber. Just Stan in the kitchen boiling coffee grounds and water together in a can on the gas stove. Me and Stan.

The house was locked down, but creaking open like a purse. Or a secret. I crawled out of the closet and into the kitchen, holding my arms against my body under my T-shirt, the sleeves dangling like the cuff of Stan's flannel where his right hand used to be.

The coffee grounds began to boil and Stan poured in a cup of cold water so they'd sink to the bottom of the tin can. Since there wasn't a handle Stan had to grip the rim with a pair of pliers Duke and Ellis had lifted from the hardware store in town. Two cups waited ready next to the stove and he tilted the can toward them, balancing it against his stump. The heat didn't seem to bother him, maybe there were no nerves where the skin creased together like an inside-out sleeve.

It's time. It's time.

I nodded as I walked across the linoleum, covered with newspapers to keep out the cold that clawed its way up from the foundation that was broken and beginning to heave. Stan said it was because it had been footed and poured above the frost line.

Stan sat back down with the rifle, working the bolt, oiling the outside of the barrel, pitted with age but worn smooth and free of rust. The stock, which used to be blond, either oak or maple, was scarred and nicked. Only the ball on the end of the bolt lever was smooth, worn and polished from years of the same motion; the palm of the hand pulling it back, pushing it forward. How many times? How many shells?

I sipped my coffee, exhaling into the cup before I sucked in the liquid with my lips. My hands wrapped around the metal. Shifting, I moved my socked toes across the newspapers, over headlines, words, fuzzy pictures that dissolved into blurry dots when you held them too close. I rubbed a picture of Jimmy Carter, face wrinkled, smile forced onto his face that looked a little too honest. "Grain Embargo . . ." it said. Grain, wheat, and corn were rotting in silos across the country. Farms were going under.

Stan caught my eye, nodding at an extra army field jacket of his and a pair of wool socks with holes cut in them for my thumbs. Under these were a pair of Lyle's old pants that he had left behind. They were too big yet for normal wear so I put them over my jeans, rolled the cuffs up, and cinched the waist with a bit of clothesline. Strange. Putting over my own someone's clothes that were so much bigger, older. They'd belonged to someone I had never met, who had driven off in his brother's car. He had run away before Stan came back from Vietnam, before Duke and Ellis found me abandoned in the car. Before Celia had Little, and had begun to love him too much and too little at the same time. Lyle. Someone I thought I would never meet, but who I knew was tall, and had been left by Pick and Stan in Minneapolis. Who had been the only one who could dunk, even ally-oop. I even knew he hated to eat kidneys . . . . And the rolled cuffs dragged at the floor, whispered over the news, the pictures.

Stan laid the gun on top of more newspapers, spread over the table to soak up the oil dripping from the joints in the action, the seam of the stock, and the barrel. I laced my sneakers and pulled two pairs of socks up and over them for warmth.

Here. Here. It's time.

He handed me a .410 shotgun that had been leaning in the corner. It was new to us. Duke and Ellis had traded it for the parking brake from their Catalina that, none of us knew how, still ran even nine years after they pulled me from the frozen car into theirs. They had ripped the parking brake out, pull-lever, cable, pad, and all from the Catalina and traded it for the gun.

I took it from him. It was light, just a pine stock and the metal tube of a barrel; the break and pin where the single shell would go. Duke and Ellis got it cheap because it shot wild. Evan, Pick's older brother, used to shoot down wasp nests from under the eaves of the old mill with it. He had emptied the shot from the shell and filled it with sand and capped the end with melted wax. The sand had worn down the barrel so now it shot out wild.

The shells, brass for Stan and red cardboard for me, lay on the table. I reached for the box.

Outside, Donovan. Never load inside.

I know.

Grabbing four shells I plunked them into the outside flap pocket that hung low at my knee.

Stan carried the rifle in his left hand. His six fingers curled around the grip above the trigger.

Get the door, he said, motioning with his chin.

I jerked at the door. I turned and pulled up, lifting it above the catch and the stripping that was always peeling back no matter how many times Jeannette complained and Stan beat it down flat again with a hammer. As I closed the door behind us we could hear Little banging his curled fists, three fingers on each, large. Knobbed and smooth like scars, or river stones, he beat them against the plaid arm of the couch. Morning sounds.

Out in the yard we realized that the cold had come. Though it had been cold before, freezing at night, skimming water in dog bowls and discarded milk cartons, it was sudden now. Crisp and certain. It was weather when you know. You *know* that the play of fall is over. We realized it had come on this day, my first hunt. The snowless grass, green and brown, crunched under our feet. Brittle. Timid.

Duke and Ellis's Catalina was frosted, all of the windows caked outside in webs of ice, the inside a smooth gray of frozen breath.

Stan put his right foot up on a rusted lawn chair, rested the 7.7mm across his knee and pushed a shell past the catch into the clip. Each one snapped into place, the copper-jacketed nose disappearing first, then the brass casing, one on top of another. Six total. Then he took the shotgun from me, holding it with his left hand he pushed the small button to the left of the trigger and broke the action open. Shifting it, he rested it on his right forearm. I handed him a shell. He took it and pushed it into the break with his thumb and grabbed the gun below the trigger and jerked it up, like whipping a willow switch against a car hood, snapping the gun shut.

He handed it over and pointed to the hammer.

Cock it back and it's ready.

I know.

I kept both my hands on it, one below the trigger where the stock began, and the other on the rest below the barrel; my thumbs were already getting cold. There was a slight wind, chiming the frozen pines together, heavy with ice, condensed there during the night. As we walked toward where the woods began beyond Duke and Ellis's Catalina, beyond Poverty, a gust came up and rattled the scraggly oak near our house. The leaves clattered together like sheaves of lead, thick and dull. Then they fell down all at once, banging like shingles down the slope of a roof, tumbling along the frozen branches and trunk to the ground.

Ahead we could see the glow of a cigarette from behind the

gray windows of the Catalina. It was Ellis, sitting up in the back
seat, the window cracked to let the smoke and steam seep from
the car. When we got closer we could hear Duke snoring, and Ellis
nodded to us, to me, the way I held the gun the right way, with
his feet propped against the headrest of the front seat. Stan
waved with his stump as he shifted the old Jap sniper rifle to the
crook of his arm. Walking past the car in front of me he shrugged
his chin deeper into the collar of his field jacket.

Still in the lead Stan stepped between the trees and skirted the
lake until it curved away from the path. Even though the houses
were still close I mirrored Stan's booted feet: heel toe, heel toe;
testing the ground before committing full weight. Indian walking
was what Ellis called it.

Behind us now, a car door opened against its springs. It must
have been Ellis headed for the house. The sound carried to us,
now deep in the trees where we navigated the path. We side-
stepped dead branches, the raised veins of broken wood underneath matted pine needles, old growth. Sidestepping, lifting,
dipping under branches and tangles of hazel brush. The car
sound had been louder than anything we spoke with our feet,
with my hands, the slap of bark and needle against skin and
cloth. The sounds of the car door, and of Ellis's cough as he made
his way to the house, wound their way along the path behind us.
They were sounds that had no place, carried no currency in the
brush and trees. Only our dance belonged. Stan and me, swaying
and dipping, threaded our way to the chosen place. It was
cadenced to fit the weave of the forest and it pulled us along
silently. Our breath slipped past and contemplated the stains and
rips in our clothes before moving behind. Stan's back, three feet
in front of me, sawed back and forth. His boots, still whole and
waterproof even though they were his issue from the marines,
picked their way up the incline that led away from the lake.

The light came stronger, freeing up the morning cold, coming
over the lake to our right, behind the trees. The cut was visible
ahead, abrupt and final where the clear-cutting had left only a
few scarred jack pines and poplars sticking through the tangle of
brush, branches and rust-colored needles, the color of slow death.

This was our spot.

Still dancing, Stan in front, we made our way to the center of the slashings. We found a stump on the low hill, looking over the entire field, toward Poverty and clear to the other side where the river hid in the trees a quarter mile away.

The morning sounds from Poverty were muted, embraced by the trees and tangles so we couldn't hear them. Only the red eye, the beacon from the water tower could be seen; peeking through the tops of the Norway pine it glowed on deeper red, darker than the approaching sun.

Stan pointed with his chin to the stump, the remains of an ancient red pine, and we sat down back to back, leaning into each other. I faced Poverty, Stan fronted the woods to the river and we sat in the morning that was waking up to us.

Resting my gun across my knees I held my hands together, pushing my thumbs through the holes in the thick wool socks, locking them together for warmth.

The wind picked up and brought us the sound of waves patting the shore of our lake. Somewhere a branch broke. Sitting and watching our breath linger and then wisp away we put the sounds together; the wind, a branch breaking, a rustle of dead leaves, sighs we couldn't quite locate. We knew the lake wasn't frozen yet, maybe tonight. As in a kid's card game we paired and discarded, matched and relinquished. A pair was never certain, only a beginning, and we weighed each sound against another. Another, looking for what might have been a deer. The only movements were our tongues against our teeth and over our lips, our toes flexing and relaxing inside of our shoes.

The night before, while Stan played gin rummy with Jeannette he spoke to me in short sentences broken by the contemplation of a run in diamonds or spades, or three of a kind with a missing nine.

Don't move tomorrow, Donovan. Don't talk.

I listened as I lay on my stomach next to the stove that was fed high but burned low with unseasoned poplar spattering water against the metal.

They're color-blind. But they can see, see you moving. Know sound too.

Jeannette cackled as she lay a card face down on the discard pile. "Gin." She lit a Salem.

And we won't smoke, not near the guns.

What?

Just no smoking outside.

I put my hands toward the curved metal, warming them.

They can smell cigarettes the best.

Thinking it around again, turning each of the words he said, rearranging the new hand Jeannette had dealt. He nodded to himself, or maybe to his cards.

As we sat on the stump still pairing sounds, listening, I thought about the eyes of deer. Color-blind.

When I had gone out to the Catalina where Duke and Ellis were drinking Colt 45 from a quart bottle, Ellis told me that they were color-blind because of rods or cones in their eyes. He told me about night-shine, which I had seen in headlights before, the red glow in a deer's eyes. I went back to the house not fully understanding.

We sat resting against each other and I *thought* the sounds together, scratching, a coyote bark, the chatter of a red squirrel. I thought them together as shades, as tones — black, white, and gray.

Black bark and red needles turned speckled gray. The grass showed up gray brown. My olive green jacket turned to the same tone as my feet, and those the same as the waves to my left. Birch bark and the unfrozen lake mouthing shades I could barely understand.

Lost in the shades, my thumbs slowly losing all sense of touch sheathed in their socks, my toes already numb, the morning drew over but refused to warm the earth enough to burn the frost off the ground. I couldn't feel my nose but I didn't dare move my head to rub it against my collar. All I could do was lick the snot that dripped down onto my upper lip, tasting the salt on my tongue. My toes had long since lost their ability to pull the texture of my socks into coherence. They pushed over and back indifferently, like looking at the face of someone you have known all of your life; passing over the features checking for something completely different in a place you could walk dizzy and blindfolded and still find your way.

Stan hadn't moved, the pressure on my back told me so: no shifts or flexed muscles along his spine; nothing I could feel through the double thickness of our coats. The light from the water tower was barely visible through the trees — the mist from the lake cut it out — and the sun was rising pale from behind the cedars. My gun lay across my legs and cut a cold line through both Lyle's pants and my jeans. My thumbs were tucked into their socks and I didn't know how I'd be able to sneak my trigger finger out.

I felt Stan shift his weight, the cords in his back bunching against the stillness of the morning. Then I heard him undo the snap on one of his flap pockets.

I didn't move.

His weight canted again but I couldn't tell what he was doing except that his left arm was raised near his face.

Here.

He whispered it over his shoulder. Trying not to move or pivot too much, I reached behind me, trying to balance my weight against his. It reminded me of the booth with the tippy rope ladder at the state fair. We all gave it a try except for Jeannette who stayed home, not believing in fairs, livestock on exhibition, and country music. It felt like the booth with the ropes and wooden rungs they called Jacob's Ladder. Pinned to the ground on one end with a singe stake and a swivel, the other end swiveled to a large pole set in the ground. All this was suspended over straw spread across the packed dirt. The trick was to climb without falling. The ladder rocked and swung, tipping anyone who didn't have perfect balance. The wooden rungs got bigger toward the middle so it looked like a giant diamond of braided rope and smooth wooden rungs. Each try cost a quarter, and it was so hard that it pissed everyone off enough to try again and lose. Even though it did cost a whole quarter, it *was* the fair, so all of us had a go at it. Duke said he would've got it if he'd been drunker. Ellis, Stan, Celia, Jackie, Violet, even Little had a go. All of us tumbled into the straw and spent the rest of the day picking it out of our

hair, finding it in our pockets, stuck to our collars, all of us except
Little. He hooked on his clawed hands, six fingers total, and shim-
mied up not even wavering, balanced perfectly. As he got to the
top he rang the bell, shaking the string knotted to the clapper and
clanging and grinning until Ellis pulled him off, holding him in his
arms and dancing a slow circle, smiling into Little who still shook
his hands in the air trying to ring any bells he could find. The prize
was two dollars so we even got almost all of our money back.

I reached back, balanced, eyes still forward, and grabbed the bottle that Stan pressed into my hand.
    What is it?
    A breath mint.
    The rectangular glass held clear liquid, sloshing in slow
motion up against the sides as I brought it close to my lips. I
smelled it and it tasted like Stan said: sweet, pepperminty, and
spiced against the cold that seemed to have reached everywhere
it could. I swallowed and it went down smooth, coating my
throat easy and right.
    The peppermint schnapps warmed me, flushed my cheeks,
cleared my nose, and stayed thick in my mouth until I squeezed
my tongue against the roof. I put pressure on Stan's back and
held the bottle out behind me. He took another sip and put it
back in his pocket.
    Settling back down again we scanned the slashing, the jum-
bled piles of limbs, like testing the integrity of the view. Our eyes
lighted on and lifted from the piles of slashings that the logging
company had no use for and, instead of burning, left as some
crude excuse for scenery. This is where the deer liked to come for
the thin shoots of poplar that sprang up everywhere.
    Nothing moved except for the tops of some jack pines left
standing, forgotten, inconsequential, useless trees. Though Ellis
told me they were a fine tree, a fire tree, living after the burn,
coming back before anything else did, while the oaks and maples
were still shy or too proud for the scorched grass.
    The boughs lying in bunches and bundles were from red pine,
sawed off and left behind. The trunks were sent away to be milled
as board lumber or pressure-treated for a new life as fence posts.

The limbs and boughs were piled but were never burned as they should have been. The laced nets of hazel brush broke through the tumble and slowly pulled those forgotten arms back into the ground. The colors, all red-rust and brown, made it impossible to see a deer's fall hide, russet and tan. Even the naked branches of living trees could have been a buck's rack.

The colors of the dead wood and the taste of the schnapps had confused me, disrupted the shades I had been working on.

I glanced down again at the .410 on my lap, trying to look with just my eyes and not moving my whole head. The gunmetal was smooth, not like Stan's pitted 7.7mm, except for the mottled tones where the bluing had been worn off. The trigger and guard were a dull gray from skin oil, too much acid taking off the finish, fingers running up and over, gracing the curved metal, the hard and gray crescent moon. Peeking my index finger out of the hole in the sock, I put it on the trigger and eyed the hammer. The pad of my finger traced the trigger from where it descended from the body to the tip where it almost met the guard. Squeeze it like a sponge, Ellis had said. Or like a lemon.

I tried to imagine it, but the metal fooled me, the stiffness of molecules, the cold, the finality of result. Lemons and sponges are too soft to imagine. Nothing happens when you squeeze them except the juice runs out onto your hand. With the shotgun, there was an invisible line, a spring only so long that was hidden somewhere in the action, shielded by the exterior.

My finger against the trigger, I looked at the hammer. Did Stan say that it was safe when the hammer was down, or if I touched the trigger, no matter if the hammer was up or down, would the gun go off? I put my thumb on the riffed spur of the hammer. I eased it back slowly and could feel the tension of the spring somewhere in the trigger housing. I pulled it back and it snapped in place raised above the firing pin.

Donovan. Over there.

I sat straighter and turned my head so I could see where Stan was pointing.

Where?

He pointed with his chin toward the woods near the river.

I couldn't see anything. Stumps that sat hunched and huddled near the edge of the trees looked the right shape but were too dark. Brush was the right color but too big, or the wrong shape.

Where?

He lifted his arm. I leaned closer so I could look down it at the same angle he was. I shrugged.

Wait here. Don't move.

He pivoted up and, bending over, took a few quick steps and disappeared behind a pile of brush.

It felt different once he had slunk into the piled scars and amputations, the morning and the stillness of it all felt different. I realized we *had* been making noises; little human ones with our feet, low sniffles. Even the quiet rhythms of outside breathing, testing every puff of air equally before eventually taking it in, over and over.

Now, it felt truly silent. I didn't know and couldn't see where Stan had gone. He had simply blended away.

I scanned the slashings now for real, from side to side and fast. It was almost as though I was looking at it for the first time.

It used to have trees, it was supposed to, had been created for them. Ellis said it all used to be trees, no slashings, not even any fields. He said the trees had been so big around and had grown so tall that the only place to get sun, where you were forced to squint, had been on the lake. There hadn't even been any brush because of the deep deep dark. Secret places, with no food for animals like deer.

The torn stumps and piled branches with Stan gone into them and me sitting, told to sit, told not to move, felt somewhere in between. It was somewhere in between coming and going, known and guessed, loud and whispered. Like when Little was little and we didn't know he could speak but simply refused to, and Celia used to bend down and rub her hands across his skinny ribs. "I love you." Silence. "I love you." More silence. A pause and "I love you" again. It was like she needed him to say it back in order for it to be true for her. I stood embarrassed at her "I love you's" until I said it back to her, which she usually ignored, or I ran outside to find Jackie, or Duke who would make me guess what was in his hand. Once, when I was nine, Duke held out his closed hand and I guessed "I love you." But it was only a rusty bottle cap, which set me crying until he pulled the Mr. Freezee that was already beginning to melt from behind his back.

The slashings were like that. Or maybe they were like something we shouldn't see, the priest in jeans at the hardware store. Like when I was ten, two summers before, and I caught Jackie and Violet naked in the summer, during the day. I had gone down to the river with some string, a rusty hook, and a handful of leftover canned corn wrapped in a paper towel. I was going to catch some rock bass. I didn't know if it would work, but Ellis had set me up, had told me it would. He had even caught one on the end of a swivel, with no hook at all. I was going to try it because it seemed crazy that those spiny red-eyed fish would eat the same things we would. I was going down to try the pool at the last bend before the river emptied into the lake. Thinking about those gulping mouths filled with teeth slanted inward, and the way they arched their fins once out of the water, I broke from the trees to see Violet and Jackie skinny-dipping, splashing each other in the shallows.

Jackie was my age, though we really don't know exactly how old I am. I saw her skin out in the sun, all of it in the sun, her hips like angled boards, pushing against her skin so it looked like she'd swallowed a huge wooden butterfly that had creaked still with its wings outstretched on either side of her belly button. She was so thin you could see the muscle by her collarbone.

Violet was different, full and hard. She had always scared me with her frown, but her body showed no weakness, no give that I could see. Her hair was jetting down her back in a wet twisted strand. If I had been older I imagine it would've *hurt* to look at her like that.

They stood up when they saw me. Jackie crossed her arms over chest, not even thinking that there was anything between her legs she should cover, and frowned a "how could you" to where I stood dumb with the string wrapped around my hand. Violet just put her weight on one leg and planted her hands on her hips, elbows out, breasts forward. I imagined her foot tapping the gravel under the water. She blew her hair out of her eyes though it was already slicked down her back with water.

Just two words.

"You. Get."

I turned, stumbling in the saw grass, and ran back along the path where I spilled all the corn to Poverty and told Ellis that it had worked, it really had, but that I had let all of them go.

Now I shivered without Stan's back to keep the cold away, and looked around the nakedness of the clearing. I still couldn't see Stan.

I looked in the trees toward the river. Suddenly I picked him out; a lighter green, olive in the dark of the pines.

Moving, moving. His own dance with the solid red pines. Where was the deer? I tried to look where I thought he was looking but saw nothing but tangle and scar.

Then I saw him stop and raise his rifle; his right arm coming up underneath the rest, forearm horizontal like he was about to wipe sweat from his forehead. His left hand on the trigger. Again, this time following the line of his raised rifle. I looked for the deer that must have been there. Nothing. Crossed arms, butterfly hips.

He shot, the sound slamming toward me a moment after I saw his body rock back. He craned his head forward through the smoke and then stood straight, turned and whistled, waving to me as he started forward.

I stood up and uncramped my legs and hefted the shotgun. It didn't feel that light anymore. It's ready to fire when the hammer's back. I eased the hammer down into the groove and ran between the brush and stumps, down the casual slope to where Stan had been taken from view at the edge of the trees.

Rounding a huge pile of brush, piled well over my head, I saw Stan standing and rocking back and forth on the balls of his feet, his arms crossed in front of him and a cigarette puffing with his breath, clamped between his lips. The doe lay on her side near his feet.

I stepped closer and saw that she was still alive. Her side heaved, slow and regular, blood frothing from a hole that looked jagged, punched through her ribs. The bullet must have passed through, or lodged in her lungs. She didn't move her head or make any effort to get up, but slowly blinked her eyes around, staring intently at the ground.

The blood bubbled and spattered like grease in a hot pan, steamed in the frost of that too cold and bare morning. It looked like thick liquid coming to boil, tomato sauce spattering as bubbles forced their way to the top of the pot. It flapped and struggled to the open air, only to bead up on her fur and be replaced by another gout.

It had to end sometime, but Stan just stood there with his arms crossed in front of him, his cigarette rising and dipping with each intake and exhale of air and smoke.

Stan Stan Stan she's still alive.

He nodded and drew a knife from his left pocket and handed it to me sheathed as he now rocked from left to right on his legs. Removing the Camel from his mouth he nodded to where the doe rasped through the hole in her side, an artificial mouth.

Bleed it. Cut across its neck.

I took the knife and pulled the blade from its sheath, noticing the smell of Neatsfooted leather. I dropped the sheath in my jacket pocket and took off my sock, flexing my stiff fingers around the black handle of the curved Buck knife. I knelt down next to the doe, the frothing blood matting the fur like the blowhole of some furry whale wetting its own back, spattering my clothes, and wetting the right side of my face. Her nose was wet with blood and grass bits, and broken pine needles stuck against the skin like an oiled pad of a dog's foot. She turned her eyes toward the ground, looking past the needles, the topsoil, the sand, clay, water, and mantle. Cones and rods, Ellis had said.

Careful. One kick'll send you to the clinic in a hurry.

I know.

Those clear brown eyes, perfect and round, eyes that could not see color, turned away as I reached behind her head and lifted it up so I could cut around her neck, across the jugular in one stroke.

A morning dove sounded from the trees and I remember being surprised at its witness, the air so cold. Morning dove. Or was it mourning dove? I could never figure out whether it was named because it sang in the morning or because its coo was so sad, wilting into the mornings, trailing off at the end. They called from the power lines by Poverty in a way that reminded me of someone arguing with someone else who was right, and who was leaving anyway. They were mourning sounds, not meant to change anything. I used to throw rocks at them out of boredom. In the summer when I nagged Jeannette for quarters so I could walk to town to play a video game at the bar and she cussed me out the door, I went outside to heave roadside gravel at the doves riding the power lines. I almost always missed, but once, carried by luck or anger, my stone hit one and it toppled to the ground without making a noise. I ran over to where it lay in the summer grass in the ditch. It blinked some, tried to fluff its wings like it was struggling with a shirt that twisted around in sleep, like it believed it was waking up instead of dying because of a small rock thrown by a small kid. I picked it up, stroking its feathers as soft as felt. It still made no sound, no mourning sound as I crushed its head between two flat rocks. Mourning sounds. Morning sounds.

I pushed the knife against the skin of the doe and drew it around. The blade made a whispering, whisking sound; toes through sand, ripping cloth. The blood, no froth or whip forced by air, deep and dark poured out. It didn't spurt or jet, but leaked steadily, pushed by its own weight and the force of muscle, bone, and fat. It was like the water escaping from underneath the dam, compressed into a channel to round the turbines. It came thick and the top currents left you guessing how deep it really was.

It continued to pour out and Stan moved closer, placing his left hand on my shoulder because he had seen me begin to shake. The doe relaxed into the ground. She let me hold her head up with all of her nervous tension seeping and steaming into the ground, ground where the trees used to grow nine feet around at the base. A place with trees that Duke and Ellis remembered, had walked through, but that neither I or the doe would ever see.

As she lay there, her life running into the ground, before Stan took the knife back so he could field gut her and remove the glands that would stink the meat, I thought again of colors.

It was only after each of us grabbed a front leg and dragged her back to Poverty that I settled down, after another shot of schnapps and after the doe's eyes had gone gray and clouded over.

We butchered her while Duke and Ellis started a fire near the Catalina so we could do up a roast. Stan and I got to have the first meat; we fried the heart in lard on the stove in our house.

It wasn't until then, until the blood was cooked from red to brown that I relaxed. Because all I could think about as the blood rivered from the doe's neck and bubbled from underneath her ribs, was that she was color-blind. As she bled out into the crisp grass and steamed into the morning air, I knew that she couldn't see the color of her own blood. The doe's blood spread in a sheet of gray in front of her own eyes, creeping ice into the center of the lake. She bled ice until she couldn't anymore.

Violet

I took to the church up until I was sixteen. It was October, Stan was still gone overseas and I was new made. I was never fat, my skin pulled tightly across my muscle. Even my Sunday dress was strained across my shoulders as my breasts grew. That October lulled by and it rained a lot. The snow came late that year, the rain stayed longer. It soaked everything. The woodpile looked limp under its patter. The sticks were piled lopsided against each other. Lyle was supposed to come over and cut and stack it with Stan gone. He didn't know how to, though. He was never around anyway. Who knows where he got the money, but that boy loved to travel. He'd go to the Cities or off to Winnipeg and just hang around. The front steps were full of sand and there was always mud streaked in front of the door. Ma would mop it every day, but we tracked it always in. The leaves were gone, September took them with little struggle, and the woods we played in all summer stood naked.

Friday it rained as I sat with my mother. She put some wood in the stove and the rain hissed down the stove pipe, breathing vapor in between the cracks in the iron. She filled the blue coffee kettle from the copper bucket by the door. It sat on the stove, struggling to warm up. We sat, not talking. I was wearing wool socks. I wore long johns and a big flannel shirt, too. When the water was hot and the coffee was done, she poured me some. It was a bitter thing. Only adults drank it, so I sipped it carefully.

"Let me brush your hair."

She put down her tin cup and went into her room and brought
back her only brush, with real bristles from some animal. She sat
me down in front of her and spread my hair out across my back.
It was long, shiny jet black, and it reached almost to my waist.
She picked up a rope of it and brushed it down in long strokes.
Over and over again she drew it out and straightened it between
the bristles of her brush. She smoothed it, pulling it into a black
river that trailed down my back. Fanning it out and drawing it
up by my waist, she let it flow between her brown fingers with her
smooth nails.

Outside the rain shot down harder, swelling the river that ran
behind Poverty. The oaks turned black and the browned grasses
were spanked flat. The road turned to mud, the ditches filled with
dirt. Everything turned and was beaten down. The peak of the
roof split the water as it closed and ran down the sides of our
house. Some rain hissed down the stove pipe as my hair shone
even blacker, slicker than before. The strokes of the brush
against my scalp pulled me closer againt my mother's knees and
my eyes shut against the gentle strain of her hands. I slumped
and leaned back against her knees, feeling their warmth seep
through the cotton. My hair now fanned out into her lap, as the
rain sheeted and danced around us. I was dozing off to sleep
when it started to thunder.

"It is only God rearranging his furniture in Heaven," Ma said.
I faded and the rain pulled me in.

The next day I awoke and the rain had left everything brown,
streaked against the sunlight I was not used to in October. Ma
left to go to town. The sun poured in through the windows of the
house, pointing out every spot of dirt and footprint on the wood
floor. I watched as the sun pushed over every grain of sand that
had been tracked in the house, each casting its shadow all the
way across the floor.

A silence settled over everything. Even the usual sounds of
the semis going by on the highway were muted. I took the bent
broom with its frayed straws and began to sweep the floor. My
hair swung against my back as I moved back and forth over the

boards. I even lifted the chairs onto the table, I got all the dirt from between its legs. I was thorough. Under the sink and the space between the opened door and the wall were swept bare. I swept the basement stairs, the pantry, and around the front step. Finally the sand and clay were corralled in the center of the room.

It was when I was trying to find the dustpan in the wood box that Lyle stuck his head in the door and asked if we had any sugar in the house. He lived with Evan and Pick down on the other side of town, though Pick was gone overseas with Stan. Lyle and I used to play together when we were little. Once he had just dipped some stray dog's tail in chain-saw mix. He took a match to the oil and gas, and the dog was off screaming around the yard.

His ma flung the door open, "Lyle, you get your little Indian ass in here." He went in and we rolled on the ground. Lyle? Lyle!! We laughed until he came outside. When he stepped out the door, both hands on his ass, we couldn't help it and we whooped some more. When we were younger and he was smaller I used to drag him around the yard by his hair until he screamed. Now he was bigger, at least six feet, and he never let me forget. His black hair was shaggy around his shoulders like a black mane and his nose was small, especially for an Indian. It made his eyes stand out and seem a deeper brown.

He startled me and my face burned because he saw me jump. It was a sign of weakness.

"Can we borrow some sugar?"

"Lyle. Don't you got any? Doesn't your ma keep any around?"

"We're out. Can we have some?"

I leaned awkwardly against the wood box, the splinters were hot against my legs. He stepped in, the ripped T-shirt hanging loose from his arms.

"What's it for?"

"Pies."

"What kind?" I didn't want to be the end of a joke. The kind of joke where he went back to his friends with a can full of sugar, telling how he tricked me.

"Apple pie. What's the big deal?" He had moved in past the front door and he was standing in front of the table, his feet were almost in my dirt pile. I was afraid that he was going to scatter it everywhere.

"We don't have a lot of it. It doesn't grow on trees and my ma isn't going to like me handing out all her sugar." The air was still, and even the dust seemed to settle slower than it had before. I heard no voices from outside anymore. The wind had ground to a halt so that not even a finger brushed the tops of the pine trees that grew up to the house. The sunlight rippled in and settled on Lyle's shoulders and hands. I could trace his pulse on a vein up his right forearm. His heartbeat was like that of the river flowing nearby, but slower.

"Here," I said, handing him a coffee can full of sugar. "Use what you need. Bring the rest back or Ma'll have a fit." His fingertips brushed over the backs of my hands as he took the sugar can from me. I turned away then, moving back toward the wood box to look for the dustpan. My skin was hot. The problem with looking white is that when I blush, everyone can tell. I expected him to leave but he stood there with the can in both of his hands.

"What are you looking for?" He watched as I turned over old newspapers and shoes, wood chips and pieces of bark.

"The dustpan. Here I spent all afternoon sweeping, and I can't find the damn dustpan."

"Are you sure it's there?"

"Would I look if I didn't think it was?" I blew the hair out my eyes but it stuck with a little sweat that had crept onto my brow. He was always cocky, and I could usually keep his head down to size, but I was trying to find that dustpan. I could hear him set the can down next to the sink and walk over to where I was.

"Here, you can just use newspaper."

"I can do it, Lyle. You can just go." He was looking over my shoulder and I could feel his breath slip past my neck. I breathed in sharply, taking some of his breath with me. It tasted like birch bark from a fresh tree. He reached past me to get the paper from the box.

"Pick's gone."

"'Course he's gone, so's Stan. We haven't gotten word from

them ever." He turned and the sunlight streaked in and hit his eyes. He stared at the ground by my feet.

"No Violet," he muttered and scuffed around with his feet. I knew he wasn't scuffing nothin', I swept it all up before.

I turned back to the wood box, looking for the dustpan. "Lyle, last we heard they was on leave."

It was getting hot, and I felt some sweat drift out of my hair and run down my back, between my shoulder blades.

He didn't say anything, but stepped a little closer. I looked down and saw his sneakers edging my dust pile. I held onto the edge of the wood box.

"I got a letter from the marines," said Lyle.

"Well? What do you mean he's gone?" The sweat was soaking into my dress and I saw that his sneakers were worn out on the back heels, the canvas worn away.

"Nothin'. He's just gone, that's all."

"It don't say nothin' about Stan?" He came up closer behind me. I could smell his breath like cedar. So sweet.

"It don't say anything." He wrapped his arms around me from behind and pulled me close. I was shaking so he rocked me back and forth. I grabbed his arms with mine and squeezed him even closer. He leaned against me. I could feel his warmth through my print dress, through his pants. The cloth pattern of roses and checks, bluebells and tiny green leaves couldn't stop any of the heat. I put my hands on the edge of the box so I could flip myself around and throw him off me. As I turned around our legs tangled because we both went down on the floor together, my dress flew around us like a fine dust.

His eyes flew wide, he realized he was trapped with me around him. My legs rested on top of his hips and he sat with his feet up against the wood box. I pulled him closer with my legs, not wanting to let him go. He pushed himself up but it just locked us closer. His head bobbed, and he looked up at me. He was crying and a little drunk. He felt my heart beat against his cheek as we began to rock against the wood box. Faster. His pants were down and he was inside me. My dress covered everything in the sunlight. It covered the wetness and trapped our heat. Faster. I was silk, and bolts of my red cloth unrolled and fluttered around us in a wind. Faster. He pulled away. As he jumped to his feet his pants came up with one hand while the other took the sugar. Grasping his pants and the sugar he ran out the door and into the sun.

I sat there on the floor awhile. Everything was still. Now, though, I picked up a faint pulse. From the sunlight, or the river maybe. I couldn't hear the trucks on the highway, but maybe their tires on the asphalt hummed a rhythm so low that I could only feel it. I looked at the floor, clean and hard in the morning sun. It looked different now. It was too bare, naked. The spots of grease and the dips where a chunk had been taken out, perhaps from a boot or a metal pail, showed through.

I sat there thinking about how many times I had walked over this floor. I never noticed the dirt ground into the linoleum. I never saw the blackened spots where coals from the stove had marked the boards. The raised sections, the sinking planks. I shouldn't have lifted all the dirt into one pile, stripping the floor. It was not mine to take. I stood up and pulled my skirt down. The dustpan I left unfound. It was a sign, my not being able to find it. I laughed out loud, the notion that we could use a newspaper to pick up the dirt. This dirt was so fine, it probably would have fallen right through the paper anyway. I took the broom and spread the dirt back out across the floor. I flung it in some places, puffs of dust streaking the sunlight. I put some dirt back under the stove and pushed some under the table. I fanned it out in front of the doorway and when I was done, the floor was so much better that I finally felt that I could sit and let the sounds start up again.

The next day it was Sunday. My mother dressed me up in my church dress, but it didn't feel quite right. We got a ride with Duke and Ellis who weren't what you'd call the church-going type. I got to sit in the back seat. The seat had a lot of springs under the cushions and when we went down the gravel road, the washboards bounced us up and down. Most of us didn't have cars, but Duke and Ellis had their Catalina that they "borrowed" from a white girl in Wisconsin. They didn't go into the church. All they did during the service was drive around the block listening to their radio, which we didn't get to listen to because my ma said country music didn't get us into the church-going mood.

The mass was the story of Job and how God put him to the test by taking away everything that was important to him. God killed Job's family and made him poor, just to show that Job would keep his faith, and that faith is the most important thing of all. It didn't seem quite right to me.

After the service we had confession. I went up to the wooden booth and pulled the curtain behind me. The curtain was purple and the booth was paneled in wood. Father Gundesohn was behind a wooden grill and I could only make out his outline. I couldn't see his face, which was clean-shaven except for his side-burns that curved down the sides of his face. Priests can't grow mustaches, but they can grow sideburns, he said.

"Daughter, have you sinned since your last confession?" I could feel Duke and Ellis driving around the block. There was dust on Father Gundesohn's shoes. I always wondered how some-one could get dust on shoes they wore every day.

"Yes, Father, I have sinned." My heart beat fast as my words slipped through the space toward him.

"And what was your sin, daughter?"

"I gave out something that wasn't mine to give."

"And what was that, daughter?" He eased the words to me, like a plate of butter being passed hand to hand.

"Sugar. I gave out my mother's sugar."

"Is that a sin?"

"Oh yes, Father, I gave out the whole can."

"I see. This is not so bad. You can always give the sugar back and ask her forgiveness."

"I can't get it back. Besides, I put the dirt back all over the floor." With that I slid out of the booth and left the church. I sat on the front steps, the ones made out of chipped cement, wait-ing for my mother to go through confession. She was at the back of the line. By that time God had quit listening and she was safe to speak. The sun beat down and it was too bright for October. Last year we had snow, why did it have to be so warm now? While I sat there Duke and Ellis drove by, slowed down, and asked me if I wanted to ride around the block with them until my ma was out too.

I sat in the back seat and listened to the radio as we rolled around the block. The song "Tumbling Tumbleweeds" was on and I wondered why we didn't have any in Minnesota. Then the football game came on; it was the Vikings vs. the Redskins. Duke turned to look at me.

"Violet. Doesn't it seem just a little off that the Vikings are in Minnesota and the Redskins are in Washington, D.C.?"

"Yep, Duke." I wondered why the dust and dirt were so small here.

"Why are the Indians there? Seems kind of stupid."

"Yeah, sure does."

"You friends with Stan and Pick?"

"Stan's my brother."

I know, but are you all friends? There's a difference."

"Yep, Duke. We all friends." He kept looking ahead as if the block were suddenly about to change. As if the stores would all suddenly disappear, or the five-and-dime would all of a sudden change into a Dayton's, complete with perfume and cologne counters.

"You'll be all right Violet. Everything's going to be all right."

On the ride back home it started to rain again. The ride was smoother, the sand parted in front of the Pontiac's wheels until it pulled up in our yard. My mother and I went inside, the rain making my white dress a dull gray before I could slip in the door. I went into my room and got into my other clothes. I hung up my dress so it wouldn't wrinkle, and then went back out into the kitchen to help my mother make dinner.

I poured the yeast into the warm water and let it sit until it bubbled. I added the flour and the salt for bread and let it rise, covering it with a wet dish towel so it didn't crust on the outside before I put it in to bake. Ma cut the potatoes for the stew and coined the carrots too. She chopped the onion and its sharp sweetness flowed through the kitchen. I punched the bread down and covered it again. I punched it too early and the dough stuck to my knuckles and fingers. I licked it off; it was salty, too much salt. I swept the skins from the onions into my hands. They were so thin, crisp like peanut skins. They reminded me of peanuts from the county fair; red and papery, I closed my hand around them and felt them crush a little. Just a little, because onion skins do that. They hold, sometimes they crumble a bit. I wondered if the skins would turn soggy and droop in the rain. Maybe they could stand dry and wet, never crumble and never become limp. I threw them in the garbage under the sink. The bread was done baking and I bent down to take it out of the oven. Ma was mixing the dough for the pies. Graham-cracker crust, apple pies.

"Where's the sugar tin?"

I was stunned, so I stayed stooped in the oven door, the heat blasting in my face, unable to answer. I feigned deafness.

She asked again. I stood up, my face red from the heat.

"I don't know," I lied.

Her eyes bunched up, and she stood with her hands on her hips.

"You gave it away. You gave it up." She turned and whirled from the room. She knew. Maybe she heard me at confession. Perhaps it was her sixth sense, but I felt she knew everything that happened. She could smell and taste everything that went on in her house. She knew my sin. Did Father Gundesohn tell her? Maybe when she went to confession God spoke to her, out of boredom, or out of friendship. Maybe his breath slipped in through the wooden grill, or under the bottom of the purple curtains, whispering to her of my deed. Maybe it was the dust all over the linoleum, spread too evenly. I don't know, maybe the sun told her, or the spirits that hide just on the other side of big trees. You can almost catch sight of them as you turn around the trunk, but no matter how fast you run, they never show themselves.

I stood alone in the kitchen while it rained even harder. With no sugar the pies couldn't be made. The only thing left to fix was the string beans. I took them from their basket and washed them at the sink. They were old, the last ones from the summer garden. They were thick and knobby, where the seeds pushed against the outer skin. Their hair was silvery and it roughed my fingers as I washed what dirt remained down the drain.

I stood and snapped the ends of the beans into the sink and put them in a bowl. The rain poured even harder, pushing against the window. The juices seeped under my fingernails and the tips of my fingers hurt. I tasted one, closing my eyes I tasted them as red. They should have been made red instead of green, full of juices and firm.

After I was halfway done I felt my mother at my side. Wordlessly, she reached into the basket, drawing out a bean. It was a long one and it was especially knobby, the ends almost pointy. She snapped off either end using her thick thumbnail; she then set it in the bowl with the rest of the beans I had snapped. She grabbed another, and another. I reached into the basket also. The rain fell. I snapped the bean and set it with the others.

わ　ふ

Lyle left the same day he borrowed the sugar and we made love on my ma's kitchen floor. I thought I'd never see him again. His leaving always brought back the tastes of sugar and salt. Other memories are harder and harder to come by, but I always wonder, as I add the sugar to my jellies for Jackie's sweet tooth, where the first sugar I gave took him. The salt he first left between my legs grew and grew until there was no hiding it. When Jackie came I gave her all of the sugar that Lyle took away. With her moods flashing back and forth, there is always full attention paid to her. Except when Little's there, the one my brother thinks is his child.

When Little is nosing at crumbs under the table or even staring at the static coming off the TV, because a lot of the time the reception isn't so good, the grown-ups take long looks at him. During a drag from a cigarette, or from over the lip of a glass, everyone stares and waits. He has a dam-break feeling. One of these days the buildup is going to spill over and bust him apart. Or maybe we just like to think so.

But the way he flits around, his hands, his word. I bake in extra sugar for Jackie. Protection. The way those three hang together. We see it, but they are blind to what he is all about. Even though we never talked about it, I think that Celia tries to hide him. The effort is wasted. Little slips in and out, either at the lake, at Poverty with Duke and Ellis, or somewhere with Donovan and my Jackie. Celia can't do it. It's an impossible secret.

When I was pregnant my mother tried to hide me at first, only taking me to church on Sundays. I sat next to her on the pew, never raising my eyes during the sermon. Even when communion was given I didn't raise my chin for the wafer, but my mother sat with her back straight and stared at the priest through the entire service. When the blood of Christ was passed I felt only the roil of blood growing inside me, so I let it pass. My mother drank deeply and I watched as her eyes groped about, always searching for the bottom of the cup, but never finding it.

When the service was over she would go and stand in the back of the line for confession, just like she always had. Only now she stood with her head bowed, as if in conversation. Then she would go into confession for a good while, until God was convinced either to save or damn her, I could never tell which one she wanted. I tried to get up once, but I showed too much by then, so I stayed hidden in my pew, content to wait until my mother came out and we got inside Duke and Ellis's car. Sometimes I would slip out of church early and ride around with them. They never said anything about my being pregnant, but Duke was always willing to ask my opinion on the status of the Vikings. His conversations grew and waned with the seasons. In the fall he'd talk about the Redskins. Then, by spring, he'd say that the Chiefs and the Braves should definitely be traded to Minneapolis and St. Paul. The only acknowledgment they gave was when they stopped at Marshall's store and Ellis bought me the grape Nehis that he somehow knew I craved.

Father Gundesohn died in the church. They said he drowned. It was only when we got a new preacher that I looked up during the sermon and stayed until the end, though I still didn't take communion.

He preached with a passion that the older priest had reserved for sermons on sin, which ranged from original to not so original in my opinion; like the amount he would like to see on the contribution plate. The younger one was from Iowa, and from his speech I could tell he knew neither women, nor very hard work, and probably was the son of an accountant or the youngest runt of a farmer. When he arrived I knew that it was God speaking to me and Jackie, not yet born. He whispered the word of God, and

I knew he spoke of Lyle and the sugar, which is another reason why I could never, ever, take the body or the blood of Christ from his hand.

I knew this from his first sermon, when he preached in a voice soft with apprehension and with a nervous quiver, from the Book of Ruth.

> *Wherever you go, I will go,*
> *wherever you live, I will live.*
> *Your people shall be my people,*
> *and your God, my God.*
> *Whenever you die, I will die*
> *and there I will be buried.*

It was then that I knew the thing that was growing inside of me was not a sin, but a thing of salt that pushed out all boundaries, and I remembered Lyle, when we sat tangled together in the dirt of my kitchen floor. As this occurred to me I lifted my head and a breeze came like the wind left by the banging front door as Lyle ran away, far away from me. I knew that whoever he was with I was with too, and the caresses he was giving to women that I didn't know were carried across space and time by the hand of God, which in this case was ivory white, with a few red hairs gracing the back of it, the nails trimmed close, and the cuticles pushed back with a penknife.

After a while though, my mother's embarrassment and repentance became too much and she refused to bring me to church anymore. I sat at home at Poverty and wrote to Stan, who, the last we heard, was in a veterans hospital in Brooklyn. Pick wasn't coming home. Duke and Ellis, instead of driving around the block during service, stopped at Marshall's and then drove out to our house. There we'd sit on their car in the sun and drink grape Nehis. I was getting fatter but my skin was continually flushed and I ate plates of fry bread with my Nehis.

My mother went to work every day at the nursing home and she never got back until after dark because we didn't have a car. The days grew long and I sat in the kitchen doing the things that she never had the energy to do: washing out a winter's worth of dust from crated Ball canning jars, sanding the water marks and cigarette burns from the pine-plank kitchen table, and soaking the beans for supper. After I started to show, I never went back to school. The school didn't give a damn anyway. And then Ma left, down to Mille Lacs, then to Sawyer, then to Minneapolis. She said it was because Dad was losing hope in Stillwater, still there after slicing up Marshall Marshall. So I was alone, pregnant with Jackie.

Sometimes I'd get up and walk a few yards from the front step where an old lilac bush struggled in the dust by the side of the road. The base was a tangled mass of sticks. Some were growing and some others had fallen off, making a network of brown branches whose pattern I couldn't figure out. The leaves that are usually my favorite color of green were coated with dust from the cars that sped down the highway to the lake. Earlier in the spring whole carloads of people would speed down to the dam with iron spears sticking from their trunks, and coolers full of beer wedged between them in the back seats. They rocketed past Poverty in a hurry to spear the suckers that ran through early May in the still ice-cold waters of the river. Sometimes there were those who just had cases of Budweiser in their trunks and they would sit on the beach until all the red-and-blue cans floated and bobbed in the waves like so many twelve-ounce buoys.

By the side of the road, unnoticed by them, grew my lilac. More and more dust stuck to the leaves, and even the hardest rain couldn't strip the leaves of their clothes. As the cars sped by and their drivers never noticed the faint purple flowers and the sickly sweet smell, they never, ever noticed or stopped for me. They never stopped by with canned blueberries or plums, with thick wax crusted around the top of the jars. They never had pans of hotdish for me, or brought me word from town. They never offered me a beer, or asked how my summer was, or if the days were too dusty, too wet, or even too in-between. They let the dust kicked up by their wheels cover their consciences and were content to drink cheap beers.

Sometimes I imagined the sounds that were to come later, in the fall: the echo of cedar sticks knocking against each other as they swept the rice stalks over canoes and flat-bottomed duck boats with peeling paint, or no paint at all. I lay in bed awake as they drove to the lake in the early morning, before the heat struck at ten. Usually their cars crunching up the gravel jarred me from my sleep. I imagined the steady hiss of gravel and the hum of pavement in time with Jackie's claws and kicks, setting up a beat no one else could hear except us. I would lie there and imagine these morning sounds out of season: the ricers scraping their canoes and boats from the backs of pickup trucks or from the roofs of cars and setting them in the water. In that hour the sound of ricing poles banging against wooden gunnels or aluminum bottoms carried for miles and beat a rhythm I imagined to be in time with Jackie's moods. But it was early June. The spearing was done, ricing wouldn't come until late August, and even berry-picking was a month and a half away. The sounds that found their way to me as I lay in the dark were hollow. It was spring after all and every sound or activity was concerned only with the possibility of its own existence. After being locked down by the snow and ice, sounds thought only that they could be, could bang and crash, that people would be able to listen and do nothing. Spring was always a selfish season. So without company I would get up and go outside to pick some lilac for my bath.

The flowers I picked were a pale purple, paler than I ever remember them being when I was younger. My skin was flushed a deep gold and I stood next to the lilac bush feeling that I ought to dust the leaves with a wet cloth, but feeling that for some reason I shouldn't. I didn't want my flowers to be noticed and maybe if I stripped the leaves of their protection, I would bring notice to the waxy green leaves and the little clusters of blossoms.

My bath was a secret, because it was only then that I allowed myself a look at my entire body. I knew that no one would stop by except for Celia, who was pregnant too. She kept to herself and sometimes I could catch her staring at me when I walked out to my lilac bush. Maybe she knew about my baths, but she had her secrets too.

I heated water on the stove in the big, clanking pressure cooker that we had gotten at an auction along with all our canning jars. When the water was boiling I would tip it into the galvanized tin washtub that was as spare and plain as a pine-board church pew. We used to have to split the firewood and use the woodstove for heating water, but one day when I was sitting at home, my mother already gone, Duke and Ellis came back to the house with my grape Nehi and a gas stove complete with a propane tank in the trunk. I couldn't believe it as they wrestled the stove and tank into the kitchen. After they left I took my first bath with lots of steaming hot water. The water wasn't lukewarm, and it was clear, pure, and bright in the morning sun.

When I was a kid I had to bathe after Ma and Stan. The water was barely warm, and that was only if you didn't move, disturbing the small currents in the washtub. The water was a dirty brown and I always felt dirtier after I swished it over my body, but with the gas stove I could heat my own water. I could keep my own secrets, not save everyone else's.

After I heated the water and lowered myself into the tub, I took the lilac blossoms I had clipped and mashed, and rubbed them across my chest and smoothed them over my belly.

I never hated Lyle for leaving me. In his absence I loved him so much that I drew everyone in who would listen to me and who could stand being a replacement, until Jackie got so big inside me that even that ended. The other men never knew of him, never any more than I did, so briefly. It wasn't that I tried to find substitutes for him. The men who picked me up in trucks or new cars were weak enough to be him.

They thought me desperate and dirty enough to let them use me any way they wanted to, but never since Lyle have I had sex facing my man. Sometimes they brought me to their houses, when their wives were off at Thursday night bingo at the community center. They used me in their own beds, the ones they shared with their wives. I think that they liked it better when they saw me kneeling in front of them and if they were quiet enough, like most of them were, I could imagine it was actually Lyle inside of me pushing out the spaces and sweating into me with a desire that I myself only felt once.

After I lay on my side, facing away from them, they curled up, nesting their bodies against mine. In this proximity their breath escaped down my neck, breath of beer, and I pretended that I was asleep. With our skin touching where the sheets had slipped, or not, where in their haste they didn't bother removing my clothes, they'd get aroused again. Still I didn't move and they slipped inside me, hoping not to be noticed. For this I loved them, too. Moving slowly so they didn't wake me up, they pushed inside me. Even when they came they tried not to quiver, but their pulsing and their quickened breath were obvious to me. Then, almost tenderly sometimes, they withdrew and rolled over to the other side of the bed, or if we were in a car they sat up and cracked the window so they could blow the smoke from a cigarette outside.

It was in that space that I missed Lyle, but I began to feel another pulse, another light opening within me. I loved Lyle enough to put him where he wasn't, and I loved him enough to let the men go when they were bored.

With Jackie inside me there was no more room for the men, and they didn't notice. In the years that followed this proved to be one of my daughter's gifts to me. I didn't need them, didn't *really* need them like the way we talk about needing men. Only one. Only Lyle. In the hot bath during the sun's strongest hours I closed my eyes and rested my back against the metal side of the washtub. The cracking and settling of my hips that occurred whenever I moved or walked up and down stairs faded away as my legs and back were loosened in the water.

The smell of lilacs was also my secret and I spread it like an oil over my whole body until I closed my eyes and imagined that the smell was actually a color. The lilac shaded me a light purple over the browns and golds that I lived in. I gave my delicate purple a white dress. I could no longer fit into the one I used to wear to church and I had no others. I gave my color a white dress that could ruffle in a wind, not hang straight down, a heavy cotton. My old dress was a fabric that had no hold of its own, and the iron in the water had given it a yellowish color. There was no fancy design, no billows in the shoulders or low neck with scallops embroidered in white lace across my chest and back. The hem was straight and there was no dipping waistline that would have drawn attention to my then-thin waist. The sleeves tapered only a little, and once when I saw Alicia Marshall at church, I looked at her sleeves and noticed that they were stitched with openings and closings like the lace doilies that old women crochet while sitting around their kitchen tables. The loops and spirals reminded me of the frost on our window panes, and the way they hung from Alicia's arms made her wrists delicate and capable of draping around a shoulder or a slim muscled waist. With those sleeves it seemed that she could hold a flower delicately and longingly — not like the way I removed the blossoms from my lilac bush out of a driving need — with a passing notice. My wrists were thick from chopping wood and carrying water for my mother, while Alicia's were mere flower stems. Her skin was paler too, from days spent sitting in the back room of her father's grocery store, where they even had an electric fan in the summer and a heater in the winter.

Alicia was my age and was the only child of her father with the exception of Ernie, her older brother, who was rough and who, since early in my life, had tried to beat me up and seduce me. Most likely in his mind they meant the same thing. Ernie always seemed much younger than he was, while Alicia acted like she was thirty and cultivated from her magazines a big-city way about her. All year round she sat in the back room, which was nothing more than the storeroom with a small wooden desk. All year round she read the magazines that they sold in the store. Her arms, good for nothing else, could flip through magazines in lazy circles, and her eyes even knew which articles to read, and which to skip over with the flutter of shiny, slick pages. When I came to the store for a bag of flour or cornmeal she would beg me with a tilt of her head to sift it into the rough cotton sacks and lift it to the scale where she would read the weight and automatically know the price. Once that was done she would go back to the fan and start paging through another magazine, and not notice when I would pull open the lid to the pickle barrel, take one out for myself, and then spit quietly and fully into the pickles. Once outside the store, I balanced the sacks of flour on my right shoulder and stuffed the smaller bags of salt, baking soda, or yeast into my pockets. With my left hand I shook the extra juice into the sand and ate the pickle as I walked back to Poverty.

The only decoration that my mother sewed out of kindness or forgetfulness on my white dress was a couple of simple pleats that lay by my hips. They seemed so obvious and they made me feel awkward. They were an open attempt to make something plain a little less so, but they did the opposite because they made something as empty as daylight, or a rumpled flour sack, look exactly like what it was. I tried not to swing my arms when I wore that dress, but kept them tucked in at my sides with my elbows bent so that they covered my pleats, but now that I could not fit that dress I wore my lilacs like a prize.

When the lilacs turned brown and dropped their flowers in June, I dropped my bath and started going over to Celia's, where she lived with her mother, Jeannette. Depending on the weather, Duke and Ellis were either sprawled out on the vast, rusted maroon hood of their car, or huddled inside with the windows cracked a bit to vent cigarette smoke and the heater on full blast. There were always cigarettes and at least a can or two of beer to be found, and if they weren't asleep they nodded to me and called me over.

Even in the years after Jackie was born Duke and Ellis were always there. Always watching. When they up and drove away, to the bingo hall, or to the junkyard, they were always there just at the right time. They drove me to the hospital when Jackie was born, and when Celia had Little, they drove her too.

They kept a keen eye out for the children. And they never told my secret. Lilacs. They must have seen me go out to the bush. They must have seen me strip it almost bare. It was there my water broke and I collapsed. Soon the car was pulled around and they carried me in. When I was in the hospital they drove over and picked up everyone else: Jeannette, Stan, and Celia. Pick was dead. My mother was in the Cities.

Now, all motion, Donovan, Jackie, and Little run around and play on the Catalina, digging holes under the wheels, crawling underneath till I nearly die thinking the car is going to drop on Jackie. I see her, scrapping in the dirt, mud on her knees, and she gets a scratch. Little laughs, but Donovan holds her hand and walks her back to me where I am, watching them from the window of the house. I watch out alone. Ma has moved away down to Mille Lacs, where her sister lives. I look out alone from the window, but sometimes I sit with Jeannette and Celia.

When Jackie started going to school, walking in the fog to the school bus, with Donovan and Little, and then with just Donovan, because the school didn't want Little anymore, I had all the hours in the house by myself. I counted, watched the clock, washed everything twice, wanting her *there*. She comes home and is indifferent, liking more to sit in the fields with Donovan and Little, talking about nothing I know. Or during the summer climbing the huge red pines at the edge of the lake, clambering over the limbs, they go higher and higher. They climb higher than Stan, Pick, Lyle, and I did when we ran loose, when we were younger. When Pick was alive and Lyle was still here. When Jackie can't reach, Donovan talks her into coming down. He finds something else for them to do, but it always takes them further away from Poverty. So far away, so high, that I worry and when I do the laundry I fold her clothes three or four times.

Lyle

I put Violet's sugar in the front seat with me after I ran back home and jumped in my brother's Thunderbird. The letter I had gotten in the mail that day was in my back pocket, and that was mine. It used to be Pick, Evan, and me. Evan was off working at the sawmill, so now it was just me. I turned the key and drove out of the yard. The car was okay. It was real bright yellow and it had rusted through in a lot of places. I was fixin' it up. Evan let me drive once in a while so I fixed up his car the best I could. Once he said it wouldn't even be running if I didn't work on it. Evan didn't know how to do shit with his hands. All they were good for was pushing logs through the rough-cut saw at the mill, clobbering someone, lifting beer cans to his mouth, or keeping Pick from thrashing me for something I really should've been thrashed for. Pick was always good with his hands and so was I, but Evan's hands could only feed logs into the chute where they were dressed and cut into rough lumber. Our wood on the reservation wasn't good enough for finished lumber anymore.

I had to go down to the end of Poverty and turn around. Duke and Ellis were sitting on their rusted Catalina. There was a six-pack of beer on the hood and a jumble of cards between them. I waved as I went around the dirt ruts that circled their car and continued up past the prefab houses of Poverty.

They both stared as I drove past. Ellis's mouth hung open and he pointed at my car. Duke jumped up on the hood of their

Catalina and shouted something at me. My windows were up
and I revved the engine, drowning out whatever they said.
Whatever it was couldn't matter much. They didn't read the letter the marines mailed me that morning; it wasn't theirs to read
and know.

I sped down the dirt road and onto the highway. When I
looked back in the mirror they were both standing up, looking
after my car. I turned, accelerated, and they left my sight as the
trees cut them off.

I turned out onto the highway. I needed to get away from the
reservation. The woods and the few stores and thousands of re-
sorts, all owned by whites, closed in on me. I almost didn't make it
out but I kept on looking over at the tin of sugar. I set the can in
the space between my legs and popped the top off with one hand.
The outside of the can was red and white, Folger's Coffee. The
inside was shiny except where the sugar came halfway to the top
in a snowy circle. It looked powdery white and I wet my finger
with my tongue, and stuck it in the grains. I held it in front of my
face as I sped past the big lake on the reservation and tried to
count how many bits of sugar were on my index finger. So many, I
thought. So many grains, how can you count them all? The wind
whipping through the car blew my finger clean and I licked it and
stuck it back in again. This time I got more sugar and I put it in
my mouth before the wind could suck it away. All those thousands
of bits, tiny squares and shapes, made my whole mouth sweet as
the creamy part of the inside of a blade of grass. Sweeter than
the cotton candy at a powwow, brighter than the white chalk of
birch bark, lighter than the fluff of milkweed in August when
Violet and I sat in the dead grass behind Poverty. We used to pull
apart the pods after the milk dried up and close our eyes, placing
the down over our lids and letting the wind sweep it into the air
before we could snatch it.

Under the taste of the sugar, around it, sneaking in from the
sides like a dog that's afraid to be kicked but yearns to be petted
at the same time, came other tastes. The grit of reservation dust
and the slippery sweat from the steering wheel carried back to
me, and from inside of it all came another taste. It was sharp as

iron and strong. The smell was like horse's sweat but bitter and sweet too. Violet's sex clung to my hand, it beat out the sugar taste from my mouth. The gentle smell of northern pike or bass we caught off of the dam was a summer smell. But that smell, it was winter. I lifted my head and the taste followed me as I glanced down to where the can rested between my legs, snugged up against the bulge in my faded jeans, and to my back pocket with the letter about Pick. I leaned way over to open the window on the passenger side of the Thunderbird and the more wind that caught it, the more it just circled and circled until I was dizzy and drunk.

I only had half a tank. The radio didn't work and I had all the windows down and the sunroof open. It was warm but the wind rushed in and chilled my skin underneath my T-shirt. The wind made the sound of falling water as it rushed past my ears and swirled around the inside of the car. I imagined driving on the bottom of the river: fish and turtles getting pulled in through the windows only to be sucked back out again. I squinted against the current as I passed the powwow grounds.

Pick, Stan, and I used to go there and play basketball during the powwows. None of us liked to dance much. We all knew how, and had danced when we were littler. Pick used to compete, fancy-dancing. Ma made him an outfit that even had two bustles and little mirrors in the center of each one, between the spokes of the feathers wrapped in bright yarn and beads she bought at Kmart. Pick used to dance a lot when he was little. My grandma gave me a picture of him in his fancy-dancing outfit. His bustle sticks out real nice and the roach on his head stands up tall, black, red, and white. The picture is black and white but I imagine his outfit looking really smart. Bright blues and oranges woven in the feathers of his bustle. He even had two sticks wrapped in deer hide with feathers hanging from the end that Stan's dad, Lincoln, made him. No fancy-dancer should be empty-handed when he danced, he said. I never saw much of his outfit 'cause someone burned our house down when I was little and I don't remember seeing it. But I got the picture in my wallet, right next to my driver's license.

During a powwow we would play a couple of games of basketball off to the side where the cement court was. Then other guys would come and play pick-up with us. No one could ever beat us three-on-three. Dressed in cutoff sweatpants and sleeveless T-shirts or sweatshirts with "Doug's Resort" or "Minnesota Vikings" across the chest, they would come for a game with the reigning champions. We'd be there all night until we stopped playing to get some fry bread at one of the booths. We'd get it with honey and butter, and Stan would get some wild rice soup and dip his bread in it. He was the fattest one of us, but he always got the rebounds. He looked as if he was just floating up to the board. His belly jiggled in slow motion and his hand arced up high to snag the ball. He was only about five-nine. Some of the guys we played against were six-five, or even six-seven and some played on the reservation varsity team. They could never get the rebounds from Stan. I was the outside shooter and Pick always ducked in for the layups and sometimes a slam dunk if the rim sagged a little low and no one had fixed it.

It was at a powwow that I got in my first fight and Pick gave me my first beer. It all happened on the same night, when I was eleven. We were sitting around someone's car in the parking field. It was about ten, the dancers were still out, and it was too dark to play basketball. Someone had shot out the floodlight next to the basketball court so it was impossible to see the netless hoop nailed onto the plywood backstop. None of us had any money to go to the bingo tent and try a couple of cards, so we were standing by a car with the radio on watching the dancers. They were doing a woman's dance.

All the guys pulled in closer for these dances so we walked to the edge of the ring and watched them go around and around in the floodlights they set up for the night dancing. It wasn't a competition so they were dancing really slow. All the mothers had their little girls out and they held their daughters' hands as they looked around. The girls were nervous but they danced almost without thinking as their mothers guided them around. Their feet two-stepped; it wasn't as showy as fancy shawl-dancing but it was real graceful and since they were going so slow you got a good look at all of the girls in their regalia.

"Hey look," Stan said. "There's Violet." There she was, dancing around with Rose. She wore a real nice white jingle dress. She turned on her little feet, looking over her shoulder before the spin.

"She could win money you know." Pick always was thinking that way.

"She's good, you guys. That there's my little sister and she's real good." Stan's eyes were glowing. We stood with our arms over the painted railing and watched them go around. He watched her dance and was smiling. I looked out at her and saw something. Her hair hung straight down her back and the lights caught it when she spun around in her circles. Her eyes lit up as her ma said something to her. Her skin was lighter than ours and it blushed under the lights and noise. There were at least a hundred rolled-tin jingles, cut from tin cans and rolled with pliers, on her dress. Her ma, Rose, had spent all winter making it. Her fingers had been swollen from bending, and the sharp edges of the jingles had cut her hands until they bled every night. The drum singing was a guest drum from Ontario, so to show they were thankful for being at our powwow they sang another push-up. The dancers were happy and I just watched Violet go around and around.

We all just stood there and soon the song was over and the dancers were coming back to where their blankets and food were by the sides. They walked back short of breath and sat down under the night sky and lit up cigarettes, the kids grabbed half-empty Coke bottles and sucked down the last bit, washing the dust from the powwow ring from their throats. Rose and Violet were walking back to their stuff when a kid about my age ran up and dumped his raspberry snow cone all over her jingle dress.

I felt my insides cave in when I saw the look on her face. She just stood there and looked down at the red stain that spread all across her shoulders and down the front of her new dress. Her mother had just finished it and all the rolled metal jingles were still shiny. The boy ducked under the railing and ran past all of the cotton-candy and popcorn booths. I turned and ran after him. Stan and Pick followed up behind me. They were slower and bigger. I was skinny and fast. I was real fast. My legs pumped as I ducked between the cars, following him to the edge of the pickups, the Chevys, and the older station wagons. I caught up to him just before he could turn the corner around the community center that stood at the edge of the powwow grounds. I grabbed his shoulder and turned him with his back to the white painted building. We stood there while people started to gather around. I was gasping, he glanced around and saw he was cornered. Stan and Pick ran up puffing and stood behind me. The boy was shorter than me and he was fat, his dirty jeans crept down his legs so he had to waddle around. He stood there glaring at me. Doug Marshall's kid.

"Ernie, what you go and do that for?" My voice came out tight. I could still see Violet's face just about to cry because she couldn't dance anymore.

"She deserved it. She was asking for it."

"No she wasn't. She was just dancing. All she was doing was dancing out there."

"Her daddy messed with my uncle. He's down in Stillwater where he belongs now." I looked at Stan and he stood behind me with his arms crossed. He and Pick were six years older than me. Too big to fight him. But they were right behind me. People were looking at us as they moved in. Everyone loved to watch the fights and even the older people glanced over, trying not to watch, but sneaking looks anyway.

"She wasn't doing nothin' to you." My fists were little balls and my eyes were narrowed.

"She's a little bitch, Lyle. Why you protecting her? She your girlfriend?" I stepped in and he tried to duck away around the corner. As he turned his head to run I clocked him right in the jaw. He stopped cold. I hit him again in the stomach. The crowd moved in closer. The boys looked at each other and they elbowed each other in the ribs, expecting a good fight.

All of us fight, but until then it had only been rolling around in the dust clawing at each other. He tried to swing at me but I stepped in and started hitting him all over. I pegged him in the back and head, the stomach, chest, arms, shoulders, knees. Soon he just covered his head and started yelling through his tears.

"All of you is the same. All of you is welfare Indians. Her

daddy never did anything for himself. Get off me. Get off me. My daddy's going to get you. You ain't worth nothin.'" I kept hitting. We were both on the ground and our clothes were full of dust. Someone was yelling.

"You ain't good. You ain't good for nothin' either. You ain't even Indian. You don't belong here." I recognized my own voice. I felt myself lifted off and Stan had his arm around me. He and Pick carried me away from where Ernie lay in the dust.

"Easy, Lyle," Stan was whispering in my ear. "Just take it easy." I was crying, wiping the tears and dirt from my face in long streaks.

"He dirtied her, Stan. He made her all dirty." My voice broke and I started crying. Stan had his arm around me and Pick was walking beside us. He jumped up and hit a tree branch with his hand.

"Did you see that? Did you see my little brother take him out? Man, that was good. I ain't seen anyone get it that good in a long time." He turned to face us. Pick grabbed me and lifted me off the ground and twirled me around in the air.

"My little brother's a bad ass. He is one bad motherfucker! Everyone on the reservation better watch out for him!" He set me down and jumped in the air again. I had stopped crying and we all walked back to the cars. Pick pulled a beer out from the trunk and pulled the tab. He handed it to me and slapped me on the back.

"You're an Indian now, bro." I took a sip and it was sweet. The dust gave way and I drank some more. Back in the powwow ring the dancers were going around again. It was a different dance but the drum carried over our heads and we all sat there by the car, listening.

I kept driving with the windows down even though the air had gotten colder. I got to the first town off the rez and I didn't want to stop. So I went into the Red Owl and bought some Cokes and some potato chips. The Town and Country Red Owl. I couldn't turn around here. Being in that Red Owl made me want to throw up, it reminded me of kidneys. The smell of cooking kidneys.

When Ma spent all of her government checks on booze, and that was all the time, we didn't have any money for meat. Once a week one of us would drive to the Red Owl, just on the edge of the reservation, and the meat department gave us a week's worth of kidneys they were going to throw out anyhow. No one wanted them but since we got them for free that's all we ate. Ma became an expert kidney cook. Fried kidneys. Diced kidney hash with onions, broiled kidneys in butter, kidney pie, kidney burgers, breaded kidneys, breaded in flour, breaded in cornmeal and deep-fried in lard, kidney pie, kidney stew, plain kidneys, barbecued kidneys, broasted kidneys. I'm not sure she ever made them the same way twice, I think that was her way of making up for the booze. But no matter how she did it, they always tasted the same. Thick and greasy, like sand mixed with cooked blood. I got back in the car and kept on driving to Duluth. I'm gonna go to Duluth, I told myself. I'm gonna go there and turn around.

The last time Pick and I rode in the Thunderbird we went down to the Cities and he left us when I was sleeping. We were all lying there by the river with this girl, Hunter. I guess we were all passed out drunk, or at least we were asleep. It was warm and the sound of the Mississippi washed over us. I was lying next to Hunter and I think she was holding my hand 'cause everything was spinning around. We woke up and Stan and Pick were gone. We figured they just snuck off to the bathroom 'cause they didn't want to piss in front of a girl. We just lay there looking up at the last few stars that stayed in the sky while the sun came up and the cars started rolling on the Third Avenue Bridge.

"Do you like the stars, Lyle?"

I shrugged. "I don't know. They're okay."

She held my hand real tight and kept on looking up. I could see her out of the corner of my eye as she stretched out next to me. She had to be the prettiest girl I had ever seen.

"I like to think that the stars are all Indians. The stars are all of us that were here before. Every time I look up there, I can see more of them. Don't they look Indian to you?"

I stared real hard at them, but the sun was coming up and I couldn't see the stars that good.

"Naw, Hunter. The ones that fall down maybe. All the other ones are white. I think we're all falling stars. How can Indians stay up in the sky?" I was still a little drunk and I needed Hunter's hand to stay down on the ground. If I let go I thought I might go rushing up there with all those white stars.

We lay there and Stan and Pick never came back. Hunter and I got in her car and drove back to Hennepin Avenue to look for them. We didn't see them anywhere. All the bars were closed in the morning and nobody had money or a stomach for breakfast. Hunter drove me to our car. No one was there either.

"Come back with me to Pine Ridge." She sat in the driver's seat and smoked a cigarette.

"I gotta find them. Maybe they went back to the rez." She pulled her hair behind her neck and leaned back.

"So they left. Come with me." I looked down the street, a few people were moving in the trash and the doorways. I opened the door and got out.

"I'll come someday, okay?"

She shrugged.

"Don't hurry," she said and raised her eyebrows.

I laughed and leaned in the window.

"I'll see you up there someday," I said, pointing at the sky. She laughed and took my hand.

"Maybe I'll see you down here too."

I nodded and started walking down the street, looking for my brother.

I had a little over a quarter tank left and I was about an hour away from Duluth. The reservation was far behind and the road ran through tamarack swamps. The frost heaves in the asphalt made the car dip at a regular rhythm. I only had three cigarettes with me. I pulled one out of the pack on the dashboard and lit it with the lighter. The wind was rushing around the car so much that the smoke and ash disappeared from the end of the cigarette.

There weren't many towns between the reservation and Duluth so I looked at all of the trees whipping past the car. They were all growing right out of the swamp. The trunks were smooth, straight. The land was flat and the ditches were filled with water.

The pavement began to dip, and I started down the hill as I got nearer to Duluth. I got over the last hill and I saw Lake Superior, flat and smooth in the distance. I put the car in neutral and coasted down into the city. It was Saturday and there were people out on the streets, maybe buying stuff for breakfast. The highway twisted down to the lake and I drove up the shore about ten miles.

I pulled off and walked to the beach. There wasn't any sand, only rocks. The little stones stopped the lake from coming closer. All the little pebbles that were worn smooth from water lay together by the edge. I stood with my hands in my pockets and squinted against the sun overhead. Pick had always hated the lake. We used to drive over there on our way to Grand Portage.

"Too big," he said. "It's too big and too cold. Can't swim in it. Can't drink it either."

There was the letter again, in my pocket, sent across the ocean. Sent by their sergeant. How did it ever get all the way to the reservation?

I wanted to jump in and swim straight across, taking in all of the cold. I wanted to dive to the bottom and hold my breath forever. I just stood there though and I started crying. Some sight, an Indian standing by the lake crying. My body shook and I tasted the salt on my face. The tears dripped down and disappeared by my feet. I looked up and through my tears Lake Superior stretched on, a salty gritty ocean that went around the whole world.

Donovan
1979

The lake out behind the house was drying up. The rocks that we used to mark where we could wade and those that showed the drop-off were high and dry. There was no rain. The air was rusting the pine trees and browning the grass, until every step you took caused something to crunch and give under your weight. So when we got the sudden hail that year, it almost broke us down. The hail started out small, the size of Chiclets, popping to the ground, and Little and I ran over to Jackie's so we could just *be* in it. We pushed it under our feet and the white chips could have been millions of pieces of gum. I wondered what it would look like if it really were tiny, bite-sized Chiclets, all rainbow colors. We got Jackie and we ran circles at Poverty, hiding under Duke and Ellis's car. We had to bend low and turn our faces to our feet because it hurt our eyes.

We twisted and chased, and Jackie kicked up her feet, scuffing her long jeans on the ground. I remember running after her as she took off for the trees, thinking for some reason that it wasn't a good idea. Little was right behind me and though he didn't say anything he had his eyes all lit up. There was lightning over across the other side of the lake, pretty far away, and Jackie ran through the jack pine, along the path that ran down to the sand. The black trunks looked like charcoal, singed from the heat of the summer, and they weren't the straight kind. They bent over double sometimes and twisted every way, as if they didn't have anything better to do, as if they couldn't do any better. Little passed me and I let him cruise by. He looked like the trees. His hands had been twisted and turned-in since the day he was born. His body bent this way and that as he flung himself between the trees after Jackie. He looked like one of those little men who live in the woods, who Ellis told me about. Tiny men, mostly spirit, who never let anyone see them, and who capture children because they love them so much.

The hail was getting a little bigger, half the size of marbles, and the jags of lightning lit up our faces as we scooped the hail from the path, mixed with pine needles, sand, and gravel. We threw the pieces in the air, but they made no difference, nothing changed, they got knocked down and mixed again. The wind was coming from behind us, moving toward the lake, so when we got to the shore there were no waves. The stones came down from the air and splashed on the surface, pushing up little spouts of water every time they hit. It looked like the water was boiling and we all stood and stared at it. Little's arms dropped by his sides and he bent down, putting his head by the water. It hissed and the wind tore even faster overhead, passing high and wide, like a train was rushing by.

Jackie's hair was blowing, just lifted a bit from the wind that snuck between the trees as she looked across the water and wondered at the lightning. Little liked the flashes and the bursts, and he knelt down with his head next to the water so he could watch the hail hit the surface. The hissing, roiling sound of the water took his eyes and held his ears as he watched the hail bubble and beat the lake. His crippled hands dug the sand and suspended his weight above the lake. I stood near the trees watching Little and Jackie, seeing the broken crooks of light across the water, and hearing the clacking of the tree tops as the wind pushed them into each other. The heat had taken all the bend out of them and they began to break and trip to the ground. Falling and chipping, they made such a sound, even the wind that caused it seemed muted and empty.

I don't know how long we were like this, the three of us watching and listening. Thinking. Suddenly the wind stopped, the hail quit pelting. The pines held still and even the lightning, now far away, looked like it was frozen. There was no moon because of the clouds, but a light, a blue and thick light lit up everything at once. I felt heavy, like when Stan and Little tackled me, throwing all the cushions from the couch on top and then on my chest, butt-first. I felt squeezed tight. There wasn't a sound, and Little lifted his head, his eyes wide and a grin across his face. Jackie quit standing with her legs apart facing the lake. Instead, she turned to me and looked in my face, asking me what was up.

A few leaves scattered down the beach, and the water lapped just a little bit. Like it was waiting. Like we were waiting. We could see the clouds now, because the hail had stopped, and they were thick like grease, growing across the sky in fat chunks. I heard the flies and mosquitoes buzz, creeping from under the ferns and the juniper. Suddenly Ellis came out of the woods right behind me. I don't know how I didn't hear him, it being all quiet. He ran out of the woods, looking up at the sky. Then he took two steps, two big steps, which made me rethink how tall he was, and stooped down, grabbed Little from the sand, and hefted him under his arm.

"Get Jackie."

I stood there, not understanding.

"Grab Jackie. Fast."

That's when I heard it. Before, when I thought it was quiet under that purple sky, it wasn't really quiet; it was a new sound. Building. The low rumble was hard to hear because it was so different from the clash and patter of the small hail, and because it was coming from the direction of the trees. From the north the wind was groaning, not very loud, but deep, like its voice was down in its throat. And it was getting faster. The rumble, like one long, low thunder, was getting faster.

I ran to the edge of the water, took Jackie's hand, and pulled her away from the lake. Ellis turned around and with Little under his arm started running back to Poverty. I pulled Jackie behind me and followed Ellis as he twisted between the trunks. Jackie was slow and she had started crying because she didn't know what was going on, so I pulled her closer as I ran and put her over my shoulder.

So the two of us, Ellis and me, struggled into the wind, which was blowing harder now, rumbling close. The trees thinned along the path and I looked to the north, from where the wind was coming. It was black, and the gusts pushed the trees in front of it. Farther behind, near where the water tower stood like a giant silver spider, it got crazy. It looked like television static, white haze. It was moving closer and closer. Not like a wall, but like everything behind it was just fading away.

The air went heavy and began to swirl and the hail started dropping again, bigger, closer together. The tiny chips that were on the ground had melted already, and the new ones were bigger, mothballs dropping and hitting the tops of our heads. As we raced for the Catalina they got bigger and bigger, until I was almost dizzy from getting hit. The white haze was getting closer, swallowing telephone poles and trees, sweeping over fields, and the sound of the wind mixed with the crashing of trees. The big white pines, hundreds of years old, were falling and booming, the sounds carried by the wind. Closer. The air felt sticky and my arms and back ached from holding Jackie, who squirmed even though she knew that I couldn't set her down.

Up ahead I could see Duke and Ellis's car at Poverty. The lights were on so we could find it in the wind. The front edge of the hail was a few hundred yards on the other side. The hail was the size of baseballs, it smashed through trees and ripped up the ground, bouncing until it lay still, covered by more of the same. It was like kick-the-can, who would get to the can first? The car was getting closer and suddenly it lurched forward. At the same time, the front passenger door swung open and Duke leaned across the seat.

"Get in!" he yelled. "Hurry up! Hurry up!"

Duke was frantic as the hail closed in from one side, just as Ellis threw Little in past the door, then dove in himself. I did the best I could, heaving Jackie in front of me, then pushing her over onto the floor behind the front seat. I grabbed the handle and swung the door shut. The pounding grew. I couldn't see past the windows, peering into the ice.

Ellis grabbed a blanket and pushed everyone down on the floor, throwing the blanket across the top. I heard crunching, and felt something on top of me. I wanted to get up and see what it was. The weight was too heavy, so I breathed the air next to the carpet, where it slipped under the seat from the front.

The sounds left, and the air that came to me was cooler, softer. The weight moved so I threw off the blankets, and glass spattered all around. Every window had been broken. The pieces of glass covered the blankets, and even a few of the baseball-size hailstones rolled off onto the floor. They were just like softballs, hard and smooth. The whole summer it hadn't rained; instead the water closed itself together, not wanting to give out gradually.

All the windows were broken in all of the houses, except the ones whose windows faced downwind. So we fell asleep in the car together that night: Jackie, Little, and me. Duke and Ellis sat in the front seat, talking about which junkyards they could steal some new windows from, and where was the best place to bang out the dents in the hood and roof. I fell asleep to their sounds. The rustle of a brown paper bag, with a bottle of Colt 45 inside, passed back and forth, back and forth. Like a cradle being rocked, the paper, the swish of the beer, and their breath combined to lull me. But I didn't fall asleep for a while. Ellis had grabbed Little, and that meant something.

He hadn't come for me; I just happened to be there. They would have left me. Like the branches buried under balls of ice, like the grass beaten down first by the heat, then by the sudden storm. I fell asleep, dreaming of being caught under something heavy, with glass coming down all around me, but they couldn't see me. They couldn't find me. They didn't want me.

～ ～

I woke up the next day and the hail was gone. It came sudden, and almost caught us, but after we collapsed in the car, surrounded by glass and blankets, it melted away in the dark. So when we woke up, there were a few small pieces of ice, the ones that were covered with the needles that they had knocked off the trees. But these too melted; once I touched them with my hand, they dissolved, a wet patch on the dry skin of my palm.

It was June, so Little, Jackie, and I didn't have school. Little and Jackie were both six, but only Jackie was in first grade. Little had been kept in Head Start for so many years, not moving up, that they didn't even want him anymore. He didn't go to school, but played around the house and in the woods by the lake until the bus dropped us off at the highway. During the year we walked the length of the dirt road to our houses and Little would run up from the lake, carried by the sound of the diesel school bus. It used to be a bus for an off-the-reservation school, but it broke down so many times they sold it to the reservation. The letters that had been sandblasted off the side of the bus still showed through, even though it had been repainted and relettered with the reservation school's name.

But it was June, so we woke late and played till whenever we collapsed. Sometimes we would get bored, kicking stones through the dust, or finding big flat rocks to skip across the water or, if they were especially flat, throwing them straight up in the air so when they sliced through the water they would "slit the devil's throat." Bored of this, sometimes we waited until it was night and we would climb up the dumpsters behind the bar in town, onto the roof. There we would wait until people started coming out and drop pennies on their heads. When we were more daring we spit. They would either not notice, or pick someone from out of the crowd to fight. Even this got boring so we used eggs, but that didn't go over so well because the drinkers had an idea that no one in the bar would have eggs and that the eggs didn't fall from the sky on their own. We got spotted and had to jump off onto the dumpsters, then into the woods where they couldn't find us because they were too drunk and too loud.

After the hailstorm we had to discover what had changed. The air felt different. It was heavy, like the perfume Celia puts on right before Stan comes over. Whatever she buys stinks up the whole house so Little and I duck out, our noses burning and our eyes red. I didn't pick up the new smell right away, maybe because of the wind. The smell was blown over the lake, or lifted up, instead of down. But by ten o'clock, when the sun got over the tops of the trees, a smell came sweet and sticky, almost rotten.

It was pine sap. When we stepped into the woods we saw that the ground, which was usually red with dead, broken pine nee-

dles, was completely green. It was a dark sticky green that covered the bottoms of our bare feet. It dripped into our hair and
when we reached to move a branch out of the way our hands
stuck to it. The hail had snapped a lot of the branches and
stripped the trunks of their bark. All the jack pines were a pale
gray, the black bark having been chipped off. The Norways and
the white pines were a creamy pale color, the wood showing right
through, the sap oozing down the trunks.

Covered with needles and sap, bark, grass, and sand, we left
the trees and the smell followed us. So I ran to the house and took
a bar of soap from the shower. We ran past Poverty to the lake,
where we rubbed our skin with the soap, and mixed it with beach
sand trying to get rid of the smell, the memory and leftover of
the hail. It marked us, like there was some turning, a switch, and
we tried to wash it off.

We scoured and scratched, standing, splashing in the water. It
was shallow way out so we waded and dove, leaving clouds of
soap in our wake. We played catch with the soap, throwing it
high and diving after it, a white square resting on the sand. When
we tried to wash with it again its surface was coated, it felt like
sandpaper. Still we couldn't get rid of the sap that clung to us.
Little didn't seem to mind. He made no effort to get rid of it. It
stuck there along with everything else, and it didn't even faze
him. He dove into the sand and rubbed it into the sticky mess.
Closer to the shore, in a deeper part where the water lilies grow,
Little took some mud and plastered it in his hair.

I needed it off. The hail, broken trees, and the sand needed to
be gone. I needed to be clean of it. So I washed and scraped,
rubbed my skin raw. I was almost done; I just got the last bit of it
off. A few places were only a little sticky, gray smears more than
anything. Then I saw the fish. At first I thought it was swim-
ming, idling over to us. It was turning side to side, its white belly
flashing when it rolled slowly one direction or the other. But it
was only the slow current, the waves underneath the surface that
brought it closer.

I tried to talk myself out of it, telling myself it was a log,
some driftwood kicked up by the storm. I didn't want to look at
it, but as it drifted closer my eyes stayed with its motion. Little

was splashing in the mud by the shore, and Jackie was sitting in the sand, shivering into her towel. I held the soap in one hand and was bent over the water, where I had paused in scooping it up into my face when I saw the fish.

It was dead, and it looked stiff like a log as it tilted back and forth. It got closer and would have bumped my leg, but I moved and it washed by me. I figure it was a muskie. Though I had never seen one, Duke talked about them. He said you never see them and all those fool tourists who come up with tackle and 100-pound test line to hook 'em are stupid. They catch thirty-pounders and stuff them on their walls, thinking they got a big one. Duke always said that the biggest ones no one ever sees; they got too much power to get caught. They're too strong. This one must have been caught by the storm. Its skin was raised and pink, the scales were beaten off its head, and one of its eyes was missing.

It must have been over five feet long. It was longer than I was tall and it just lazed by. Stiff. It was carried by the current, beaten, killed, and gone. It didn't seem right. It was supposed to be too strong, that's what Duke had said, and Ellis had nodded. But then Ellis had scooped Little off the ground and left me and Jackie to fend for ourselves.

The great fish rolled and bumped along the sand by my feet, and I moved my leg so it wouldn't touch. I couldn't afford to let it. It turned its empty socket toward me, then its one good eye, which had clouded over. I saw all this through the water, straight down. It turned its good eye at me and I swear it was looking at me. Looking. It seemed to say one thing, Little's one word, as it eyed me and was gone, carried away by the water back out to the middle of the lake, which some say is hundreds of feet deep. Its eye told me one thing, the one word that was always ringing in my head. You.

The Reservation
1978

After nine years of northern living Paul had become used to snow in October. He had come to expect it, even though initially the early and sudden winters had startled him.

The poplar and birch started turning in August, shimmering gold, branches of tumbling yellow coins. So soon, he had first thought. So soon. It happened fast, while the lake water was still warm and the days humid. Paul hadn't thought to pay attention to the color of leaves. It hadn't occurred to him that the color of leaves and the direction of the wind marked anything at all. He took no notice when the wood ticks, which plagued his pale legs as if he had grown scores of moles, disappeared suddenly in mid-August. He never looked out to see that the thrush, the towhees, and killdeer were nowhere to be seen. When the lakes quieted and turned in upon themselves, covered with algae and sudden growth of lake scum in backwaters, Paul missed this most obvious sign of the impending fall. Even when the swamp tamaracks changed from a waxy green to a sudden shower of yellow needles Paul failed to take notice because he had been raised on a farm where trees were to be worked around or, preferably, gotten out of the way. They were to be cut down, chopped up, burned, and then forgotten.

As he was growing up, what Paul experienced as the descent into winter had been marked by a change in activity, the shift between different categories of chores. If he had paid more attention he would have sensed a change in the texture and thickness of the wheat and corn. He hadn't noticed this either because he had crept to his room as often as possible and engaged in a silent fruitless war against the house in which they lived, the house that harbored no love for either him or his parents.

While Paul was fighting it out with the house that looked like it was going to cry tears of frustration from the scratched glass of its front windows, Paul's father was busily engaged in trying to make payments on it while crop prices were dropping and taxes were rising. To make matters worse, his only son wasn't fit to work because of the listless way he sat in his room and did God knows what. After years of dragging Paul from his attic room to prop him up in front of a rake or a pitchfork, of begging him at least to muck out the horse's stall; after years of this, Paul's father had finally given up on his pale, soft son. It had taken more of an effort to get Paul to pick rocks from the fields or to do some other equally mindless chore than it took simply to do it himself. Paul's father had given up.

Except sometimes the task required at least two people. When there was absolutely no way Paul's father could do it himself he climbed the creaking stairs in his meticulously oiled boots and knocked on Paul's door. He dragged his feet up the wooden stairs and the wooden planking that shrank back from the risers squeaked out warnings to where Paul lay in his room. Paul's father couldn't believe that it had come to this; that he had to knock and ask permission to enter a room for which he himself had paid. To make it worse, the squeaks and echoes of the recalcitrant house announced his presence, and yet he still had to bring his callused hand to the thin door and ask permission to enter.

Paul's father had paid for the door, jamb, trim, hinges, supports, studs, paneling, wiring, subflooring, flooring, carpet, paint, rafters, tar paper, shingles, and nails. He had paid for it all with years of backbreaking work. Paul's father had herniated a disk, and had dislocated his shoulder while studding the bull. Paul's father got up before first light and went to bed after the nighthawks were out catching dragonflies, and for what? So he could climb noisy stairs to ask his son's permission to enter the room whose roof he had reshingled so the same son wouldn't be wet?

Most of the time it was too much to bear and his poor white pride kept him from asking permission to enter and then asking for help. It was a ridiculous turn of events. But still, when he walked into Paul's room, he knew that whatever he was walking into certainly didn't belong to anyone but Paul. A pale yellow light always hung under the raftered ceiling like silo dust. Everything in the room was ordered and neat. The floor was an even level surface devoid of any sort of carpet or throw rug even in the winter when the drafts seemed to come through the boards themselves. Despite these things Paul's father wasn't quite sure what marked it as different, what stamped it as a space in which he had no influence or control. Something did. Maybe it was that he had never been inside the room when Paul wasn't there.

Upon entering, Paul's father had always seen Paul on the bed under the window. He was either reading from the Bible or some other book thicker than a two-by-four, or staring out the window at the paper-wasp's nest that clung securely under the soffit. Paul marked his place, his milky freckled skin glowed in the sunlight while his slender hands whispered over the moth-eaten pages he was staring at intently. Paul commanded the cramped corner of the attic room in which he chose to fight a detailed and tedious psychological battle with the house, whose only weapons were physical. Paul thought he had the advantage.

When Paul's father asked him, asked him to please come out and pitch hay from the truck into the mow, Paul stood and stumbled about. Paul hesitated and mumbled because he experienced this as the house getting back at him in one of the only ways it could, a way no one but he could identify and fight. Banging into the bed frame or a chair like a paper-wasp tapping its head on the skin of its home, Paul marked his space by bumping around the edges without disturbing the order of anything.

When they went out the front door together, Paul's father headed straight for the barn, but Paul stood blinking in the bright sun like a mole. Paul's father turned impatiently in the dust, afraid if he left Paul's side Paul would wander off or disappear back into his room. Finally Paul would notice where he was standing and step off the front step into the yard. Paul's father didn't know it, but Paul was still waging war with the recalcitrant house, a war in which Paul's father was on the house's side. Paul's step into the yard marked his defeat, the house having won again. Picking up his pace, he made his way with his father to the barn.

It was only then, after seeing the baled hay, seeing the stubbled fields and the canvas tarp thrown over the tractor, that Paul realized and knew that fall had come.

Fall had always coincided with his arrivals at college and then at the seminary, so when he moved to northern Minnesota his awareness of the seasons was thrown into chaos. There was no change in his activity or his duties that would show him that another season was coming. He had the same schedule, saw the same people, and ate the same food, most of it from cans. He also learned quickly that calenders had absolutely no meaning in relation to the seasons in the north.

So Paul had come to expect that more often than not it would snow before Halloween. After the first snow, what Paul experienced as the long, dreary, and formless winter would begin, where he would sorely miss the absence of any exciting or permanent structure, and that at first threatened to drive him mad.

During his second winter in northern Minnesota, Paul had been awed by the way the cold and snow shouldered their way into every crack and weakness of northern life. Paul had seen mailboxes and steps, walkways and low bushes buried under layer upon layer of snow until they were no more than formless lumps. Small dogs and large mutts were lost in the drifts and cemented to the snow by their body heat. They remained frozen until April and May, when the smell of rot revealed their location.

By February Paul thought that spring had come because the snow stopped. Paul thought it was over. He soon learned that the winds that swept down from Medicine Hat, Alberta, were gearing up for the push, the last turn of the vice handle between whose steel clamps everyone and everything was held. The winds closed in, sat back, and waited. Out of curiosity or a perverse desire to see how things broke apart, the cold sat heavy and waited with a patience much greater than that of men and nations. Deeper than the snow that had come before, the wind's idle and tempered patience cracked metal pump handles, burst pipes, froze deer solid as they curled into sleep, and cemented car tires flat on the bottom so they would thump along for miles down the highway until the motion warmed them up.

The cold hushed all sounds bigger and deeper than the human voice that weren't made by the cold itself, and in the void whispers careened around the corners of rooms and one could hear the snap of eyelids as people blinked away the tears already turning to ice. Outside zippers rattled and seemed to cause the ice to boom on the lake. Each foot, no matter how gently placed on the hard white earth, crackled in the snow so that even the flakes that had fallen so gently the month before were crushed under the weight of the cold.

Paul had thought since the snow didn't come anymore that the winter was over. When he realized that it was only the cold that stopped the snow he searched for something to hold onto, for something he could trust.

As he sat at his kitchen table organizing his sermon, leaning back in a rickety white chair, and looking out of his picture window, he found nothing. The hedge of wild rose was buried under the snow that had been scraped from the road. Across the iced road he saw his church, the tallest building for miles with the exception of the water tower blinking in the distance down by the frozen lake. He looked to the church for some comfort. Paul sipped some coffee and searched the clapboard building for something he could use as a handhold so he wouldn't be buried under the snow, erased by the bitter bite of wind that blew over a thousand miles of prairie from the Canadian Rockies. Paul tried and tried. But when he looked to the steeple he knew it was devoid of bells, emptied of sound except for that of swallows who nested there during the spring and summer. Paul knew it was just a shell with a sharp point, perched on top of the pathetic little church with no purpose whatsoever.

He looked for the windows, but they were on the sides of the church, hidden from view, and he knew that even if he could have seen them they were nothing but flats of lead, crusted with frost. The only stained-glass window was in the back of the church, set in the wall behind the altar. It had been purchased and shipped in from Chicago back when the church still thought that missions were possible and worthwhile enough to spend a large amount of money on. They attempted to outdo the Evangelicals, whose church used to stand next to the bar but had burned down many years before, and had never been rebuilt.

Since the stained glass was on the back of the building Paul couldn't see that either. When he first preached in the church he noticed that the back wall was a poor place for the stained glass since it faced west, so the window would never catch any sun during the morning services. Once Paul had changed the time of mass just so that the sun would shine through when he reached the end of his sermon. He was preaching about the heavenly rewards of earthly work, and he raised his hands as he finished, having timed the length of his sermon to match sunset as it was listed in the *Farmer's Almanac*. But he had neglected to consider that tall pines grew up to the back of the church, and as the sun went down they took in its final light, and Paul was stretching his empty, soft hands out to the five people who had bothered to show up.

Since Paul could not see the stained glass from where he sat in his cold chair, staring out of his kitchen window, could not latch onto the empty belfry, he tried to embrace the entire structure so as to save himself from drowning in the formless north. Only he didn't know where to grab onto the church; the drifted snow and the white church walls had been fused together by the wind and the cold so that he couldn't tell where one ended and the other began.

The trees were no help either. Even though the evergreens were the only things to have kept their form in the winter hush, they offered Paul no help. For miles the pines stretched, tall and proud in self-competence, losing no color or shape. Yet there were so many of them, so many that Paul couldn't tell them apart, couldn't distinguish one from another. Even the row of spruce next to the nursing home offered no relief. The top halves of the trees had been sawed off because they interfered with the power lines, which sagged too low overhead. They offered Paul nothing; even in their pathetic state as amputees they refused to die.

Paul was at an impasse that threatened to dislodge him from his precarious hold in the far north until he traveled to Mankato, Minnesota, for a church conference. While he was in that unremarkable and boring town something extraordinary happened to him: he was walking along, enjoying the knowledge that underneath the ice upon which he walked there was a real concrete sidewalk, and he happened by a B. Dalton bookstore. There in the window he saw his salvation, priced at $7.98:

Architectural Wonders of the World
– A Pictorial Collection –

A book of photographs with a little bit of accompanying text describing each architectural wonder, it sat behind the window of the bookstore along with a multitude of cheap novels and next to a hardcover edition of *All the President's Men.*

Paul went in and bought it immediately, not for the dramatic and poorly written text, but for page after page of glossy pictures depicting enormous and intricately built structures: the Sistine Chapel, the Cathedral at Salisbury, the Pyramids at Giza, the Great Wall of China, Monticello.

He gave the pages a few flips, and satisfied that he had made the right decision, he buried the book underneath his socks, underwear, and extra pair of slacks in the bottom of his beat-up cardboard suitcase.

He could think of nothing else all weekend. While he sat with a stiff back listening to various undereducated and overly wordy ruminations by nameless priests on Vatican I and II in the prairie river town of Mankato, he thought of the large heavy pages, of buildings, of flying buttresses. He thought of the pages in full color of buildings and places that mattered, not knowing that the only structure that had mattered in Mankato, the mass gallows, had been taken down in 1862 after thirty-eight Lakotas had been hanged because they were starving and their Indian agent had told them that they should "just eat grass."

When Paul got home he made himself some tea and sat at his

kitchen table (the only table in the pink rectory) and stared at the photographs until dawn. He would have continued but his hands had begun to shake and his eyes burned.

Paging through the book became his ritual. He would wait until after the first snow and on Halloween he would fill a bowl with butterscotch wraps and Jolly Ranchers so that if someone came by to trick-or-treat he wouldn't be caught unprepared. No one came by. No one stopped on his front step for Halloween candies. So, just as he had come to expect snow before Halloween, he also had come to anticipate that he would spend that night alone and in silence.

With a basket of hard candies that would never be eaten, and his book of architectural wonders of the world in front of him, Paul had come to take great satisfaction in his contests with the formless landscape that greeted him with a toothless grin after the first snow. Each Halloween Paul would start at the beginning of the photo book and page his way slowly to the end. Skipping the introduction, of course.

The Pyramids at Giza, Monticello, the Great Wall of China, the Corn Palace in Mitchell, South Dakota — all of these were in the book, but his favorite was the photograph of the Cathedral at Salisbury. The old yew tree in the courtyard, the vaulted ceiling: it took his breath away. The columns lined down to the left of the pews reminded him of the double row of trees planted as a windbreak, and Paul took great delight in the knowledge that the stone supports would last longer than any tree and were designed to hold the roof up, not the wind back. Paul liked the fact that the columns, like the three-hundred-year-old yew tree in the flagstoned courtyard, had a specific purpose, there was no duplicate, and nothing else would do. Windbreaks weren't like that; any tree could stop the wind. There was nothing specific about windbreaks and to Paul that meant that they were desperate and weak.

Paul had become accustomed to snow on the ground in October. He had come to expect it, just as he had come to open his picture book on Halloween, after the first snow. When in 1978 it didn't snow before Halloween, he was thrown into doubt for the first time in almost nine years. There was no snow, there was no ice, and the water slapped freely at the shore of the lake. He set out the candy and then couldn't decide whether or not he should open his picture book. It wasn't time if there was no snow. Paul wasn't sure if the book would lose its power if he opened it when there wasn't any snow, but he wanted to nonetheless.

He washed two coffee cups and set them upside down next to the sink. He took a step toward the bookshelf in the living room and then stopped himself. He vacuumed the living room with the clanking Eureka vacuum cleaner that he purchased secondhand and that, no matter how often he changed the belt, always gave off the smell of burning rubber. He still couldn't decide whether he should open and turn the glossy pages. Paul took his vestments from the closet and, turning the shower on hot, he hung them from the shower-curtain rod to steam out the wrinkles.

He fixed himself a cup of tea with a new Lipton's bag, and while it was steeping he took the vestments from the shower and hung them on the refrigerator handle so the hot air blowing from underneath would dry them out slowly.

Placing his cup of tea on the gold-speckled white-surfaced Formica table, he strode into the living room and pulled the book from its place on top of his shaky bookshelf and carried it back to the kitchen.

Paul settled himself into one of the white chairs, and taking a deep breath he opened the cover and turned to the first picture past the introduction.

The sound of breaking glass boomed through the kitchen and the front door rattled in its frame.

For a second Paul stared at the picture of Monticello in front of him, as if the sound had crept out from between the pages and slammed him in the face. The eggshell dome and the arbors of lily and bougainvillea stared placidly at him, frozen in spring purple and green. Paul snapped his eyes up and looked around at his neat, orderly kitchen. Every cup, each chair, and all of the dish towels were in their proper place. His frock was still hanging from the refrigerator door.

The kitchen window in front of Paul was intact and the overhead light glared in the thick glass, so Paul knew that it too was intact, yet it blocked his vision out into the yard. Paul jumped up, then slowed, reaching the front door quietly. He opened it and broken glass pattered onto the linoleum floor and the wind came through the jagged space where the storm window used to sit in the screen door.

Paul opened the screen door and, lifting his black-shoed feet over the glass, he stepped outside. He didn't think or expect that he would find out why it broke, but he felt deeply that he had to try. It wasn't that he was unused to structural catastrophe; he had grown up surrounded by it. It wasn't that he didn't expect things to collapse and break around him, but of all the parts of the still-pink rectory Paul needed to know why it was the storm window on the screen door that had broken. Paul had to know why the storm window had gone because it was the only part of the rectory, the only piece of his home of the last nine years that he had purchased, picked up, and installed. It was the only aspect of the rectory that he had fixed, that he had marked; and it broke on Halloween.

Outside the air was clear and the wind clattered the stems of his wild rose hedge against one another. A dog barked in the distance and a car door slammed. Paul squinted and looked around his small front yard. The light sprung from the lamppost in front of the church on the other side of the street casting crazy shadows along the hedge and grass that, although it hadn't snowed yet, were a brittle brown from the recent frost.

Paul didn't see anything unusual. Looking down at his feet he pushed a large shard of glass around with the toe of his shoe. He looked closer and saw yellow fluid and the crushed shell of an egg mixed in with the glass. As he bent closer he heard someone giggle from behind the jack pine in the corner of his yard. Paul paused. The giggling got louder.

"Shut up," came a whisper from behind the tree.

The laughing continued.

"Jesus Christ."

"Shut up, Jackie."

Paul started moving toward the tree. Whoever was behind the tree started shouting.

"Run, Don! Run!"

Three figures sprang up from behind the black-barked jack

pine. Two of them smashed right through the hedge of wild rose, the third ran straight for Paul.

Paul tried to back up, but the leather heel of his shoe slipped on the wet grass and he fell over onto his back just as the figure reached him and they both toppled together onto the brown grass.

Whoever it was was shouting as Paul struggled to get him off. "You! You! You!"

Paul grappled with both of the child's arms. He tried to grab hold of Little's hands but they were slick with dew and there weren't enough fingers to grab onto. The two who'd run were back, trying to pull Little off Paul.

"Little, c'mon!" They jerked him up and away from Paul and started running again.

As Paul lay there on his back in the wet grass of his front lawn on Halloween night with his kitchen light streaming through his broken storm window, Paul found the resolve to speak.

"Don't move!" He actually yelled, and his voice didn't even crack.

They stopped running.

"Come here," Paul said firmly, in his most Moses-like voice. The children turned and walked toward Paul into the light.

Paul saw that it was two boys and a girl, all Indians. The oldest boy was tall and came with his hands shoved in his pockets, his fine black hair was ruffled and his thin face was red from the chilly night. The girl had her arms crossed in front of her and her chin pointed straight out. The way she held her head reminded Paul of the female traditional dancers he had seen at a powwow. Actually, Paul had only been to one powwow and the sounds of the drums and the poise of the dancers had scared him so much that he left the grounds right after grand entry and sat for the rest of the day inside the church.

The youngest, the one who had shouted and jumped on top of Paul, was hugging the older boy around the waist. His hands were fused into claws, which made it look as if he was two fingers short on each hand. He grinned at Paul and buried his face in Donovan's T-shirt. He held on tight and swiveled his head to look around. When his eyes caught the lamplight from the kitchen they looked damp, likes pebbles under water.

Paul's breath clouded in front of him and he could feel the dew seeping through his polyester pants and into his powder blue JCPenney boxers. Both of the older children were looking down at him, waiting for him to speak.

Paul scrambled to his feet and brushed the back of his pants off with the palms of his hands.

"All right," he said, clearing his throat, "why did you do it?" Paul tried to think of something else to say.

"Accident." It was the girl who spoke.

"Accident," the older boy explained.

"You."

"Shut up, Little." The older girl frowned down at the boy.

"We was throwing eggs, that's all. That sure must have been one hell of an old window."

"Actually, it was brand new," said Paul. He imagined that the dew made it look like he had wet his pants.

"Oh," said Jackie.

"Why did that one," Paul pointed at Little, "why did that one attack me?"

"He just does that," said Jackie. Donovan's hands were still in his pockets and he looked down at his feet.

"He does?"

"Yep. He does it to me all the time."

"But he doesn't know me."

Donovan just shrugged his shoulders.

Paul was getting dizzy. His butt was wet, he could see his breath, it was Halloween and instead of snow, three strangers and a broken window stood on his front lawn. He needed to sit down. He needed his book of *Architectural Wonders* now more than ever.

"Let's go inside and straighten this out."

They shrugged.

"You," said Little.

They shrugged again at Paul in explanation.

Paul led the way, stepping over the eggshell and broken glass. He heard them scattering glass on the walk with their feet.

"Holy shit, it *really* broke."

"*Shut up,* Jackie," whispered Donovan, "he's a priest."

"Like he's never heard anyone cuss before."

Paul pretended he couldn't hear them as he stepped into the house.

Little still clung to Donovan's shirt as they entered the white kitchen. Paul pulled out a chair and sat with his back to the refrigerator; Jackie and Donovan stood in the doorway not moving, just swaying with Little's tugs at their waists. Between the children and Paul, between them on the table, *Architectural Wonders of the World* lay open to a two-page color print of Monticello, the dome the color of eggshell against the light blue of a spring sky.

Paul felt better. The squareness of the table, the ample light, and the catalog of structures all helped him mediate the presence of three guests in the kitchen at once and the destruction of his storm window.

No one spoke. Paul clasped his hands on his lap. A dog yelped down on the highway. The oil furnace below them in the basement hummed as it pushed warm air up into the house. Paul could hear his alarm clock ticking from beside his bed in the next room.

Jackie looked up at the ceiling.

Paul felt he had to do something. If he didn't he thought he might get stuck, he might be always looking at them where they stood in the doorway. He shifted in his seat and wiggled his crossed foot. The chair gave out a little squeak.

Tea, he thought. He uncrossed his legs and stood up to fill the kettle and light the burner. As he turned the faucet knob and began to fill the kettle with tap water, Little began to scream.

It was high-pitched. It tore out of his lungs and his body shook. Paul dropped the kettle on the floor. Jackie and Donovan grabbed hold of Little. His neck whipped his head back and forth and his knees snapped in and out, locking and unlocking.

Paul ran over to them.

"What's going on?"

"How the fuck should I know?" shouted Jackie.

Little raised his hand and pointed out to Paul.

"You! You! You!" He shouted and screamed over and over. Sweat beaded on his forehead and nose.

Paul moved to the side, to get out of the way of the claw jutting straight from Little's body, to get away from the words. Little kept on pointing ahead, toward Paul's vestments where they hung from the fridge handle.

Donovan tried to pull Little's arm down but it was frozen, stuck like a stick through lake ice, pointing at the black garments and the starched white collar. Paul's robes hung there intact, perfectly formed like a two-dimensional priest preaching from the refrigerator door. Little kept on screaming.

"You! You! You! You!"

His voice ripped higher and higher until his wet-bright eyes rolled white and he collapsed on the floor.

"We gotta get him out of here," said Jackie as she stooped to grab hold of Little's limp body.

"Yeah. Yeah, you're right." Donovan reached for Little's other side.

"Wait. I'll call your parents."

Paul stood with his arms hanging down. He didn't move. Neither Jackie nor Donovan said anything to Paul as they lifted Little in their arms.

"Let's get an ambulance." said Paul.

Donovan pushed against the screen door with his back and he and Jackie made their way outside. The door closed behind them and Paul could hear their feet crunch over the broken storm window.

The kitchen light was still on and the room glowed white. The coils under the fridge kicked in and Paul's vestments swayed as the warm air rushed by them. Paul couldn't hear Donovan and Jackie as they carried the unconscious Little down the lonely road to the bar.

Moving slowly, Paul shuffled over to the refrigerator and shut off the kitchen light. In the dark he sat down in one of the chairs. It gave out a groan.

Outside he could hear four car doors slam. An ancient motor turned over twice and caught. The wheels crunched along in the gravel and then faded in the distance.

In front of Paul in the dark lay the *Architectural Wonders of the World* open still to Monticello. Paul reached out and touched the pages but there was no texture. He could feel no wood or brick, he could smell no magnolia or tulip. There was just the whisper of skin over paper as Paul reached out in the dark.

At Poverty, Duke and Ellis lifted Little from their car and put him on Jeannette and Celia's couch. Donovan and Jackie fell asleep on the floor beside the rough and torn couch, and they slept as Jeannette covered them with a tattered quilt that smelled of wood smoke and early mornings in the woods.

IV

Just Another Night Sound

Donovan
1980

It's hard to notice sometimes what the world is trying to tell you. What you should have noticed a long time before, standing there in front of you, whispering your name, warning you. Like a sideways look you'll get from someone at a powwow. Just standing there, in midlaugh at someone's stupid joke, you swing your head with the smile still on your face and you catch someone's eye, and he thinks you're laughing at him. Before you know it, it's you and him rolling in the dust kicking the shit out of each other. Just for that look.

So I should have learned my lesson about leaving the ground, should have known somehow. I read a bunch of mythology in English class. There was this one about the strong guy, Hercules. He was strong, the baddest guy around, but he had to wrestle this other guy who never ever lost, because his mother was Mother Earth, and so long as his feet were on the ground, no one could beat him. Well, Hercules just picked him right up and strangled the shit out of him with his feet just waving and dangling in the air. No one thinks I think like that or that I remember stuff. People figure I don't put things together.

"Slow Donovan. He's got a good heart." Since I'm so quiet they say I don't think much. I can tell you now, I just listen. I feel tuned into everything. Sometimes I lie all quiet at night and I concentrate just hard. I can pick up on everything going on at once, everyone buzzing and moving, thinking, feeling, and talk-

ing. The whole world can be going through me like an electric
shock. I'll feel close to everyone and everything but I can't touch
or something will break. After I run I feel all tingling, but I have
to go off by myself. If someone touches me I'll dust into sand or
turn into a swarm of bees.

I figure I'm like that giant Hercules fought. As long as my feet
are in the dirt or on the grass, I'm okay, but as soon as I'm separated, forget it. All of us skins are like that; close to the earth.
Soon as we leave it though, we're on our own. Soon as we leave
the reservation, there's nothing to stop anyone from picking us
up off the ground. That giant, the whole earth was his mother
but she couldn't help him even if he was just a couple of feet
away from her. Celia always said that I got no common sense,
don't know my limitations. I do, but mine are different from
everyone else's. It's just that she couldn't help me when I was on
the top of that water tower that one time, no one could. It was
only me and the sky, Mother Earth so far below.

Once Little figured out about the water tower across the lake he
wanted to climb it. Bad. He didn't say anything. He would run
out of our yard, then Celia would send me after him. He'd be
standing by the lake just looking up at it. It looks like a big silver
spider, with its legs touching the ground, holding its belly way up
high. At night he would look up at the red light that blinked on
and off.

One night he woke me up and pulled at my arm until I stumbled out of sleep. It was cold for April and I just stood there for a
while, not really knowing what Little wanted. He ran around the
room until he found both my shoes, then he put them on the floor
in front of me. Then he grabbed a sweatshirt and threw it so it
hung over my shoulder and down in front of my face. I put my
shoes on, still real fuzzy and tired. My sweatpants were twisted
halfway around from sleeping so I straightened them out and
Little grabbed my arm and dragged me out of the room.

The moon was out. I can remember it rising big over the lake.

"Should we get Jackie?" I asked.

He didn't respond. He took my arm and started leading me to
the path along the lake to town.

"Let's get Jackie," I said. I was half asleep still. "She'll want to come."

He shook his head, and pulled me in between the trees. There wasn't even a whisper of wind. The moon bounced off the lake, but the black-barked jack pine and hazel brush ate it up. I couldn't see very far ahead, but Little pulled me over the roots and rises without a wrong step. I looked to my left as we made the curve around the lake, keeping the lights from town in view so we wouldn't get lost by taking a side path or a deer run. Our breath caught the moonlight and whisked over our shoulders as we picked up speed down the path.

"Christ, Little. Slow the fuck down, this ain't a race."

My breath was coming short. Little looked over his shoulder and grinned crazily. Little pulled me along the path until we reached the edge of town. I turned to walk up on the shoulder of the road but he jerked me back, cutting behind RJ's Hardware, paralleling the lake. We passed Marshall's store.

"Where we going, Little? I'm tired and I'm gonna turn around."

He took off running down to the lake.

"Shit," I said. Picking up speed I ran after him. I could hear the water. There weren't any waves, but on still nights you can hear it, like it's sucking at the shore.

"You better not jump in," I yelled. "'Cause I'll kick your ass if I have to carry you home wet."

He stopped and was staring up into the sky. It wasn't till then that I caught on to what Little wanted to do: the water tower stood above us. The way he looked up at the tower, then back at me, sent shivers down my back. The moon shone on his teeth.

I shook my head.

"We are not going up there," I said.

Duke says that I shouldn't blame myself, that all I did was what I knew best. He said that other powers were in control, different spirits that control stuff, and that sometimes we just gotta go with 'em. But I know that all I did was follow Little when he started climbing up that water tower. It was like his touch was on me, pulling me along on a black string behind him. I wanted to get away, but he kept me with him. It was like any other time we were together. I could never shake his touch. Sometimes when I was mad and I got off into the woods or I started alone to the store, he'd follow me, not letting me go by myself. He could tell these things real good. Even when Ma's had me watching him all day and he'd pissed me off too many times. He would come to me and hang on my pants pocket, until he just washed over me so I couldn't even frown or yell anymore.

The rungs started a good eight feet off the ground so Little jumped up and grabbed on with his knees and arms. I don't know how he hung on, because I guess the county or someone else greased the pole and the rungs of the ladder with about an inch of axle grease. It was supposed to keep us kids from climbing it, but Little just stuck on somehow, until he reached the rungs. I stood there as he clung to the first few rungs of the ladder. He looked down and motioned me to come up. He was covered head to foot with the black stuff: it slicked his face and hair, worked its way through his clothes. He was just a speck of blackness clinging to the ladder. He was a patch of shadow waving me up after him. I walked up to the support and clung on with my knees and wrapped my arms as far around the thick metal as they would go, embracing the black.

The rungs were greased too, so we looped our arms around as we went up, our sneakers slipped all the time until we wedged them between the rungs and the metal support. As we climbed up, the lights from town got smaller, but it seemed like the moon never really moved at all. It was like we were stuck, we never really got closer, but the ground kept on falling away from us so that if we let go, we'd hit the ground even harder.

The top of the tower was rounded and the rungs went right to the top where the red light was blinking. You ever notice how those things seem kinda soft and peaceful looking when you look up at them from the ground? Well, right next to it, it was bright, blinding us. Like blood in our eyes. It turned us into ghosts and the grease looked like blood when the light shone on us, sticky and slick. The light flared on and off.

I don't like heights too much, and being up there all sticky and smelly made me even sicker than if I'd been drinking real cheap 3.2 beer. I sat with my back to the light, pressed up against it real close so it was a hot pain, fire in the middle of my back. I shut my eyes 'cause I didn't like the way it made Little look. He was all shimmering, a dancing blood, as he moved and jumped on the top of the tower.

I remember sittin' there, wanting to keep my eyes shut just hard, but they were saucers, pointed toward Little, as if the power behind them would keep him from falling off the tower. I was scared out of my pants that he'd fall off and I wouldn't be able to catch him, then I'd fall off too. I was concentrating so hard about not falling that I didn't see Little bend down in the red light and open the hatch that led to the inside of the water tower. I wanted him not to fall and prayed so hard that he would stay on top of the tower that it never occurred to me that he would go inside the tower.

It's funny now that I think about it; I don't know if he slipped 'cause of the grease or if he just jumped in. Anyway, I never thought about him drowning. I mean, would you think about someone drowning two hundred feet off the ground? I ran to the edge as he disappeared and looked into the little hole that he had opened up on the top. It was dark in there and water was flying out. You'd think it would be all calm in there, a dark lake way above the city, but water was rolling, rolling over everything. I yelled down, but didn't get an answer. Little was quiet anyway. He jumped, that's all I can ever guess for sure. But think about it. Doesn't it make sense that the water supply was the best way for him to be in everything? Touching, filling, completing everything with holes in it. Now every person that got city water would be with him.

I can't remember how long I was bent over that hole just staring down. I never cried later or nothing, and I can't remember crying then, but when I shut the cover my face was dripping wet. The wetness dripped and rolled, beading off the grease that covered my face, rolling off my face and slipping down to the ground below. I felt like that man of the earth that Hercules fought, lifted and separated from my mother and from the living down below, all while the water strangled the life out of me. The black grease became part of my skin as Little swirled around and around below me. Even if he could have screamed, I don't think he would've. I don't remember any sounds either, just water moving, and moving, swirling above my head as I sat there. It was almost dawn when I climbed down and there was no noise, no cars, no yells, no fights.

I stumbled in the house and went to my room. There finally, I fell headlong and black into bed.

You

He comes staggering whip-drunk across the road, black shoes scudding the frozen tar. You'd see him if you looked harder out your winter window, hear him if you just sat still . . . .

But there is no sound anyway. The wind bangs mute into his drunken tilt. Snow crusts up against the crumbly cement steps as he takes them slow, wooden. One at a time the smooth soles slip.

He leans against the closed door, hands scooping lint from the dark nose of his pants pockets. Butterscotch wrappers, skullcrackling in the northern wind blow yellow down the empty bone-tight road.

With red knuckles he turns the knob and staggers in leaving no tracks, no mark of passage. The door clicks shut, the same wet smack as a bird's wing being broken. The only sound except for the steady scrush of a bristle brush on the floor in the front of the church.

Wind grips the panes and skulks bitching under the eaves and the blistered caulking, but can't come in as he takes his first loose step down the aisle.

She is there on the floor next to the mop and bucket. Dirty rags hug the pine boards like used condoms in the ghost glow of the February no sun.

Dust bums listlessly in the stilling air. He takes another lurch down the aisle. There is no wind in the church. Remember? Nothing but another step closer, grinding his way along the aisled open toward her wringing and washing in the front of the church.

Celia isn't looking but knows — the cough, the gentle clearing of phlegm like he is pushing brush from his way on a grown-in path, his tottering step and the crack of his knuckles — and waits without turning her head or brushing back her curtain of hair hanging toward the wet floor.

He leans close to her and asks with whiskey-thick breath:

Did you, my daughter? Did you?

Did I what? Softly. Not turning, just watching the brush sink slowly in the soap gray water.

Father Gundesohn jerks his head away from what he was about to say and instead squats down. His shoes make no sound on the wet wood as he unsteadily swivels his bulk nearer.

The bucket, brush, and rags lie useless, the water slugging to a still in the bucket. It tips sideways as he falls on her. Wet gray filth scurries over and over the pine church floor that merits no washing.

Celia is on her back, dress dragging limp in the spilled mop water. My God! She is crying my God as he fucks her on the dirty floor. Sand is everywhere, tiny bits of sand; between the folded lip of the bucket and the smooth smooth floor, scratching the smallest of lines in thin fabric, in places where it will never go away. Never, while he slams into her so hard they slide over the wet slick floor and her head wedges under the first pew. She feels herself bleeding into the sand and onto his black trousers, not even pulled all the way down, where it is soaked up, leaving no color, no trace except for smell that will disappear once it dries. Neither the sheriff nor the coroner will notice.

You did. I know you did. Father Gundesohn is crying into her shoulder.

In the still still church the wet scramble frays and splits, ducking in between the pews only to die out somewhere along the floor, where there is no light and only dust.

Outside the town is quiet.

He stands up, gasping, snot dribbling out of his nose. His hands bunch the trouser fabric together to keep them from falling down, knuckling tight as if the very threads would come unraveled if he let go.

He turns around, away from where Celia is still lying on the floor, and Jeannette is standing there with cold steaming off her coat. She yells, full of a mother's fury, and her yell spills him over in a clean arc. His body is rigid with shock, eyes are open as he jumps back in surprise and slips on the wet floor. As he falls he is still white-knuckling his trousers with both hands. Such a simple line, nature's purest motion.

The wooden stand supporting the baptismal urn stands forgotten to the side like some awkward teenager at a high school dance. The jointed corners are sharp, very carefully seamed.

You can see it now: there isn't much sound — a minute pop — as the corner accepts the hollow at the base of his skull. Not much at all; a click, a deep shudder runs through the length of the oak stand and into the floor.

He lies tangled with his downed polyester trousers warping his legs underneath him. His left thumb stutters against the black, tap-

ping in Morse what happened or maybe signaling the fluttering rhythm of his heart so that the two women who stand over him now can see that he is still alive.

Outside a pickup truck coughs past, the exhaust falling out on the iced road to skate behind the rusted tailgate never quite catching up and then disappears into the now still air.

Pick up your things, Jeannette tells her. Pick 'em up, damn it! Before he wakes up.

While Celia wipes the floor down and throws the rags in the bucket, the other one kneels down next to him. Jeannette still has on her coat. Careful not to bump him or drag her coat sleeve over his red skin she tucks in his shirt and, freeing his cold hands from their station on his crumpled trousers, zips his pants, trying not to look at or touch the tumescent flesh between the metal lips of the zipper.

His breath comes out sharp and she stops, there is a spot of blood on his pink fingernail. His thumb has stopped moving.

She continues to zip them up and quickly buttons them.

Celia is standing above now, shivering in the church air, squinting in the low light toward her mother.

Go get snow, Jeannette says. Wait. Here, use this, she says, shrugging off her coat.

Celia starts toward the front, confused.

Use the back door, she says.

Celia turns around and walks stiffly past the unconscious man and to the back. Pushing the door open, she holds it with her foot and scoops snow onto the bulky wool coat. Her hands go numb and the cold bites its way through her ripped dress.

She holds the edges of the coat together with one hand as she jerks the door shut. The jacket is full of snow and it bumps against her leg as she hurries back to where her mother still kneels next to the unconscious priest.

Now pack him, she says, grabbing the coat and spreading it out. Pack his mouth full.

They both grab handfuls of snow, melting a little, and push it past his pink, baby-soft lips into his open mouth.

More, Jeannette says, her lips slammed into a tight line.

More, she says, putting her shoulders into it like she is kneading bread.

She takes smaller pinches of snow, thumbing them deep into his nose, the crusty flakes lightly scratching his skin. Celia knows they are killing him. She leans on his chin to crack his mouth open wide for another fistful.

More. More. Until it is melting on his face like sweat. His thumb is silent, and his mouth cannot close for all of the snow, pushing his cracked lips into a wide white grin. His eyes are closed like he is dreaming, the snow in his nose and mouth glowing in the musty church light, as if everything is lit from within him. A gentle, fuzzy landscape resting just inside his drunken wet skin. Some miniature vista with moving figures and textures and depth, like a glass ball with winter scenes and flakes of snow falling, falling, and falling to rest, perpetually, along the glassy slope.

They stand up and Jeannette grabs the baptismal urn and tries to tip it gently, but is too old and weak. Celia rushes to her side, and together they do it, lowering it carefully onto his chest as if they are covering a sleeping child with a well-worn blanket.

He doesn't move as they step back and walk backwards to the front of the church. Jeannette is stroking her daughter's hair, and pulls her closer, putting her coat on her shoulders.

They reach the door and, peering through the church, they can only see half of his shoe sticking out from behind the first pew. They scan the gloom, looking for movement or a sign of betrayal, but the church is calm.

Jeannette pushes Celia out first and shuts the door.

Outside the town is quiet as they cross the road in the dark. A car turns from the highway and into town, shuddering its cold way toward them. They recognize the big Catalina's sounds and bulk and stand under the jack pine in front of the rectory across from the church, the windows blackened. Nothing is moving except for the car growling slowly along the slicking road. It stops and they get in, the car-door slam echoing across the small reservation town. Just another night sound, disappearing into the winter air.

Paul
1980

Paul waited for the bus. Wedged into a plastic seat, behind the built-in arm complete with a small television on the end, he waited. The dead screen of the television greeted him, and the soft plastic chair caused his back to sag and ache. He was uncomfortable. He was uncomfortable because he had to choose whether to pay twenty-five cents for fifteen minutes of viewing, or to get up and move to a new location, either directly in front of the click-clacking Arrival/Departure bulletin or outside the Winnipeg bus depot where it was April. Where it was spring.

Although it was spring, it was a northern spring. This meant that it was a time caught between the clutch of winter and the heat and openness of summer. It was a time when one remembered how bright, how unbelievably bright and warm the sun was. After the pewter and tin of northern winter skies, the tree-scraping clouds hung low, the brown-bare trunks of trees, the dull sounds of movement diminished by acres and miles of snow — after all of this, the strength of the sun and the heat of dark colors had to be relearned. The air — one could actually feel it, rolling over bare arms and lifting hair; one could feel its currents and even know the origins of that invisibility, know whether it had just lain next to dark earth so it was warmer or whether it had come from above.

When a breeze struck up one could know the effect of the sun. The frost line three or four feet below had gone out, as anyone could tell. The smell of the earth was back, the smell of dirt.

With it came the smell of moving water, musty, quick, and alive. It was a northern spring and even though it was warm and the invisible wall of frost four feet below the surface of the earth had melted away, the dirt, the ground, was cool, even cold. So northern springs were an in-between time, between frozen and warm, between below and above.

Paul too was caught between wanting to go outside and wanting to stay, feeling compelled to watch the departure time of his bus slowly crawl its way to the top of the black bulletin with its flipping numbers.

He wanted to go outside because he knew what he would find. He had known as he had boarded the bus on the reservation and headed north to Winnipeg. After his nine years at the reservation and its crumbling church, he had stepped up onto the Greyhound and sat on the cushioned bucket seats, staring through green-tinted windows as the bus headed north, past the tree line and into the northern prairie of the Red River Valley.

As the bus had rolled over the dipping highway he had seen that the fields had been turned for the first time of the season. The shoots of spring oats hadn't appeared yet, and the raised furrows of sparkling black soil glistened and looked smooth and long in their ordered rows. He had known the depth of the trenches, had known the curving edges of the fields as the tractors rounded and headed back for another pass. He had known how his feet would sink into soil, loosened by newly sharpened blades and the exuberance of a farmer's desire to get an early start, daring the frost.

He could tell by the rows, how they lay straight, how the crust of decaying stalks was split evenly by the discs, that the farmers had dared the frost and won. There had been no new passes. He could see them engaged in other chores, reshingling their houses or perhaps wedged underneath their pickup trucks, tightening clutch cables. He had known from these activities that the first planting had been a success.

Through the green-tinted windows of the Greyhound bus he gauged the quality of the soil by its color, and by the smell that managed to push its way past the air-conditioning and the antiseptic smell of the rest room with its chemical toilet at the rear of the bus. The spring smell, the smell of newly turned rows and a winter's worth of thawing manure, had managed to find Paul where he sat with a single suitcase in a window seat. He was bothered by no one. No one sat next to him, or near him for that matter. He had placed his suitcase on the seat next to him so nobody could have occupied that space if they had wanted to, and no one had wanted to anyway. Not that he'd noticed. Not that he could tell.

He had been looking at the rows whipping past the windows, and smelling the soil, noticing the ditches high with water that actually had a current. He had been remembering his father talk of this soil, of Red River soil. Richest in the world, his father had said. Richer than the Nile overflows, no stones, no clay, and no sand. Just pure loam. Paul had been remembering that his father had never actually seen this new Canaan, as he himself never had. But here it was. Just a few miles to the north and west of where he had lived for the last nine years, in a small house with a breezeway to a garage that remained swept and bare his entire stay because Paul had never had a car and had never used the space to store boxes of old newspapers or plates, or outgrown clothes of children.

As the green tint glazed everything that swept before his eyes, Paul had known he was leaving. For good. Forever.

As the bus rumbled over the worn blacktop and dipped down into the farmlands north of the reservation, Paul had known that spring had come, that winter had finally unclenched its fist, that the trees swaying outside of window light of his small kitchen would no longer explode in the middle of the night. The moisture trapped in the fibers and hollow runs within the trunk, frozen by the fingers of cold that took hold of anything or any-one stupid or careless enough to show weakness or fault, would no longer snap and blast twenty or thirty years of growth in a night's work of cold weather and high winds.

Paul had known that he would no longer wake to find the bowls and pots in his own sink skimmed with ice. He would no longer find the felts in his Sorels stiff with frozen sweat. As he sat in his seat he had seen a tractor that he knew needed a clutch box because of how it jerked around the corners of the field. The spring sun had arced through the green glass. He had known that the key to the church door would no longer freeze and break in the metal puzzle, that the wine for the Eucharist could now sit in its bottles without having to be wrapped in newspapers, straw, and an electric blanket so that they wouldn't ice and shatter, spitting glass into the rough timber supports in the basement of the clapboard church. The church that always needed a new coat of white paint.

It was spring now, and the water ran free in the river and lapped against the pebbled shore of the lake. It was spring, and already the gear boxes and engine blocks from ancient diesel tractors were being loaded into pickup trucks so that maybe, with a little bailing wire and even less money, maybe they could make it through another year.

This knowledge was the most painful kind; the kind that sat on his brain, and could be called up with ease and fluidity. These were beautiful knowings, though it seemed that they graced his perception only when there wasn't a thing to which he could apply them, not a single situation in which they could be put to use. They idled around behind his eyes, and begat other memories, knowledge of things that were past, had been done. Those things were gone. He had turned his gaze to the toes of his shoes, though they were thrust under the seat in front of him. He had pulled his legs back and seen the predictable scrapes and marks on the caps of his shoes. He had seen the white marks of salt that had worked their way into the leather from the sidewalk in front of the church; stains that reminded him of dried semen on his blue cotton sheets. He had looked back out the window and seen a hawk riding spring currents in the sky. Paul bent forward and tried to catch the sun behind its tail to see if it was a redtail hawk. He had craned his neck, trying to secure the halo of lapped feathers.

It was the end of nine winters and nine springs, with their painful births of sudden frost and last-minute storms.

After the bus ride of long vistas of turning soil, the short stretch of city streets as they had passed through Thief River Falls, they coasted into the station in Winnipeg. Now, as he twisted in his seat trying to decide between the black panel with white-tiled numbers and the outdoors where it was spring, he had to make up his mind.

Picking up his suitcase, he turned his hip so as to pass from behind the blank television screen. He stood and, with his battered brown cardboard suitcase in his left hand, he walked the few steps that brought him in front of the clacking panel, showing his bus as the second to the top.

He sat down, this time in a seat without a television, and nodded to the man sitting next to him because he had bumped the edge of his suitcase on the man's shin.

"Sorry," said Paul.

"It's all right," the man said, smiling, "I got another one."

Behind him he heard the sound of video games and the occasional grumbling roll of a pop can tumbling out of a machine.

Paul looked around, looked for the numbered gate from which the panel above him said his bus was leaving. He gazed around, and a pang — the pang of suddenly realizing that he might have misread the time and missed his bus — caused him to crease his forehead and whip his neck in all directions for a clock. Paul had never worn a watch.

"If you're headed to Thompson, the bus ain't left yet."

Paul turned to the man sitting next to him. He was Indian and tall, over six feet. He was thin, but had wide shoulders and hair that shagged around his ears.

"Thanks."

Paul settled back into his seat, pushing his suitcase an inch further beneath him with the heels of his black work shoes, shoes he'd had to order from Sears.

The man had his legs crossed straight out in front of him, and the cuffs of his jeans bordered his tennis shoes just above the tongue, comfortable and perfect in a way that Paul could never seem to fit his own clothes.

"I was just up there myself."

The man yawned and locked his fingers together, flexing his arms out in front of his face. Folding them in, he glanced at his watch.

"Really," said Paul.

He wanted to ask more, know more. But the man looked over

to the ticket counter, then back over his shoulder to the row of three battered pinball machines that stood in a row before the double glass doors leading outside to spring.

"It's beautiful up there. You gotta grow into it, but," he shrugged, "but it's really something else." He trailed off, and glanced at his watch again.

Paul looked up at the panel and saw the numbers and letters flip to show that his bus was leaving next. The announcer rasped from the tinny loudspeaker that his bus would be boarding in five minutes. Anxious about missing it, about losing his ticket, about not finding room for his single suitcase, Paul patted the breast pocket of his black nylon windbreaker and tested the latches on his suitcase. He reached back and felt that his wallet was still in place, and knew from their weight and gentle sag to the left, that his keys and change were still in the front pocket of his beige slacks.

Paul looked at the numbers above him once more, and just to be sure, he stood up and walked over to the doors above which was painted the number of his departure gate.

There was no line to speak of. Few traveled up that way, and if they did, they had the sense to do it by train. But, as a rule, Paul despised trains, and secretly viewed them as a dying form of transportation. He handed his bag to the man by the side of the bus and watched as he threw it under the silver-sided doors.

The air smelled of diesel exhaust that beat out all smell of spring, and he handed his ticket to the blue-sweatered driver who held a Kool in one hand as he greeted the passengers and handed them back their baggage stub. With the smell of blue diesel exhaust Paul stepped up the three steps into the bus without looking back.

It was like this:

The bus pulled away and headed north with Paul believing that he knew about the spring, that he knew what he was leaving. He never knew, as the fields gave way to tundra, the moss that ran to a depth of three feet and in all directions.

He never knew, because he left too soon. He never knew as he stepped off the bus and walked away from the small town of

Thompson and placed his feet on the moss with its base of permafrost that had never, ever melted, even before the last glaciers that swept through ten thousand years before. Even before that, this ground had been frozen.

Those glaciers had carved the basin that held the Red River and its black soil, glistening as it was freshly tilled again. Another season, another year.

He never knew, because when he placed his feet down on the moss, that space of earth, that tenderly nursed life would die and not grow again for a hundred years. In this he thought he had finally found resolution.

It was like this:

Back in the Winnipeg bus station Lyle uncrossed his legs and looked at his watch again. He was impatient, and longed to see the black-and-white sign by the side of the highway that would tell him that he was finally home.

He crossed his legs again and stretched his long arms out behind his head, pushing his ribs against his white T-shirt and pointing his toes inside his leather Nikes.

Lyle was impatient for his bus to come, though he knew it would. He wanted to see it, the wind in the red pine at Poverty. He chafed against his plastic seat because he wanted to smell lilacs and trade insults with those he had left ten years ago. Ten years! he thought. Hell of a long time. Lyle shook his head, his black hair waving about his ears.

Soon the bus did come, and Lyle boarded and headed south. Finally. To see the little girl named Jackie he didn't even know was his daughter. Soon, as the air grew warmer and warmer, soon he would see Violet, grown ten years older. And, Lyle thought, this time. This time I'll carry her to her bed. This time I'll undress her and cry at seeing her breasts, her curved thigh. I'll cry when I hear her speak. And I'll laugh when we've both stopped shaking.

Donovan

The June after Little's drowning broke over us in a way we will always remember.

The days were clear, and the sun continued its long travel across the sky. And though it was hot, the tall trees, red and white pine, shut out enough light to keep our houses cool. Even when sometimes the heat became too much, a few clouds would appear from the sides of the sky and partly hide the sun, tempering its power from a blistering heat to a gentle, constant warmth.

At night it rained. Dripping from shingled roofs and metaled hoods, it gave us life, devoid of the batter and fury of summer storms. When it did storm, the claps and peals sounded in the distance, never touching and striking the trees or our homes. We would sit then, down by the shore of the lake, and toe the sand, ruffled only by a slight wind, a distant tendril of the rage that had been carried somewhere else. Those wisps of air current were enough only to lift a few hairs, enough only to make us pull closer to one another; me to Jackie, Violet to Lyle, who had finally come back. This is what the nighttime rains brought us, so we knew it was for us. Finally.

By the end of July the blueberries and raspberries were ripe. We all went together out in the bush behind Poverty. Ignoring the raspberries and their thorned stalks, we collected the blueberries in one-gallon plastic ice-cream buckets. We picked them in a lazy way, more to be out there in the stands of jack pine with

245

holes of sunlight streaking onto our shoulders than to pick for food. We filled our buckets and canned long into the night, playing hearts around Jeannette's kitchen table. Sometimes, far into the evening, with the patter of rain pulling long lines down the screen door, Stan and Lyle would speak in quiet voices about Pick. Casually, gently, they allowed themselves to remember him. In the lamplight, in the streak of rain coming through the door, and in the steam and bubble of simmering berries, they drew out past things that Jackie and I had never heard, that had been kept apart and down. We sat and listened, sharing the stories told in an unrushed but steady beat between these two men. That is what the summer brought us.

By August the chokecherries were ripe and the night rains had stopped. No one pulled the tart clusters from the springing branches. Instead, we sat on steps and hood, talking slowly as the night sounds settled around us: fish-flies bumping into the porch light, a dog's bark that ran across the lake's smoothed surface; a blanket of doings and goings-on that we usually weren't privileged enough to hear. But the summer had opened up to us and we had been let in.

Sometimes Lyle and Stan would take me to the basketball court at the high school or the powwow grounds and we would play in the spray of car light.

As August drew on, the usual dog days' summer dust was nowhere to be seen. There was a clarity of vision, a crisp detail that comforted us and cloaked us in a way the dust never could. We knew we were finally equal among the pines, along the lakeshore, and with the river.

It was in late August that I visited Stan at the fisheries where he had worked for the last eight years.

The fishery wasn't much more than an insulated wood shack set along the river above the dam. But the cement floor was cool compared to the gravel road I had walked to reach the one-room building.

Long concrete tanks lined one wall, where walleye fry swam and darted in the fresh river water pumped continuously through. Stan sat with his back to the tanks that weren't connected to his job. He turned his head as I blocked the sun's slant through the doorway. He got up and pulled a metal folding chair, identical to his, from behind the door and set its rubber-tipped legs carefully on the cool, level surface.

I sat down next to him and he opened a Coke for me that he had kept cold in the cement tanks behind him.

With the door open and a single bulb hanging low overhead, we sat without talking and stared ahead.

This is what I saw:

A row of five tanks of glass, like huge upside-down mayonnaise jars. Each of them must have held fifty gallons of water. Suspended in each jar was a cluster of translucent, stringy globules, the whole bunch of it the size of a large turkey. It looked like blond tapioca pudding, minute curves and circles, a gelatin sphere of spheres suspended in temperature-controlled river water.

They were fertilized fish eggs. And I sat there with Stan watching them.

The sound of water trickled behind us. We had taken off our shoes and the concrete floor cooled our feet, taking out the sweat and aches, pulling the tension deep down into the earth.

The August afternoon sunlight slanted in the door. I leaned closer to the thick glass tubes.

There were thousands, millions of eggs clustered together in the cold water. They were clear ovals with gently arced membranes, like tomato seeds. I knew they must be pulsing, beating, eating. There were millions of vessels leading to millions of hearts, clinging together but separated by clear shells of mucus. The capillaries and nerves were smaller than the smallest hair. We watched them together that August day.

I leaned closer.

Peering through the one-inch-thick glass of the central jar, I saw something.

A bubble broke, a current no bigger than a pea waved out from the cluster of eggs like an aquatic sun-flare, lasting for less than a second, traveling less than half an inch. A small cloud of wet pollen, particles of shell.

Then another.

Another.

I got up and stood next to the tank, my eyes almost resting on the glass.

Another. The smallest of disruptions, nerves firing before the eye, sending out slivers of flesh from the home of curved tissue. I saw a dart, a silver flash, secrets collapsed in empty balloons of tissue the size of a seed, of a kernel of corn.

The eggs were hatching. A tail pushed another shell apart, shimmering shiny muscle never before used, its width less than a pencil lead, a feather of cartilage. It was thinner than onion skin, thinner than the outer surface of the eye. Another egg erupted and the tiny fish sat dazed next to the towering column of eggs. I could see the heart, a red pulse the size of a single raspberry capsule. The spinal cord, hair-thick, was alive with the electricity of message.

Another. Another. I couldn't keep track of them all. Soon there would be more and more. There would be too many to count, too many to know.

David Treuer is Ojibwe, and is a member of the Winnebegoshish Band of Northern Minnesota. He graduated from Princeton University in 1992.

This book was designed by Will Powers. It is set in Monotype Bodoni by Stanton Publication Services, Inc., and manufactured by Edwards Brothers, Ann Arbor, Michigan, on acid-free paper.